THE
DARK ARK

THE DARK ARK

JOHN LEIFER

The Dark Ark

For information about this title or to order other books and/or
electronic media, contact the publisher:

Earhart Press
P.O. Box 6136, Overland Park, Kansas 66207
www.earhartpress.com

ISBNs:
978-0-9995655-6-8 (print)
978-0-9995655-7-5 (ebook)

Printed in the United States of America

Library of Congress Control Number: In Process

CONTENTS

CHARACTERS

Randall Hawkins: Commanding General, NORAD

Colonel Marsetti: 2nd Space Warning Squadron, Commander

Carl Perkins: Head of Secret Service detail

Commander Hart: Mission commander, former SEAL, CIA operative

Dr. Elizabeth Wilkins: Runs the scientific team of the CIA and married to Hart

Mary Conner: FLOTUS

Deputy Director O'Hara: Daily ops command, National Military Command Center

Bill Martin: Secretary of Defense

Mr. Stinson: Director of National Intelligence

Joe Sanford: Chairman of the Joint Chiefs of Staff

Colonel Mike Jackson: Squadron leader

Allan Hatfield: Vice President

Wei Hai Zhao: Chief Scientist aboard the Prometheus

Jane Graham: Senior scientist aboard the Prometheus, formerly with USAMRID

Captain Seward: Captain of the Prometheus

Carole Hubbard: Lead geneticist

Martin Houser: Scientist

Buck McMasters: Lab security officer

Marvin Kahn: Deputy Director of Operations for the CIA

Mark Adams: Commanding Officer, Naval Base Guam

General Anthony Cosgrove: Andersen AFB

Charlie Harbinger: Secretary of the Navy

Tom Linfield: Director, CDC

Lt. General Mark Scott: Head of Joint Special Operations Command

Li Qiang Chow: Area Director

Commander Huan: Director of Chinese Naval Operations, Spratly Islands

Marta Hopkins: Second in command, CDC and rare disease expert

Elijah Obaji: Molecular biologist, CDC

Graham Nielsen: Geneticist, CDC

Carl Hodges: Data expert

Captain Mike Anderson: Second in command charged with securing scientific team

Staff Sergeant Juan "Paco" Ramirez: Underwater demolition expert

Lieutenant Tommy Lamott: From South Boston and with the attitude to prove it

Jason Harding: A hardened war fighter from Macon, Georgia

Roman Sitarski: A former SEAL and John Belushi doppelganger

Bob Bridges: Member of Anderson's crew

Ronny Good: Member of Anderson's crew

Joaquin Alvarez: Sniper assigned to Anderson

Sammy Latourno: Sniper assigned to Anderson

Christopher Hamil: Captain of the USNS Mercy

Kevin Taylor: Helicopter captain

Brigadier General George Solomon: Commander, Andersen AFB

Chief Master Sergeant Ketchum: Head of logistics at the airbase in Guam

Andy Peterson: Helicopter pilot

CHAPTER 1

Incoming

IT TOOK ONLY SECONDS for NORAD Headquarters to be transformed into a scene of utter chaos as early warning signals flooded in from a network of missile detection sensors located across the globe. A torrent of men scrambled to their stations seeking to first validate, then mitigate the potential threat of attack.

One man remained unfazed by the flashing red lights and deafening warning klaxons. He was Randall Hawkins, NORAD's Commanding General. As he sat in the heart of the action, his posture was relaxed, his freshly shaven chin cupped in his right hand. After more than thirty years in the business, he had learned to take such events in stride.

"The comm line is open to Buckley, Sir," a female airman announced. Buckley was the Air Force base that served as home to the 460th Operations Group, responsible for missile warning and missile defense.

In an unruffled voice, heavy with a languid Texas drawl, he responded, "I need Colonel Marsetti on the comm."

"I'm on the line, General," the Commander of the 2nd Space Warning Squadron responded quickly.

"What the hell is going on, Tony? I've got all kinds of lights flashing and sirens blaring. It's hard for a man to think with all this ruckus."

Though Marsetti was physically unremarkable, standing a mere 5' 8" and weighing 150 pounds, he, too, was unflappable.

"General, our sensors have detected a missile launch from a silo proximate to the eastern coast of Iran. We will have confirmation within minutes, Sir."

"I don't need confirmation. We neutralized the Iranian threat . . . or don't you remember?" he added coldly.

Marsetti didn't say anything, letting the slight pass, knowing it wasn't personal.

Hawkins continued, "It has to be that damned Space-Based Infrared System acting up again. I've told you I don't trust it, and I'm not about to call the president and put our nation on full alert just because one of your toys is broken."

He could hear the muffled sounds of Tony Marsetti conferring with his staff before he responded.

"It's no malfunction, General. We can now confirm the launch with high confidence. Its heat signature suggests an ICBM," Marsetti added.

Hawkins straightened in his chair. "Put it up on screen!" he shouted at the sergeant manning the video control console in the center of the sprawling command complex. As the ten-foot-high, ultra-high definition screen came to life, a column of data began to scroll down the left side of the screen, while a satellite map of the Iranian coast appeared on the right. Just north of the Indian Ocean, a glowing red circle near the port city of Chabahar indicated the precise point where infra-red sensors had picked up the initial launch signature of the missile. A bright yellow line depicted its trajectory.

"Get NMCC on the comm," Hawkins ordered. The National Military Command Center at the Pentagon was the nexus of control for any retaliation measures. "I want them up to speed should the president choose to respond."

As Hawkins barked orders, gigabytes of data generated by the Integrated Tactical Warning and Attack Assessment Network were being fed into a Cray supercomputer. Capable of one quintillion calculations per second, the machine triangulated the precise location of the missile, its trajectory, speed, and altitude in real time.

"Holy Mother of Christ," Hawkins whispered as he stared at the geographic coordinates for the presumed target. He prayed it did not carry a nuclear warhead, but his gut told him otherwise. If his instincts were correct, less than thirty-eight minutes remained before the water of the Potomac would be brought to a boil and Washington would be consumed in a conflagration that would make the Civil War torching of Atlanta look like a marshmallow roast.

Hawkins picked up the hotline to the White House. A computer-synthesized voice responded requesting his identification code.

"Four, two, niner, niner, bravo, sam, glory, adam, charlie, charlie, alpha, delta."

"Name and rank?"

"General Randall Hawkins."

A moment later, a live voice instructed him to hold for the president.

President Jonathan Conner skipped the pleasantries. "Do we have a situation, General?"

"Sir, we have a confirmed ICBM launch in southeastern Iran. Our preliminary analysis of the trajectory indicates that the target is Washington, D.C."

"What is your confidence level, General Hawkins?"

"Approaching one hundred percent, Mr. President."

"How much time until impact?"

"Thirty-six minutes, Sir." Wanting to interject a ray of hope, Hawkins added, "We don't know for certain the nature of the payload."

"I think we can guess, don't you?" Conner didn't wait for a response. "I want you to keep me informed of any change in the projected trajectory or time until impact. Understood?"

Conner needed to act, and act now. He summoned Carl Perkins, the head of his Secret Service detail.

Perkins was the consummate Secret Service agent: no immediate family, an almost rabid devotion to the office of the presidency, and an unflinching willingness to lay down his life for his country. Perkins knocked once, then entered the Oval Office.

"Carl, I'm implementing DEEP DIVE," Conner said. DEEP DIVE was the protocol requiring the president, First Lady, and a select list of governmental officials be sequestered in a subterranean bunker in the event of an impending attack on Washington. A separate group, including the Vice President, would be airlifted by Marine 1 to Raven Rock Mountain Complex near Blue Ridge Summit, Pennsylvania—ensuring that a critical mass of top-ranking government officials would survive whatever attack might be coming.

Perkins nodded in acknowledgment, then spoke a quick series of orders into a miniature lapel mike. A few seconds later, a swarm of agents flooded the West Wing. As they fanned out in search of their assigned senior leaders, Perkins took Conner's arm. "This way, Mr. President," he instructed him, steering him towards an elevator.

Conner stopped mid-stride. "I want you to locate Commander Hart and Dr. Wilkins and bring them to me. You have thirty minutes, Mr. Perkins. Then I want the White House locked down."

Perkins hesitated, suspecting Conner was not in the most receptive of moods. "I don't know if that's possible, Sir," he said at last.

"It damn well better be," Conner shot back. He resumed walking, Perkins following on his heels.

Commander John Hart was Conner's go-to person in emergencies. A former Navy SEAL, Hart had spent much of his career running black ops in sewers and gutters across the world. He was one tough son of a bitch, but even John Hart was vulnerable. A recent encounter with a .50 caliber sniper's bullet had ended his military career and almost ended his life.

Elizabeth Wilkins was Hart's partner professionally and personally. More recently, she became his wife. An expert in bio-warfare, Liz was well known in the intelligence community as well as in the upper echelons of government.

Per Conner's instructions, the White House was soon on full lock-down, with all personnel confined to their offices so they would not be a hindrance to the agents as they worked to complete their directive. In under three minutes, POTUS and everyone else on the Members of the DEEP DIVE list were loaded into a little-used elevator that was hidden in plain sight. It looked like nothing more than a large storage closet.

"What's going on, Jonathan?" an anxious Mary Conner asked her husband after being escorted—without explanation or apology—from a meeting with the wife of the Canadian Prime Minister.

"The Secret Service are just doing their job, Darling. I'm sure it will prove to be nothing more than a drill, but we can't take any chances." He strove to stifle his own anxiety as he forced a smile.

She knew better.

There were no floors or levels indicated on the elevator's control panel—just a keypad into which Perkins entered a code. As the door closed, a synthesized voice instructed the president to approach a camera mounted behind the glass panel for a retinal scan. After Conner's identity was verified, the elevator began a precipitous descent, finally coming to rest one hundred feet below street level. Deep enough, in theory, to survive the explosive force of a nuclear weapon.

Conner wasn't interested in testing that theory. As the doors opened, he turned to Perkins. "Take the First Lady to our quarters, Mr. Perkins." He turned towards the remaining group, which included the Secretary of Defense, the National Security Advisor, and the Director of National Intelligence. "Let's get moving," he ordered. "We don't have much time." He then set a fast pace towards the Situation Room.

Once everyone was seated around the expansive oval table, the president instructed an aide to bring up the video feeds from NORAD. A collective rush of anxiety swept through the group as the missile's trajectory was projected on the screen. It terminated in the sky above Washington.

"General Hawkins," Conner's voice summoned the attention of NORAD's commanding general, "I am in a secure bunker with members of my staff and Cabinet. The Vice President and others are en route to Raven Rock and will be patched through once on-site. But based upon what I'm looking at on-screen, we don't appear to have the luxury of time to wait for our colleagues' input. We must act now."

"Agreed, Sir. I have Deputy Director O'Hara at NMCC on the comm with us awaiting your instructions. I've also taken the liberty of raising the alert level for our interceptors. As you know, the normal sequence would be to activate missiles at Fort Greely in Alaska, with Vandenberg being our fallback."

Conner looked over at Secretary of Defense Bill Martin, who gave him a confirming nod.

"What happens if neither set of interceptors scores a hit, General? What then?"

"Then we are in trouble, Sir. We'll be relying on air-to-air missiles to strike an object moving at close to Mach 20. It will be like trying to shoot a bullet with another bullet."

"Deputy Director O'Hara."

"Yes, Mr. President."

"Launch the interceptors."

"Yes, Mr. President. They will appear on your screen as soon as they clear their silos. Each missile will be staggered at 15-second intervals, with its time to intercept appearing next to its trajectory. Right now, I'm estimating 12 minutes to launch."

"I'm muting our line, Mr. O'Hara, but we'll be able to hear you." Turning to his Director of National Intelligence, Conner continued, "I'm praying we intercept those missiles, but if we don't, I want to know what to expect, Mr. Stinson."

Before Stinson could begin, Conner's aide appeared at the door. "Forgive me for interrupting, Sir, but I thought you would want to know that Commander Hart and Dr. Wilkins are en route and should arrive within five minutes."

"Thank you," Conner said, as an almost visible sense of relief washed over him. He nodded for Arch Stinson to continue.

Meticulously groomed, every inch of Arch Stinson communicated sophistication, from the tweed jacket that dated to his professorial years at Yale to the manner in which he lifted his chin as he spoke.

"Based upon our intelligence reports, we believe that the Iranian warhead is identical to the ones we destroyed earlier. If so, it's a boosted device of North Korean design with an estimated yield of 300 kilotons."

"How in the hell did they pull that off right under our noses, Mr. Stinson?"

Stinson didn't need to respond; Conner already knew the answer. The North Koreans and Iranians were united in their hatred of America and more than happy to engage in technological cooperation that served to advance the destructive capabilities of both nations. As a result, Iran acquired boosted fission devices, while North Korea received advanced missile delivery systems from Iran.

This hellish marriage transformed two minor league players into formidable adversaries, capable of mass destruction.

"But I thought the Israelis had destroyed all of the Iranian silos known to contain nuclear warheads," Conner argued.

"We all thought that, Mr. President." He paused. "You were asking about what will happen if that nuke explodes, Sir. I will defer to General Sanford, who is an expert on the impact of such a weapon."

In sharp contrast to Stinson, Joe Sanford was a bull of a man, a career Marine without an ounce of fat on his body. His style matched his physique, blunt and aggressive. It had served him well through multiple tours of duty in Iraq, Afghanistan and Syria. Wounded twice, Sanford was the recipient of two Purple Hearts, the Distinguished Service Cross, and a Silver Star.

Though he had detractors, there was unanimous agreement that if the U.S. ever got into a serious shooting match, Sanford was the man to lead the charge. He'd been appointed Chairman of the Joint Chiefs of Staff by Conner two years earlier and had been unanimously confirmed by the Senate, a rarity in an era of bitter partisan divide.

Sanford stood to address his boss. "We've conducted elaborate computer simulations depicting the impact of a 300-kiloton nuclear device detonated over Washington. For the purpose of modeling, we assumed an aerial detonation at an altitude of 1,500 feet directly above the Pentagon.

"As you can imagine, the results were catastrophic. In a microsecond, the bomb would release more than 250 million calories of electromagnetic energy in the form of a brilliant flash of light capable of vaporizing people midstride." He paused to let his words sink in.

"In seconds, the fireball at the center of the blast would expand from less than a yard in diameter to more than a mile. The temperature at the core would be thousands of times hotter than the surface of the sun. As if that weren't enough, a blast wave, accompanied by tornadic winds with velocities as high as five hundred miles per hour, would follow. After that . . ."

"General," Conner interrupted him, "I want to know what the models show in terms of damage."

"The Pentagon would be crushed by the force of the blast. Within one to two miles of ground zero, an area that includes Arlington, Pentagon City and numerous other densely populated areas would look like a dystopian nightmare. The asphalt pavement atop our streets would flow like hot lava, cars would burst into flames, and buildings would be leveled by the shockwave. Within hours, virtually nothing would remain of Washington but ash, dense smoke, and rubble." He paused and stared into the faces around the table.

Although what he was describing was horrific, none of it came as a surprise to the people in the room. They all knew the consequences of a nuclear blast.

"Even at a distance of three miles from the epicenter," Sanford went on, "hundreds of thousands of people would be severely injured through a combination of thermal burns, ionizing radiation and flying debris. Anyone unfortunate enough to have looked directly at the flash would suffer blinding retinal damage. Most of these casualties would be consumed by the fire that would engulf Washington and its suburbs. The total body count could easily reach 500,000 within the first few days."

As he was concluding his summary, Hart and Wilkins appeared at the door of the Situation Room. Conner interrupted the General long enough to greet the couple. "Thank God, you're here," he said, hugging them in an unusual break from etiquette.

It had been months since Conner and Hart last spoke. Hart had returned from his final mission, one in which he served as a military advisor to the Prime Minister of Israel at Conner's behest. At the time, the Jewish state was under siege by the combined forces of Syria, Iran, Russia, and Hezbollah, collectively known as the Syrian Coalition.

What had begun as simultaneous attacks on the Golan and Gaza had quickly escalated. When Iranian missiles loaded with Novichok-V rained down on Tel Aviv, Conner surmised that nuclear weapons might follow and knew that the deployment of a nuke would draw the U.S. and Russia into a world war. That's when he dispatched Commander Hart to counsel Abraham Rabinovich.

Working hand-in-hand with the Prime Minister, Hart crafted a plan to eliminate the Iranian threat, beginning with the destruction of their ICBMs. Not one to remain a safe distance from the field of battle, Hart insisted on leading one of the ten Israeli Special Forces teams assigned to destroy hardened Iranian silos.

After planting explosive charges deep within one silo's support structure, Hart's team raced to a Blackhawk helicopter which stood ready to extract them. The Commander was the last man to board, but not before a sniper's bullet struck him mid-chest. The hot metal eviscerated one lung and tore a gaping hole in his back. The team hoisted his failing body aboard, while a medic pumped him full of morphine. It was an act of futility. No one survived that kind of wound. Not even John Hart.

Somehow, Hart made it as far as a MASH unit in Iraq, where a cardiothoracic surgeon awaited his legendary patient. Despite the surgeon's skills, midway through the operation, Hart coded. He lay lifeless on the operating table for more than two minutes while efforts to resuscitate him proved futile.

As Hart hovered near death, it was not only his body that was transformed by that bullet. So, too, were his psyche and soul. It was during that time that he felt the touch of God. Though he had long ago stopped believing in a divine force, there it was in the form of an undeniable, brilliant and transformative light. His life would be spared, but no longer could he be in the business of killing.

It would take months of recuperation for Hart to regain even a modicum of strength. Throughout his convalescence, he thought about the many men he had killed, his near-death, and what he clearly understood to be God's intervention. When he finally returned to the states, he knew he could no longer lead troops into battle. And so, with regret that he could no longer serve his country, Hart had submitted his letter of resignation to President Conner.

"Have you been briefed?" Conner asked as he gestured for Hart and Wilkins to be seated.

"Yes, Sir. The agent that picked us up gave us a 30,000-foot view. Although, we would welcome an update."

"General Sanford, would you please provide the Commander and Dr. Wilkins with a short synopsis of what you just shared?"

The General summed it up in a sound-byte. As he was finishing, the video screen and comm line suddenly came back to life.

Sanford pointed to the monitors. "We should be close to seeing the first volley of interceptors depart their silos at Fort Greely."

As if on cue, five circles appeared sequentially on the map, followed by dotted lines showing their matched trajectories. An "X" depicted the projected point of interception, and a countdown clock showed the elapsed time until impact for each of the five interceptors.

It felt to Conner like the air had been sucked out of the room as a deathly silence overtook the assembled group. It was finally broken by the voice of General Hawkins counting down the time until impact.

"A miss," he growled in frustration, as the first interceptor flew by its intended target.

Over the next minute, the four remaining interceptors all failed to engage the ICBM.

"Mr. President, I'm afraid it is now up to Vandenberg," Hawkins informed the Commander-in-Chief.

"Understood, General. We'll be back to you."

Conner turned to Sanford. "General, how long until Vandenberg comes on line?" Conner asked somberly.

"About three minutes, Mr. President."

All faces were directed towards Conner. There was a distant look in the president's eyes. As he spoke, his tone was soft and reflective, more suited to a private conversation with his wife than a war room.

"If you're wondering what is going through my head at this moment, I'm thinking about my grandchildren," he said. "They're probably at recess on the playground right about now. As many of you know, they go to school in Arlington."

Heads nodded in affirmation.

"I am also picturing photographs that I saw many years ago. Black and white photographs of schoolchildren in Hiroshima shortly after the bomb went off. Many of them were burned beyond recognition. Other children had hideous wounds, their skin sloughing off in sheets. Can you imagine the sheer terror those children must have felt? It must have been . . ." The president stopped, closing his eyes.

After a moment, he re-opened them and looked around the table. "Well, so much for my façade of implacability," he said with a self-deprecating smile.

"Everyone in this room has been blessed with a good life. That's not to say it was without hardship, but blessed, nonetheless. If it is comfortable for you, I hope you will say a prayer for all of our children and our children's children. May they be so blessed."

The solemnity of the moment was broken as General Hawkins' voice boomed through the speakers. Three minutes and seven seconds had elapsed since his last communication.

"Same drill, ladies and gentlemen. You will see five overlapping circles representing our interceptors. The missiles are hot and will be airborne momentarily."

The first missile streaked heavenward to an altitude of 120,000 feet, coming within fifty yards of the Iranian ICBM before failing to detonate. None of the four remaining missiles came close.

A sense of dread swept over Conner, pulling him down like a riptide. He fought to dispel it, to hold onto hope. That was his sacred obligation to everyone who was counting on him. He took a deep breath and slowly exhaled.

"So, General Sanford, what are our chances of knocking this damn thing down with an air-to-air weapon? Didn't you say it was like trying to hit a bullet with a bullet? I sure as hell hope the pilots are good shots."

"We have a chance, Sir," the Marine responded, stone-faced. "With your permission, Mr. President, I am ready to give the order to scramble a squadron of F35s from Joint Base Anacostia-Bolling. They're on the tarmac, loaded with our newly developed SM-3 Block IIA interceptors."

"I thought that system had yet to be tested, General."

"That's correct, Sir, but it's our best option. The missiles are programmed to detonate when they reach a defined kill zone for the missile. If they successfully obliterate the warhead, there will be some fallout from the weapon's core, but not a nuclear detonation."

"I pray you're right, General. Give the order. How long before the F35s are in position?"

"Four minutes, Mr. President."

"You're cutting it awfully close, aren't you? That leaves only two minutes to impact."

"Yes, Sir. Mr. President, I have the squadron leader, Colonel Mike Jackson, on the comm. May I patch him through?"

"Do it."

A moment later, Conner could hear the roar of Jackson's F35 engines on full afterburner.

"Colonel, this is Jonathan Conner. You've got a room full of people praying for you."

"We appreciate that, Sir. We won't let you down."

"I sure as hell hope not, Colonel. We'll leave this line open so we can follow you in real time."

"Understood, Mr. President."

With that, Jackson radioed the rest of squad. "Gentlemen, the comm line has been patched through to the White House. You've got a room full of people, including the president, counting on us. Let's not let them down."

"Yes, Sir!" each member of his squadron sounded off.

As the squadron broke through 60,000 feet, General Sanford spoke. "Colonel, you should be seconds away from deployment of the SM-3's."

"Understood, Sir."

"Gentlemen, fire on my command." The Colonel's eyes were fixed on the plane's targeting computer. A moment later, he shouted, "Fire!"

"The birds are hot, Sir."

Conner's shoulders were hunched with tension as the missiles screamed upwards at velocities exceeding two miles per second. The screen showed the missiles appearing to lock on to the incoming ICBM.

This time, they didn't miss. With a flash, the threat of nuclear annihilation disappeared from radar.

Triumphant shouts erupted in the room.

"Congratulations, Colonel Jackson," Conner said, the relief evident in his voice. The shadow of death had just passed over Washington, D.C.

CHAPTER 2

A Grim Warning

THE JUBILATION THAT FOLLOWED was short-lived, as the sober reality of what had just transpired sank in. Conner let out an audible sigh as he closed his eyes, lowered his chin, and folded his hands.

Those individuals near to the President could see his lips moving as he whispered a prayer of thanks. When he finished, he opened his eyes and turned towards the room full of people.

"By the grace of God, we have a world to return to, a world largely unscathed by the desperate acts of madmen. Now it's our job to determine what constitutes an appropriate response, knowing that the eyes of the world are upon us."

Joe Sanford stood up and addressed Conner. "Sir, our response should be immediate and in kind. It will send a message to Iran and to anyone else who dares to threaten America that nuclear provocation will result in cataclysmic retaliation."

"What are you suggesting, General, that we nuke Tehran?"

"That would be a good start, Mr. President."

"I understand the desire to strike with overwhelming force, but our response must be a just one. The Iranian people are not complicit in this attack. They have branded the theocracy as enemies of the state and returned their nation to democratic rule. If we retaliate against them, they will once again become victims of the theocracy. That's my perspective. Arch, I'd like to hear your point of view."

Looking deep in thought, Arch Stinson slowly rose to his feet.

"This is not the kind of matter that lends itself to a rapid resolution, Mr. President, and yet I understand the urgency you must feel. I believe we have two priorities, the most pressing of which is to eliminate any remaining threat from the missile silo at Chabahar."

"Are you suggesting that there may be more missiles armed with nuclear warheads?"

"That is a possibility, Mr. President. The silo should be immediately rendered inoperable."

"Commander Hart, do you agree with Mr. Stinson?"

"Yes, Sir. And I'm eager to hear the DNI's second priority."

"Well, Mr. Stinson?" Conner inquired.

"As you know from a prior briefing, we have corroborated intelligence regarding the location of Iran's shadow government. They are ensconced in a small complex of buildings located in a sparsely populated area approximately forty miles west of Zahedan, a city of more than half a million. It's about seven hours by car from Chabahar."

"How confident are you in our intelligence?" Sanford asked. "I thought Zahedan was a Sunni stronghold. Why would a Shia government in exile select a region where their people have been targets of suicide bombers in the past?"

"Because no one would think of looking for them there," Stinson replied.

"What do you suggest we do, Arch?" Conner inquired.

"I would respond in kind."

"You mean you'd nuke them."

"Yes, Mr. President. Just as a modest nuclear-armed warhead would be used to destroy the missile silo at Chabahar, a more substantial nuclear weapon could be deployed to eliminate all traces of Iran's shadow government lurking within the broadly defined area we have identified. Since it is thinly populated, from a civilian perspective, collateral damage could be kept to a minimum."

"Commander Hart, what are your thoughts?"

"While respectful of General Sanford's position, I favor the strategic response outlined by Mr. Stinson, with one addition."

"And what would that be?"

"I believe that President Putin needs to hear from you, Sir. The Russians have watched this entire event play out, undoubtedly hoping that their greatest nemesis would be dealt a fatal blow. Rather than indulge in regret, they may elect to capitalize on our perceived vulnerability by calling for a first strike. In fact, that debate may be going on in the halls of the Kremlin as we speak."

"That would be mad!" Conner responded.

"Yes, and we have to hope that the threat of mutually assured destruction remains a potent deterrent. Still, I believe that a few carefully chosen words from you could eliminate the threat altogether."

"Sir, if Russia was going to seize the moment and strike, I believe they would have done so while the Iranian missile was in the air and all of our resources were focused on defending against it," Sanford argued.

"With all due respect, General, I believe that President Putin is unpredictable and could still strike without warning," Hart responded.

Turning to an aide, Conner instructed her to open a secure line to the Kremlin and to alert him as soon as President Putin was on the phone.

He then returned his attention to the table. "I want that silo obliterated before we find ourselves tracking another incoming missile. Then I want those bastards in the desert nuked. You've got five minutes to nail down the details while I deal with the Russian president. Get on it."

"President Putin is on the line, Sir," the aide informed him. Pointing to a wall-mounted monitor, she added, "A voice analysis of the conversation will appear in real time on this monitor. You will be able to see when Mr. Putin is being deceptive."

"Arch," Conner called out, "I assume the Russians have the same capabilities?"

"That would be a reasonable bet, Mr. President."

"Well, put him through," Conner instructed the aide.

"Good afternoon, Mr. President," Putin said in thickly-accented English.

"President Putin, I'm afraid I don't have time for pleasantries. I trust you just witnessed the attempt on the part of your ally, Iran, to destroy our nation's capital."

There was a brief pause for translation, after which Putin quickly interjected, "Yes, our satellites picked up the infra-red launch signature."

Conner studied the monitor closely for any signs of deception, but the green line-tracing representing Putin's voice remained flat.

"That was the first we learned of the threat," Putin added. "You know, of course, that we would never sanction such an action, President Conner."

The trace-line shifted from green to red as it began dropping precipitously from the baseline.

"I'm not certain what or whom to believe, Mr. Putin," Conner replied, though the voice analysis had made it clear to the president. "Whether you explicitly authorized the attack or not, you have been complicit in bolstering the military objectives of the Iranian theocracy. Surely you would not argue that point."

"We have allies, just as the United States as allies. Imagine how you would respond, President Conner, if the Russian government held you accountable for the actions of a rogue group operating in Turkey or Israel."

"Are you asking me to believe that you and your compatriots were not salivating at the idea of Washington in ruins? That has been an objective of your country since the very formation of the Soviet Union. Today, Russia almost achieved that goal—and without the need to fire a single shot."

"Come, come, Mr. President, the Cold War ended decades ago. Furthermore, you crushed the Iranian theocracy. So I fail to understand your point."

Conner looked over at Sanford, who was angrily jabbing his finger at the monitor and mouthing the word "LIES!"

"We believe that Russia is continuing to support Iran's shadow government, waiting in the wings, so to speak, until the theocracy is returned to power."

"When you say 'we,' I assume you are referring to a handful of hawks within your inner circle, men who are all too ready to incite a war. We both have this fringe element within our governments. So far, we have both done a good job of keeping them in line. I trust each of us will continue to do so."

"That's the reason for my call. There's a point at which the strength of their argument will overcome the call for restraint. I urge you not to do anything that might be construed as capitalizing on America's vulnerability at this difficult moment. We both know the consequences of such action would be catastrophic. I'm asking you to keep your powder dry, President Putin, when we strike Iran in retaliation."

"I trust your response will be measured, President Conner," Putin replied.

"There will be no mercy for people who have perpetrated such a horrendous act. Just as there would be no mercy for any government that interceded to support them. Goodbye, Mr. Putin." With that, Conner disconnected the call and addressed the room.

"As we already knew, the man's a liar. That aside, I trust I have given President Putin sufficient reason to discourage any type of action against our country. I wonder what his advisors are telling him at this moment."

Hart said, "If they are using voice analysis, they're telling him you are a man of your word and will make good on your threat."

"I hope you're right, Commander. Now, let's move on." Conner turned to the group. "According to my watch, the five minutes I gave you to formulate a plan are up, so tell me how you believe we should respond."

Joe Sanford was first to speak. "One of our guided missile frigates, the USS Georgia, is within easy striking distance of Chabahar. She's carrying conventional and nuclear-armed cruise missiles that allow for variable yields. A single nuke, set to a micro-yield, will forever end the threat from that silo, while largely sparing the port city."

"Arch, do you agree with Joe?"

"Yes. And I believe we cannot afford to waste another minute."

Conner nodded. "Destroy the silo."

With those three words, a nuclear strike was put in motion. Orders were delivered electronically to the captain of the USS Georgia, who removed a sealed envelope from a safe in his cabin, then delivered the launch codes to his weapons control officer. Within minutes, the missile was ready for deployment.

"General, can you give me video coverage from the point of launch?" Conner asked.

"Yes, Sir." An image captured from high above the deck of the Georgia appeared. Conner watched as the cover on one of the ship's launching tubes slid back. With a belch of smoke and fire, a Tomahawk missile became airborne. A few seconds later, the perspective shifted to an image being fed from the missile's nose-cone camera.

"How long?" Conner asked.

"It will take approximately twenty minutes before the missile reaches Chabahar."

"That gives us time to discuss our next step," he said, turning towards Sanford.

"General, there cannot be any survivors. I want everything within twenty square miles of the purported hiding area to be scorched earth. Can you make that happen?"

"Yes, Sir. Based upon your objectives, I would recommend that we deploy an SLBM. We have an Ohio-class sub, the USS Nevada, on station in the Persian Gulf. She can fire a single Trident D5 missile with a yield approaching 400 kilotons. It will be programmed to detonate at a height of 1,500 feet over the desert. Since our target is in the heart of the Kavir-e-Loot desert, collateral damage should be minimal."

"How long will it take for the SLBM to reach its target?" Conner asked.

"Traveling at 19,000 miles per hour, a matter of minutes."

"Commander Hart, are you in agreement with this plan?"

"Yes, Sir. It is the just response you spoke of earlier."

Liz, who had been silently observing, was apoplectic. "A 'just response'?" Liz exploded, shooting her husband a withering look.

Conner turned toward Liz. "Perhaps you'd advocate for a more tempered approach, Dr. Wilkins?"

"If I may speak frankly, Mr. President?"

"I believe you already have, my dear."

Hart's eyebrows lifted in anticipation and concern about what his wife might say.

"Retribution is not the hallmark of a strong democracy. Justice is. And contrary to what General Sanford and others may think, we are not living in biblical times when justice was doled out eye for an eye."

"Your point being?" Conner interjected.

"You are in the process of neutralizing the threat. Why not simply round up the rogue elements of their former government and charge them with crimes against humanity?"

Conner looked around the room, then back to Dr. Wilkins. "I appreciate the spirit of your comments, Doctor, and I would have expected nothing less from you. But I have to send a clear message. And I have to ensure the complete destruction of the remaining heads of government, a group bent on our annihilation."

He looked around the room. "Unless there are further objections, the retaliatory strike, as outlined, will proceed."

"Mr. President, please, there has to be another way," Liz implored.

"No, Doctor, in this case there is not."

Liz lowered her head in resignation. "Yes, Sir."

"Mr. President, I have the Vice President on the line. He is secure at Raven Rock."

"Patch him through."

"Are you alright, Mr. President?" an anxious-sounding Allan Hatfield asked.

"We're fine, Allan, though I hope never to repeat the experience. To that end, we have reached a consensus regarding our response, which should negate any possible further attacks."

"I'm listening, Sir."

Conner summarized his conversation with Putin and outlined the strategic strikes he had authorized in eastern Iran.

As the president was speaking, Hart realized that there would be one remaining vestige of the theocracy after the attack: the Ayatollah, who, though presumed dead by most Iranians, sat in solitary confinement in an Israeli prison.

CHAPTER 3

There's Something in the Water

THE ULITHI ATOLL IS COMPOSED of forty small islets located 360 miles southwest of Guam amid the Caroline Islands in the western Pacific. Lurking beneath the calm, sapphire blue waters of the Atoll's twenty-two-mile-long lagoon is a graveyard for the rusting hulks of warships lost in the final battles of WWII. There, too, lie the remains of Japanese and American sailors trapped aboard their vessels. A naval graveyard with a sparse population and no ports, Ulithi Atoll was the perfect place to hide the Prometheus.

Named after a Greek Titan who was considered to be the protector of mankind, the Prometheus was a one-of-a-kind naval vessel. It measured nearly 400 feet in length with a beam just under 100 feet. Its trimaran, three-hulled design provided maximum stability for a ship capable of exceeding forty knots on the open sea.

But it was not just speed that made the Prometheus formidable; it was the ship's stealth-like radar signature. It turned it into a phantom, unseen and unheard. Its long bow resembled the serrated blade of a spear, which swelled mid-ship to form a square enclosure housing the crew and laboratory facilities.

This floating enigma was home to a staff of fifty naval personnel complemented by twenty scientists, each of whom had signed on for a two-year stint. The scientific team, headed by Dr. Wei Hai Zhao, was divided into two functional areas: a Biolevel-IV (BL-IV) lab on the ship's starboard side, and, on the port side, the immense data-processing systems needed to power the team's research.

Due to the extraordinarily sensitive nature of the work, which included research into novel pathogens, the ship remained far from populated areas. Thanks to an on-board greenhouse, the Prometheus was virtually self-sufficient. When additional supplies were needed, autonomous naval vessels ferried them under the cover of night.

It was a quiet, moonlit night, just shy of 0:00 hours, when Wei Hai Zhao slipped quietly out of his cabin. The bulk of the ship's crew were fast asleep, allowing Zhao to move unseen through the empty corridors. His soft-soled shoes made no sound as he descended a flight of stairs, then negotiated the long hallway leading to the Biolevel-IV laboratory. He had less than fifteen minutes to complete his mission before a bell would chime signifying the end of a shift. Then there would be people everywhere and he would be seen.

When Zhao reached the entrance to the lab, he swiped his ID card, then picked up a phone connecting him with Security. It was the one human contact that was unavoidable. A video camera transmitted his image.

"You're working late, Doctor," the MP said. It was more a statement than a question. As chief scientist and senior molecular biologist, Zhao managed all projects related to novel organisms, in addition to his supervisory responsibilities. He had unrestricted access to every area of the laboratory.

"Just checking on my work. I'll only be a minute." As he explained himself, the electronic bolt was retracted, and Zhao nodded in thanks and hung up the phone.

Entering an airlock, he donned a bioprotective suit complete with an independent air supply that provided absolute isolation from the pathogenic environment he was about to enter.

The laboratory was dark; the only illumination came from the glowing LEDs on equipment used to monitor the status of various life forms. He flipped on the master light switch, instantly bathing the lab in the eerie green glow of fluorescent lights. He was grateful there were no cameras in the lab to transmit or record the clandestine work he and his team did there.

Zhao walked over to a small stainless steel refrigeration unit and carefully opened the door. In it, there were racks upon racks of glass vials, each bearing a barcode identifying the contents. He reached down and removed a rack from the lower shelf and set it gently on a lab table. He extracted a single vial containing approximately ten milliliters of a milky-looking suspension, which he placed in a small padded pouch. He returned the rack to its home and proceeded through the decontamination unit.

"Turn off the lights," he muttered to himself, taking a quick look around the lab to make certain he was leaving no trace of his presence.

Once in decontamination, he removed the padded container from his pocket and held it carefully, his eyes tightly shut, as powerful ultraviolet light washed over him. When the process was completed, he stepped into the airlock and removed the bioprotective suit. Before re-entering the security camera's range, he slipped the container under the waistband of his pants.

As Zhao exited, the guard called out to him via a speaker, "Have a good evening, Doctor."

"Thank you. You, too," he answered, before disappearing into the night.

The next morning, Zhao rose with the morning sun. It was 06:00, and an angry, orange sky transformed the surrounding sea into a fiery cauldron. A fire within Zhao raged as well. Nothing could dull the intensity of his determination. He had a job to do, one he had spent a lifetime preparing for, and he was about to take the first step. He watched through the porthole in his cabin as the color slowly faded as the sun climbed into the sky.

After dressing, he opened the top drawer of his built-in wardrobe and carefully removed the vial of liquid he had appropriated from the lab the night before. He held it up to the light, turning it between his fingers as he contemplated its remarkable destructive power. He smiled as he slipped the vial into his left trouser pocket and walked out the door.

Zhao descended the same flight of stairs he'd taken the previous evening. But, as he went below deck, he did not stop at the first level. Rather, he continued down two levels to engineering.

"Good morning, Sir," a sailor greeted Zhao as he approached the restricted area. He pointed at the scientist's lanyard. "You know the drill, Doctor. I need to scan your ID."

Zhao held it up long enough for the guard to read the barcode with a handheld scanner. After a second, a green light flashed up, clearing him.

"If I may ask, Doctor, what is the purpose of your visit to engineering?"

"The water in my cabin has a funny taste. When was the water purification system last checked?" he asked with an air of authority. The water on the Prometheus was provided by a state-of-the-art desalination unit.

The guard walked over and removed a clipboard hanging from a hook on the wall. "Two days ago, Sir. It's not due to be checked again until Wednesday."

"Well, I'm sure it's nothing, but if you don't mind, I'd rather not wait until Wednesday. I can take a sample up to the lab and check it now. We don't want anyone getting sick."

"Of course not, Sir."

"I'll have them run a quick screen on it." He waited for permission to move on.

The guard stood aside. "You will let me know if the lab finds anything?"

"Of course. Thank you, Bowman Taylor."

Zhao walked the length of a corridor until he reached the door marked "Desalination System." Opening it, he was relieved to find the room empty. He scanned the ceiling from corner to corner, looking for surveillance cameras, but failed to detect any.

Confident no one was watching, he removed a pair of thin, latex surgical gloves from his right pants pocket and fitted them snugly over his hands. Next, he extracted the vial from his left pocket while, with the other hand, he opened the access door to the system. He peered into the still, cavernous pool. It was the only source of drinking water aboard the Prometheus.

Zhao lowered the vial until its lip hovered mere inches above the surface of the water. Then he upended the vial and poured the contents into the reservoir. It took only seconds to disappear.

CHAPTER 4

A Punishing Blow

"THIRTY SECONDS TO DETONATION, Mr. President," General Sanford called out as a count-down timer was superimposed over the satellite image on the monitors. "The screens will go off-line the instant of detonation," he explained. "We should regain our feed a few seconds after the blast."

No one moved. The only sounds breaking the silence were the mechanical clicks of the countdown clock and the hushed breaths of those watching.

When the clock reached zero, the monitors went white as they lost the signal. After what seemed like an eternity, a new image began to take shape, pixel by pixel. General Sanford had been right. Through the dense smoke and expanding fireball, Conner could make out an immense crater where there had once been a missile silo.

"That's one threat you will never have to worry about again, Sir," Sanford commented.

"Let's hope we are equally successful with the next shot, General," Conner replied. "How close is the Trident to its target?"

"General Hawkins, switch the input to the satellite feed tracking the SLBM, and give us a time to detonation," Sanford ordered.

The tight arc of the Trident II appeared on the screen. From its launch point somewhere in the Persian Gulf, it was plummeting towards Zahedan at more than five miles per second.

"Forty-one seconds, Mr. President," the General advised.

Conner's arms were folded tightly against his chest. He felt no remorse for his actions. He wasn't murdering innocent civilians. He was putting down a pack of rabid dogs. Conner knew that his actions were morally defensible. However, had the target been a direct hit on Zahedan, rather than on the desert west of it, an estimated 500,000 Iranians would have been incinerated, and the international outcry would have been instantaneous and deafening.

"Ten seconds to impact," Hawkins advised.

Once again, the monitors lost their signal before slowly coming back to life. But unlike the smaller detonation in Chabahar, a massive, roiling fireball soon filled the screen, followed by the formation of a towering mushroom cloud that was already stretching towards the upper limits of the stratosphere.

It was as if the gates of hell had opened and destroyed everything in sight, Conner thought in wonder.

As the mushroom cloud passed 20,000 feet, the ground destruction became apparent. Even the battled-hardened generals were awed by the force of the explosion. It was equivalent to 30 Hiroshima bombs.

No one spoke until Conner asked, "Could there be survivors?" directing the question to General Sanford.

"No, Sir. However, if someone miraculously survived the blast, they would die from the radiation. That you can count on."

"And a collateral damage assessment, General?"

"That will take some time, Mr. President, but based upon the intelligence estimates we are receiving at this moment, the numbers will be extremely low. The weather remains stable, so there's little risk of a more broadly dispersed fallout plume."

"That's good," Conner sighed. Turning to the broader group, he added, "I hope that we never again face a threat as terrible as what we faced today. I'm grateful to each of you for the role you played in protecting this great nation of ours. I've been informed that we are going to be confined here for some time; long enough to verify that any residual radiation is below the threshold to harm us. I will be meeting with a number of you to discuss what we have learned from this experience. But, for now, I suggest you go and relax and perhaps offer one more prayer of thanks for today's outcome."

Little did Conner realize that another storm was brewing on the not-so-distant horizon.

CHAPTER 5

Blurred Vision

Jane Graham raised her head from the binocular microscope and blinked repeatedly in an effort to focus her eyes. She'd been peering into the device for hours without a break, and her body was finally rebelling.

It's just fatigue, she told herself, as she began to look around the room, shifting her gaze from nearby objects to more distant ones in an effort to validate her hypothesis.

"Are you alright, Dr. Graham?" asked an observant colleague working at an adjacent lab table.

"Yes, of course." She turned towards the woman, forcing a smile. "Just a little eye strain. But thanks for asking."

But things weren't alright. Not only was she experiencing a significant decline in visual acuity, but suddenly objects appeared to be duplicated and overlapping.

"My God, I'm having double-vision," she murmured with mounting alarm. Dark thoughts began to swirl in her normally calm mind. Her chest heaved as she fought against a sudden wave of anxiety that robbed her lungs of air. "Surely not," she told herself, in an effort to squelch the notion that she might somehow be contaminated with a biologic agent.

Not wanting to further alarm her colleague, the stalwart microbiologist forced another smile. Then, quietly, she exited the lab and proceeded through decontamination. She removed her bioprotective gear and steadied herself before moving towards her cabin. With each passing minute, she felt more symptomatic.

As she struggled to push back her fear, the former USAMRID scientist began to refine her hypothesis regarding the nature of her symptoms. She could be experiencing anything from an aneurysm to a transient ischemic event. None of the options heralded a positive outcome.

Then an even more insidious thought broke through her consciousness.

She prayed that a self-examination would relieve her mounting anxiety and lead to less devastating conclusions.

Graham walked straight into her bathroom until her body was squarely aligned with the framed mirror over the sink. With her gray hair pulled back in a tight bun and no make-up, the neurological deficits were plain to see. She covered her gaping mouth with her hand, terrified by the bilateral weakness evident in her facial muscles and drooping eyelids. She tried to swallow, but her mouth was as dry as cotton. But what was most ominous was that something was robbing her of breath.

"It's just anxiety," she repeated over and over like a mantra, but it wasn't very convincing even to herself. As someone who possessed an encyclopedic knowledge of micro-organisms, it didn't take her long to make sense of her symptoms. They read like a textbook definition of botulinum poisoning. But how on earth was that possible, she wondered.

If true, it would mean that she been exposed to the toxin excreted by the bacterium *clostridium botulinum*, a toxin so deadly that as little as 75 billionths of a gram could prove fatal.

Graham knew there were vials of the toxin stored in the lab, but she had no clue how she could have possibly ingested it. She was meticulous in her decontamination procedures and had no memory of having worked with the bio-agent in recent days.

For the moment, the source of the exposure would have to be secondary to her survival. With her symptoms progressing, Graham knew she had to summon every fiber of inner strength in an effort to preserve her life. But with no known anti-toxin for the particular strain of botulinum found in the lab, her options seemed almost non-existent. Her only hope might be a mechanical ventilator which could take over for her soon-to-be paralyzed diaphragm.

Leaving her cabin, she walked haltingly towards the bridge, stopping every few feet in an effort to catch her breath. What normally would have taken a matter of minutes seemed to take an eternity. As she passed crew members, she noticed that they, too, appeared to be exhibiting varying degrees of neurotoxic poisoning.

Always the scientist, Graham attributed the variation in intensity of their symptoms to the amount of botulinum they presumably had ingested, as well as the time that had elapsed since ingestion. She wondered what could have created this calamity.

"This is an unexpected pleasure," Captain Seward struggled to smile as he greeted Graham.

"Can we talk in private, Captain?" her words were slightly slurred.

"Of course." Seward gestured towards a small conference room used for executive briefings.

As she stepped forward, Graham suddenly collapsed into a chair, causing Seward to lurch in an effort to break her fall.

Alarmed, he asked, "Are you alright?"

Eyes closed, she muttered, "No, I'm not alright." She sat motionless for a few seconds before slowly opening her eyes and staring at the Captain, trying to bring his image into focus.

"I'll be okay," she lied. "But tell me how you're feeling, Captain."

"That's a strange question to be asking me. I'm far more concerned about you at the moment."

"There's a reason I'm asking. I need to know if you're having any visual difficulties or trouble breathing."

The implications of Graham's questions were not lost on the Captain, who hesitated before responding.

"Yes. But I assumed it's nothing. Just some respiratory virus."

Graham lowered her gaze. A single tear coalesced in the corner of her eye, as an image of her family popped into her mind. The thought of not seeing them again was devastating. She'd missed so many life events, always convincing herself that duty came before family. She'd skipped her nieces' and nephews' graduations, was MIA when her mother passed away, and delegated caring for her aging father to a younger brother. Guilt weighed heavily on her.

"What has you so upset, Jane?" the captain asked, dropping the formalities. "I've never seen you like this."

"I've been experiencing a number of symptoms that don't correlate with a viral infection. Some of my symptoms are neurologic and may be attributable to a toxin."

"Remember, I'm not one of your scientists. What exactly are you saying?"

"I'm saying that the crew may have been exposed to high levels of botulinum toxin. If I'm right, we're going to be knee-deep in casualties, if not fatalities."

"Who else knows about this?"

"No one. You're the first person I've spoken with. But if my colleagues in the lab have been exposed, it won't be long before they reach the same conclusion."

"Isn't there a vaccine onboard?"

"There is no vaccine for the variant of the toxin housed in the lab," she said in a defeated tone.

"What about an anti-toxin or an antibiotic?"

"No, only mechanical ventilation can counter the respiratory paralysis. That sometimes forestalls death long enough for a victim's body to recover."

She hesitated, afraid to ask the next question. "How many vents do we have in sick bay?"

"One."

"One!" she exclaimed in shock. "No, please tell me there are more in storage. With all of the personal protective equipment aboard this ship, there's only one respirator?"

"I'm afraid so," Seward responded.

"Then, in all likelihood, the Prometheus will be our tomb."

"It can't possibly be that bad, Jane," he said, but she took no reassurance from his words.

She pulled a tissue from her pocket, dabbing at her eyes. You've got to keep it together, she told herself, fighting the emotions that overwhelmed her.

"How in the hell did this happen, Jane?"

"I don't know. But I'm betting someone was doing his or her very best to kill us."

CHAPTER 6

The Rodeo

THE LAYOUT OF THE SUBTERRANEAN BUNKER reminded Liz of an ant colony, complete with an elaborate network of passageways that linked the various functional areas within the shelter. At the center were operational command, communications, and security functions. From there, spokes radiated outward to form a ring of pods housing medical and recreational facilities, living quarters, food service, and even a school for the occupants' children.

This hub and spoke design incorporated tall, wide corridors constructed of gray sheetrock, the monotony of which was broken by vibrant backlit images of nature. Liz paused in front of a photograph of El Capitan, studying it while listening to the subtle meditation music playing in the background.

"I know what this reminds me of," she said. "The tunnel at O'Hare. All we need is a moving sidewalk."

"Sarcasm so noted," Hart responded.

"Come on, who are they trying to fool with this crap?" she said pointing to an image of Washington awash in cherry blossoms.

"We dodged a bullet, Liz."

"That's an interesting phrase for you to use."

"I would have thought you'd be grateful that someone tried to instill a little brightness into what could easily have been a drab, post-apocalyptic world," Hart responded. "Remember, Darling, this place was not designed for weekend getaways. It was designed to serve as the semi-permanent living quarters for those individuals and their families deemed vital to the survival of our nation. All while the air above remained too poisonous to breathe."

"Yah, yah, yah. You sound like you're reading from a government travel brochure. Now tell me honestly, doesn't this place get to you?"

"What do you mean?"

"I mean being captive in this contrived world, ten stories underground, where even the transition from day to night is simulated by computer."

Pointing once more to the photograph, she added, "I don't care how high the ceilings are or how captivating the photographs, it feels like the walls are beginning to close in."

"Try spending three months at sea submerged in a submarine." Hart chuckled at the thought of his wife aboard a Trident. "This is heaven by comparison."

"I'll take your word on it."

"I think a workout will do us both good," Hart said, as they arrived at their destination. He reached for the glass door of the athletic facility, opening it as Liz stood in awe.

The 60,000-square-foot gymnasium was unlike anything she had ever seen. Not only was there every imaginable type of exercise equipment, there was also indoor tennis, an Olympic-length pool, aerobic studios, and even a computer-simulated driving range.

"Just wait until you see the locker room," Hart said. He had toured the facility once shortly after its renovation several years before. He gestured to a door marked 'Women's Spa.' "There should be an attendant in there to help you. I'll see you on the treadmills in a minute."

Liz's jaw dropped as she walked into the high-end spa. The lockers were mahogany and the fixtures granite. "Our taxpayer dollars at work," she thought, not noticing the female attendant advancing to greet her.

"You must be Mrs. Hart," the attendant said with a smile that quickly faded as Liz corrected her. "Actually, I'd prefer *Dr. Wilkins*."

The attendant lowered her gaze. "My apologies, Dr. Wilkins. I just wanted to welcome you and say that I'm at your service if you need anything."

Suddenly aware of how abrupt she must have sounded, Liz softened her tone. "I'm so sorry. Please call me Liz. I'm afraid that being down here is affecting me more than I realized."

"I understand, Ma'am. Being ten stories underground does take some getting used to. Would you like me to arrange for a massage? It can be for two if you would like to include the Commander."

"Thank you, that's very kind. I'll let you know. But right now, I just need to find a locker, and then the treadmills. Maybe after a good workout I won't feel quite so confined."

Hart had already broken a sweat by the time Liz stepped onto an adjacent machine. She glanced over at the LED display indicating his speed and incline. Her husband was an animal, running at a pace approaching 10 miles per hour on a seven percent grade. She wondered how that was possible after having his lung function cut in half by a .50 caliber bullet.

"My God, you need to slow down, Cowboy! You're going to have an MI!"

"Am I that feeble, Darling?" he responded, only half out of breath. "If so, maybe you ought to have this old gray-muzzled dog put down."

"Very funny. I didn't mean that. I just don't know how you can keep up that pace after being wounded. You're lucky to be alive."

"It's all in here." He prodded his skull. ""It's not the body that limits us, it's the mind. That was drummed into me during SEAL training. It was the only way to survive."

"So, what's going on in that mind of yours right now, John?"

He hesitated before responding. "I was remembering what it felt like to run cross-country in high school, pushing myself as hard as I could in an effort to clear my head. It was a dark time, Liz. A very, dark time."

"You mean in the years following Matthew's death?" Liz said sympathetically. Matthew was Hart's younger brother who had tragically drowned in a pond on their Montana ranch. It was an event that forever changed Hart's life: a moment when he had been fully responsible for his 7-year-old brother but became distracted by the opportunity to take a shot at a prairie dog. He'd left Matthew alone just long enough for the boy to slip off a dock and fall into the brackish water. When Hart returned minutes later, Matthew was nowhere to be seen.

Hart increased the speed of the machine, pushing himself even harder. "I really don't want to talk about it, Liz," he said, keeping his eyes on his feet and refusing to meet her gaze.

"It wasn't your fault, John. It was an accident. Besides, you were a child yourself."

"How can you say it wasn't my fault? Don't you think that Matt would still be here if I hadn't left him alone?" His tone was now laced with anger. "My parents certainly thought so, and they never let me forget it."

"And that was unspeakably cruel of them, John." Tears were now streaming down her face as she thought about the burden of guilt her husband's parents had placed on his shoulders. A burden he would carry for the rest of his life.

"You loved your brother, and I know you would do anything in the world to bring him back."

"You're right. I would do anything." Hart nodded in acknowledgment, then slowed his treadmill long enough to reach over and touch his wife. "It's my burden to bear. We all have something, Liz."

"I just wish I could lighten your load, sometimes. Maybe it would help to talk more about our families. I think there are some demons, on both sides, that need to be exorcised."

"Okay, Dr. Freud, but from where I stand there are no demons, beyond Matt."

"What about Cory?" she asked. Hart's older brother had died in the Twin Towers.

A look of exasperation flooded his face. "Don't go there, Liz. You've stirred the pot enough for today."

"But you couldn't have helped him, John. Cory, along with three thousand other innocent victims, was murdered by Al Qaeda. You've got to accept the fact that some things are simply beyond your control."

"Like your willingness to respect my boundaries? I told you, I didn't want to go there."

She put a finger to her lips, kissed it, then touched it to his cheek. "You're right, I'm sorry. Is my apology accepted?"

"Sure," he said unconvincingly, then resumed his run in silence.

After 45 minutes, Hart slowed the treadmill to a crawl and allowed five minutes to cool down. Liz followed suit.

"Why don't we go back to our room and take a shower?" she suggested. "Then I'll give you a quick check-up and make sure everything else is working. That's assuming you really have forgiven me."

"I don't hold on to things, Liz."

"Oh my God. I can't believe you really said that, but I'm going to take you at your word. Are you up for a little rodeo? Maybe some calf roping?" Liz asked with a beguiling smile.

"You know I'm not into bondage, Darling."

"Oh, you're no fun. Now I suggest you move that butt of yours. This girl has plans for you."

✲

Liz watched her husband step out of the steaming shower and dry himself. At 6'4" and two hundred fifty pounds, the Navy SEAL was a unique specimen. His body formed an inverted pyramid with a small waist giving rise to massive shoulders. Hart's neck measured more than twenty inches in circumference and led to a strong, handsome face with intense brown eyes. It was those eyes, those brooding, soulful eyes, that had won her heart.

He walked out of the bathroom and into the bedroom, his hair still wet and a towel wrapped tightly around his chiseled abs.

Liz was waiting for him, lying seductively on the bed wearing a black lace negligee. It left just enough to his imagination.

She stood up, slipped the spaghetti straps off her shoulders, and let the wispy garment drop to the floor. All that remained was the tiniest pair of panties Hart had ever seen. He could feel his heart pounding in his chest, its pace quickening as he imagined what it would feel like to be inside of her.

"You look down-right dumbstruck, Commander," she whispered seductively. "I didn't mean to throw you a curve."

"I guess I just didn't expect you to look so sexy a hundred feet underground during a nuclear attack," he marveled.

"Well, I told that Secret Service agent I wasn't leaving the condo until I had the bare essentials, particularly since it might be our last night together.

"So, are you just going to stand there in awe, or are you going to join me?"

Hart walked eagerly over to her, but Liz raised an outstretched arm to stop him.

"You sure you still have the energy after that long workout?" she teased her husband.

"You can let me know in an hour or two," he responded, scooping her up in his arms and pulling her into a long, deep kiss. Sweaty and panting, they separated just long enough to catch their breaths. As their lips touched again,

Liz reached for the towel still surrounding her husband's waist. She tugged it free and it fell to the floor. She ran her hand over her husband's muscular butt before rolling onto her side.

Picking up on the cue, John began to caress her long, shapely back. His hands were like magic, working every muscle before finding their way down to her waist. His right hand followed the deep crease in her bottom, as if it was a roadmap to even greater pleasure, eliciting a soft groan.

After a few minutes, Liz turned so she was flat on her back. John's hands moved to her breasts while Liz's hand moved down to his groin. She began touching him softly.

Now it was Hart who was moaning, louder and louder.

"No, not yet, Cowboy. I want you inside of me," she said as she released her grip and invited him to become part of her.

He started out slow and gentle, but that didn't last. Before long, it was a frenetic dash to the finish. With one last, loud groan, John's body tensed, then went slack.

The couple basked in the calm afterglow that followed. John held his wife tightly, Liz's back fitting like a puzzle piece against the front of his body. After a moment, Liz craned her neck to look at her husband.

"How long do you think we'll be stuck down here?"

"Long enough for another rodeo, I hope," Hart muttered with a grin.

"Seriously, John."

"Seriously, Elizabeth."

She hit him with a pillow. "Can I have a straight answer?"

"We should know something in the morning. My guess is the president will clear us to go topside sooner rather than later. What would you like to do tonight?"

"I was thinking maybe a movie. I hear they have a pretty extensive library of DVDs."

"Sure. How about something light?"

"Like *When Harry Met Sally*?" Liz cooed. It was her favorite movie of all time. "What were you thinking?"

"*Dr. Strangelove*," Hart responded.

Eight thousand miles away, the crew of the Prometheus were dropping like flies from the devastating effects of botulinum toxin. Jane Graham was using every bit of her remaining strength to identify the source of the exposure. It would be her final act of duty.

CHAPTER 7

No Mercy for the Living

EACH STEP OF THE JOURNEY from the bridge back to the lab was slow and laborious, as Jane Graham struggled for breath. "What's the point in suiting up?" she asked herself, as she entered the decon unit. But she wasn't yet willing to acknowledge defeat, and she donned her bioprotective suit anyway,

She opened the airlock into the BL-IV lab and was greeted by an overwhelming scene of panic. Her normally calm and quiet lab was now in chaos. Several people were sprawled on the floor. Others were doubled over in pain. Some were crying out for help.

She stood frozen in her tracks, unable to process what she was witnessing.

Carole Hubbard moved swiftly over to her. "Are you okay, Jane?" Hubbard asked.

Graham simply stared back at her.

Taking hold of Jane's shoulders, Hubbard shook her gently. "We've got people dying," she said, trying to break through to her colleague.

Finally, Graham's eyes came back into focus.

"It looks suspiciously like botulinum," Hubbard went on, "but we can't imagine how something like that would happen."

Graham nodded in acknowledgement, then began to look around the room. At least a dozen of her colleagues were slumped over in their chairs. Even through their bio-protective face-shields, she could see the telltale drooping of the victims' facial muscles. Clustered to one side were a handful of researchers, who moved en masse to talk to Graham and Hubbard.

"Where is Dr. Zhao?" Graham asked with urgency.

Hubbard spoke for the group. "He left some time ago. He said he wasn't feeling well and was going to his cabin to lie down."

"Carole, are you still logged onto the system?"

"Yes, though it's about to log me off."

"Pull up the barcode identifying the vial of botulinum-H, please."

"Of course," Hubbard replied as she placed her hands on the keyboard and began to type. "But why, if I may ask?"

"I'll explain in a minute."

"0638921. Do you want me to write it down?"

"No," Graham said as she moved towards the refrigeration unit where bio-active material was stored. The toxins were in sealed vials and arranged sequentially by number. Rotating one of the vials, she read its code: 0638920. Next to it: 0638922. She double-checked before turning back to her colleagues.

"We have a problem."

"No shit, Dr. Graham," the words came from Martin Houser, a mercurial scientist and resident pessimist.

Graham ignored him. "Look around," she said with a sweeping gesture. "Everyone is displaying similar symptoms: drooping facial muscles, difficulty breathing, but with no overt sign of infection. What does that tell you?"

"Dr. Hubbard already identified the symptoms as botulinum poisoning. None of us disagree with that assessment. So, rather than play twenty questions, Dr. Graham, why don't you tell us what we are going to do?" Houser responded.

Jane could feel the vitriol rise in her gut, but now was not the time to let this asshole have it.

"Dr. Hubbard is correct, the symptoms are unmistakable," she stated definitively, then paused. "And a vial of toxin is missing from our inventory."

"The vial of Botulinum-H?" Hubbard asked.

"Yes," Graham responded.

"So, we're going to die; is that what you're saying?" Houser growled.

"Thank you for that constructive observation, Dr. Houser. Now if I can make a recommendation, why don't you keep your mouth shut while the rest of us try to deal with this emergency?"

Houser shut his mouth with a snap.

"I'm not sure how you're connecting the poisoning with the missing vial," Hubbard said. "Are you suggesting that this was a deliberate act of sabotage? If so, by whom and why?"

"I don't have the answer to who or why. Only how. The only viable scenario I can think of is that it was a purposeful act of poisoning. I know that doesn't help us much."

"Does the captain know?" The question came from Buck McMasters, the lab's security officer.

"Yes, I told him shortly after I became symptomatic. He's showing symptoms as well, though not as acute. He said he would report our situation to Naval Command once we were in a position to apprise them of our planned response."

"Planned response?" barked Houser who, it seems, couldn't keep his mouth shut any longer. "The only thing you should be planning is your funeral. I suggest you take any remaining time and write your own obituaries."

"Lieutenant McMasters, remove Dr. Houser from the lab and see to it that he is confined to his quarters."

'I'd be delighted to," said McMasters, gripping hold of the now ranting scientist's arm in a vise-like grip and pulling him towards the airlock.

When a modicum of peace had returned to the lab, Graham spoke earnestly to her colleagues. "I'm afraid I can't see a way out of this. But maybe, together, we can think of a solution that has so far eluded me."

But there were no solutions to be had. As the minutes ticked by, Graham and her colleagues became progressively more ill.

It wasn't long before the botulinum toxin brought everyone to their knees, including Jane Graham. She never made it back to the bridge to confer with the captain. Graham died in the lab with her colleagues, slumped over in her chair like a lost raggedy doll.

Back in his cabin and without a clear path of action, Seward elected to ride out the storm as long as possible before calling in the cavalry. He knew there was a standing order to scuttle the ship in the event of any type of catastrophic event; anything that might threaten to reveal the secrets aboard the Prometheus. But the thought of destroying his ship gnawed at him. So he decided to wait, wait until he could wait no more.

CHAPTER 8

Retribution

THE SHIP'S SICK BAY, a narrow room lined with six gurneys separated by flimsy curtains, was soon filled to capacity. Within hours, it was overflowing. Those individuals experiencing a more delayed onset were forced to seek solace in their bunks. It would become their last resting place. Most would die within twenty-four hours of falling ill.

Zhao, who had feigned illness, was safely ensconced in his cabin, armed with a sufficient supply of untainted water to last several days. He listened to the agonized groans of his colleagues, their unanswered pleas for help reverberating through the walls. It would be only a matter of time before their bodies began an irreversible shutdown, as the toxin began to paralyze the muscles in their diaphragm and pharynx. When that happened, they would all slowly asphyxiate.

Unfazed, Zhao reclined in his bunk, his head propped up by a stack of pillows and a smirk upon his lips. Dangling from his hand was a small gold locket. It was an heirloom from his mother and a reminder of his cause.

He carefully pressed his fingernail against a nearly invisible crease in the metal, opening the locket and revealing a tiny sepia-toned photograph of a man in uniform. It was his grandfather, Wei, after whom he'd been named. The photo had been taken at the time of his induction into the Chinese Army and showed a man standing tall and proud, blissfully unaware of his fate.

Six months later, his grandfather was captured by the Japanese in Manchuria and imprisoned in a camp under the leadership of General Shirō Ishii, commander of Unit 731 of the Japanese Imperial Army.

Zhao remembered his grandfather's nightmarish stories of human experimentation in which men were tied to posts as explosives laced with a cornucopia of bacteria were detonated in close proximity. The shrapnel would pierce the POWs' legs and buttocks like butter, depositing pathogens deep within their wounds. Within days, the blockhouses were rife with the overpowering stench of wounds festering with gas gangrene, anthrax, and glanders. The prisoners were forced to endure raging infections until they begged for a merciful end to their suffering. In response, Ishii ordered his staff to perform live vivisections on hundreds of men. Their screams echoed through the camp, a sound his grandfather could never exorcise from his mind.

Yet Wei had somehow been spared this horror. "It would have been better to die," his grandfather would often say later, perhaps out of survivor's guilt.

Like his medical counterpart at Auschwitz, Joseph Mengele, Ishii methodically collected reams of data to power Japan's burgeoning biological warfare division, information that proved to have tremendous value. With it, Ishii negotiated a grant of full immunity from the

United States government, which was in the early stages of developing its own bio-warfare capabilities.

Though more than seventy-five years had passed since Ishii's exoneration, the injustice suffered by his grandfather and the Chinese people was front and center in Zhao's mind. There was a tremendous debt to be paid by the United States for its complicity in sparing Ishii from justice, and Zhao planned to help collect it. He revered his grandfather, and he knew how proud the man would be of his grandson at this moment.

Zhao had taken the first step—more like a giant leap—towards ensuring China's preeminent role in controlling the biological destiny of man. Whatever secrets the Prometheus held would soon be within his grasp. So, too, would be one of the most dangerous biological weapons ever concocted. China would not fall victim to the West or any other nation. It would soon ascend to its rightful place as the most powerful nation on earth.

With a cold smile, Zhao snapped the locket shut.

It took less than two days for the sounds of the dying to give way to silence. Zhao slowly opened the door to his cabin, peering left and right, before stepping out. Tucked into his boot was a thin titanium stiletto. He began walking cautiously towards the bridge, stopping every few steps to listen for evidence of survivors.

As he entered the bridge, the communications room was to his immediate left, its heavy metal door open. Captain Seward was seated with his back to Zhao, oblivious to his presence.

Zhao moved with the grace of a jaguar stalking its prey as he inched towards the captain. Seward's eyes were trained on a computer screen. Clearly impaired by the botulinum, Seward seemed to be struggling to complete a transmission.

Just as the captain hit send, Zhao pressed a button on the handle of the stiletto, causing the razor-sharp blade to lock into position with an audible click. The captain turned in the direction of the noise.

"What are you doing here?" the words slurred from his mouth as he struggled to stand.

Without answering, Zhao grasped the muscular man by his hair, pulled his head back until his neck was taut, then slid the blade across the captain's throat. With a gurgling scream, the captain slithered to the floor. He lay there, blood pumping from the wound.

Zhao shoved the captain's body out of the way and took a seat facing the large computer monitor. With two clicks, he was able to bring up Seward's message. It was directed to Naval Intelligence:

> *Ship appears to be contaminated with a toxin thought to be botulinum of unknown origin. The crew has succumbed to the agent. I am the last survivor. Unclear whether it was a deliberate act of sabotage or inadvertent contamination from the lab, though sabotage appears most plausible. Suggest immediate intervention to preserve data or scuttle ship. Please advise.*

Zhao berated himself for not dealing with the captain sooner. A distress call to the U.S. Navy was the last thing he needed. Though he was eager to get to the lab, Zhao knew that he first had to notify his handlers that his mission had been a success and the Prometheus had been taken over.

He sent a coded message that began with the ship's coordinates and concluded with the need for rapid intervention in order to download petabytes of data from the ship's information repository before the Americans sank her.

He stepped over the growing pool of blood pulsing from Seward's neck and headed for the lab. Within minutes, he was in the decontamination unit donning a protective suit. Once fully isolated from the external environment, he opened the airlock and prepared to enter a stark world where the only surviving organisms were in refrigerated storage.

He moved towards a group of storage vessels that had been cooled to -195 degrees Celsius by liquid nitrogen. They were home to the Prometheus's most lethal microorganisms: chimeras. These novel life forms resulted from a devil's brew of genetic material recombined using synthetic biology.

Chimeras were Zhao's passion and had been the focus of his research since joining the staff of the Prometheus. He took great pride in having birthed a new virus formed by pairing critical genetic sequences from the rabies virus with the SARS genome. The result was a devastating neurological killer that was transmissible by air and thus highly infectious. Until today, it had been his proudest accomplishment.

After removing a half dozen vials, he stopped and studied the sample culture in his gloved hand. As he rotated the tube between his thumb and index finger, it slipped from his grip. He watched in disbelief as it dropped to the ship's steel floor, shattering into tiny bits.

Horrified by his carelessness, Zhao instinctively began to pick up the shards of glass. He stopped dead when he heard the ominous hiss of air escaping from his pressurized bioprotective suit. The sound was coming from a paper-thin slice that traversed one gloved finger. A wave of indescribable terror swept over him. He felt faint and steadied himself against the edge of a lab table. "Breathe," he coached himself. "There's no blood," he said, trying to reassure himself. But he knew better.

His orders had been clear: remove the chimeras, as well as the hemorrhagic fevers, then abandon ship, leaving the critical job of data retrieval to his compatriots. Every instinct urged him to abandon the viruses and head straight into decontamination. But that wasn't an option. So, exercising as much caution as possible, he secured the additional material before entering the airlock.

After being thoroughly doused with a potent disinfectant, Zhao closed his eyes as intense ultraviolet radiation flooded the surface of his bioprotective suit. Only then could he remove it and examine his finger. An almost imperceptible red line ran perpendicularly across his finger.

"Maybe I'll get lucky," he prayed as he exited the lab on his way to the bridge.

Re-entering the communications room, Zhao studied the stark white corpse in front of him. As if it was all a drama, he spoke to the corpse, quoting an apropos admonition from Sun Tzu: "The opportunity to secure ourselves against defeat lies in our own hands, but the opportunity of defeating the enemy is provided by the enemy himself."

Zhao paused, then added, "Retribution, Captain Seward, sweet retribution." He kicked Seward's body savagely before turning his attention to the computer monitor. He was hoping for a reply to his earlier transmission, but there was no response.

There was, however, a message to Seward from Naval Command indicating that a rapid-response team was en route from Guam.

"An F-18 could be here in minutes," Zhao admonished himself, "and probably with orders to scuttle the ship." To remain onboard would not merely be futile, it would be foolhardy. Zhao took one final look at the Captain, then left the bridge and walked mid-ship to where a cluster of lifeboats hung suspended, ready for deployment.

CHAPTER 9

Amazing Grace

"Can you give it a rest, Sweetheart?" Mary Conner asked her husband, whose constant pacing was wearing on her nerves. "Even the threat of nuclear annihilation didn't agitate you as much as this 7:00 a.m. briefing."

"I'm not agitated, Mary. I just want to get top-side and back to work. I damn well better hear the words 'all-clear' this morning."

"Or what, Jonathan? You'll pace some more? Be grateful there is still a top-side to return to, and be mindful that your staff are doing their jobs."

"Point taken," he said, as he stopped moving and settled into a chair near the foyer. No sooner had he exhaled, letting the tension flow out of his body, than there was a knock on the door. As Conner opened it, a Marine Colonel saluted.

"Good morning, Mr. President. I'm here to escort you to the situation room. If you'd follow me, please."

Conner couldn't fathom the need for a military escort one hundred feet underground in the world's most secure facility. It wasn't as if there were terrorists lurking around every corner or even an irate Republican ready to even a score. But the colonel was simply honoring protocol, so the president followed him dutifully.

"Good morning, Mr. President," DNI Arch Stinson said, acknowledging Conner's arrival. "I believe everyone is present. With your permission, I'd like to proceed with our assessment."

Conner scanned the faces in the room, taking his own attendance. Satisfied, he nodded. "By all means, and I hope you have some good news for us, Arch. I'm starting to get a little claustrophobic."

"You know we have medication for that, Sir," Stinson offered, eliciting an exaggerated eye-roll and headshake from the president. Shifting gears, he pulled up the first PowerPoint slide.

"We have been monitoring atmospheric and ground-level radiation using both land-based sensors and aerial reconnaissance ever since the missile was destroyed. It appears that our interceptors performed admirably. They vaporized the incoming warhead."

"By *vaporized*, do you mean that there are no residual traces of radiation?" the president asked incredulously.

"I wouldn't go that far, Mr. President. The radiation signature for Plutonium 239 is clearly evident at higher altitudes, generally above 30,000 feet. The good news, however, is that prevailing winds are out of the west, and they're carrying the last vestiges of fallout towards the sea." As he spoke, Stinson brought up a weather map depicting the flow of air currents over Washington, followed by a slide simulating the debris trail moving off-shore.

"We've redirected all flights that were on a trajectory to enter the debris field. That area will remain closed to air traffic for the next forty-eight to seventy-two hours. After that, it should be smooth sailing."

"If this stuff is going to be dumped in the ocean, don't we risk contamination of the food supply?" The question came from the Secretary of Homeland Security.

"There's a small risk, but remember, we're talking about twenty pounds of plutonium being vaporized and its oxide being deposited across a thousand square miles of ocean. It would be a fluke for a measurable amount to end up in the belly or flesh of a fish. Even so, we'll be monitoring the water, as well as what fishermen are harvesting from it."

Conner was pleased. "It sounds like we got away with it, Mr. Stinson—no real damage, no long-term consequences. I can't say the same thing for the perpetrators. General Hawkins, do you have an update for us?"

"Yes, Sir. Nothing remains in the Iranian desert west of Zahedan, nothing but a lot of glass where the sand was fused by the heat of the explosion. All of the structures occupied by the former theocracy were reduced to rubble. The former missile silo in Chabahar is now just a gaping hole. No one could have possibly survived at either location."

"Any updates on collateral damage?"

Sanford rose. "Close to zero in the desert, as anticipated. Chabahar, however, did sustain damage. We are still waiting on exact numbers, but we anticipate casualties in the range of fifty to one hundred."

"That's much higher than I was told might happen, General," a clearly perturbed Conner remarked.

"I understand, Sir, but I'm not sure what choice we had, Mr. President."

"What type of aid are we providing?"

"A MASH unit has been established outside of the hot zone. It's being staffed by specialists in radiation exposure, as well as our best reconstructive surgeons and burn care experts. Beyond our medical interventions, we've transported extensive decontamination equipment to the area along with the troops needed to implement it."

"What about world opinion? How are we being treated in the media?" Conner directed his question to Stinson.

"As you would expect, Mr. President," the DNI replied. "Most of the free world views our actions as unfortunate but necessary."

"What about those who think our actions were abhorrent?"

"The overt criticism has come from a small group of our adversaries, including non-state actors, such as the United Islamic State. They're transmitting live feeds of the injured from Chabahar."

"What about the Russians?"

"Not a word. They've been silent since your phone call with President Putin. They've even put a ground hold on their long-range bombers, suspending their normal maneuvers. I don't think they will enter into this morass, Sir. Not after what you said to him."

"I hope you're right." Conner returned his attention to Stinson. "Are you ready for me to sound the all-clear, Mr. Stinson?"

"Actually, Mr. President, I would be more comfortable waiting until tomorrow morning to ensure there are no major shifts in the weather pattern. I believe my colleagues are in accord with this recommendation."

Conner watched as heads bobbed up and down in confirmation. "Then, unless the situation changes significantly, I'm returning to work as usual at 07:00 tomorrow morning and trust that I'll be accompanied by everyone in this bunker."

"Understood, Mr. President."

Before the group dispersed, Conner added, "Just one more thing. The First Lady and I have asked the White House chaplain to lead a short prayer service. I don't care what God you believe in, or if you believe in God at all, but I hope you'll take a moment to give thanks for the countless lives spared. The ecumenical service will begin at 11:00 hours."

Conner intercepted Hart as he was preparing to leave. "John, it looks like we have a little time on our hands. Mary and I would love to have you and Liz sit with us at the service. That is, if you plan on attending."

"We will be there, Sir."

"If Liz agrees, I also hope you'll join us for dinner this evening. We don't get to see enough of you these days, and I'd like to take advantage of your time while we have you captive."

Hart smiled. "We'd be honored, Mr. President."

ⅅⅉⅅ

A few minutes before 11:00, John and Liz approached a small chapel located in the far reaches of the vast underground labyrinth. Above its doors were the enduring symbols of five of the world's great religions: a crucifix, a Star of David, a crescent moon, a lotus, and the Hindu symbol *Aum*.

The sanctuary was lined with seven wooden pews, each comfortably seating ten people. The walls were decorated with elaborate stained-glass panels, each section illustrating a different story from the Bible. The entire room glowed with the warm light of candles, illuminating the pulpit and aisles.

President Conner was standing beside the front pew, his back to the altar. As John and Liz entered the sanctuary, he motioned for them to join him and the First Lady. While Liz and Mary caught up on the details of their respective lives, Conner, not one for small talk, pursued a very different conversation with Hart.

"You know, you chose an interesting line of work for a religious man, John," Conner said bluntly.

"I understand why you would come to that conclusion, Sir."

"You do believe in God, don't you, Commander?" Conner asked.

Surprised by the president's abruptness, Hart took a small step back.

"I didn't mean to throw you a curve ball, John. I thought it was a pretty simple question."

"It is simple, Sir, to many people. The truth is, my experience in Israel was life-changing in more ways than one. I'm still trying to make sense of it all."

"You can't make sense of God, John. That's why they call it *faith*."

"Yes, Sir. I'm working on it."

"It can't be easy to believe in a God that would allow the kind of suffering you've endured."

"Suffering, Sir? The wounds have healed."

"No, I didn't mean your injuries. I meant the loss of your brothers. Those wounds never heal."

For a moment, Hart was tempted to tell the truth. To tell the president how he really felt. But he stopped himself. He had to show he was strong and nothing could dent him. Even a memory. Was it bravery? No. It was survival. It was the only way he could get through a day. Not wanting the president to see how much his hands were trembling, he stuffed them in his pockets.

"We all have burdens to carry, Sir," he muttered at last. "That happens to be mine. Whether I believe in God or not, has little bearing on my past."

"It may have a huge bearing on your future," Conner said with a warm smile. "Just something to think about, John."

A small choir composed of Cabinet members and Congressional leaders began to sing *Amazing Grace*. As Hart listened, his lips began to move in synch with the choir: " . . . And saved a wretch like me," his voice barely audible.

Conner reached over and placed his hand on his friend's shoulder. He too was singing, "I once was lost, but now am found, was blind but now I see."

Though the service was relatively short, the message was profound: An overwhelming darkness had threatened to enshroud the nation's capital, but through the grace of God, it had been overcome by the light.

"Have faith, John. It's the only way to bear life's heaviest burdens," Conner whispered to the commander as they prepared to leave.

CHAPTER 10

A Floating Casket

"I'M SORRY TO DISTURB YOU, SIR," the lieutenant said as he handed a message stamped 'Top Secret' to General Mark Adams, Commanding Officer at Naval Base Guam. It was from Secretary of the Navy Harbinger.

Adams, who had just sat down for a relaxing lunch at the base's outdoor café, scowled and stuffed the message in his pocket. He then dismissed the lieutenant.

"I'll be right back, Becky," he said to his favorite server. Standing up, he pushed back the wicker chair, then sought out a private refuge in the restaurant.

Adams pulled the message from his pocket and quickly read it. He then read it twice more just to be certain.

"God damn black projects," he muttered, as he hustled towards the door. "Sorry, Sweetheart, duty calls," he called to Becky on his way out.

Adams didn't break stride as he entered his office and barked an order to the lieutenant: "Get General Cosgrove at Andersen on a secure line."

Minutes later, the phone in Adams' quarters rang. "I have General Cosgrove on the line, Sir."

"To what do I owe this pleasure, Mark?" the congenial Anthony Cosgrove began the conversation with his old friend.

"What do you know about the Prometheus, Tony?"

"Are you kidding me? Nothing other than the damn thing is parked about four hundred miles south of here in the Caroline Islands. My boys know better than to fly anywhere near her. Why? What's going on?"

"Some kind of black project that I'm not privy to."

"Give me a break. You run the largest fricking naval base in this part of the world. What do you mean 'not privy to'? Are you suggesting that it's classified above your pay grade?"

"I'm just giving you the facts, Tony. Now, let me tell you why I'm calling." Mark Adams' tone was suddenly serious. "I just received a message from Secretary Harbinger. It appears that the Prometheus may be in trouble."

"What kind of trouble? Like taking on water?"

"No, like a biological outbreak or some type of poisoning."

"When did this happen?"

"A couple of days ago. Don't ask me why the ship's captain chose to sit on it for so damn long, but we've got to make up for lost time."

"Oh shit. I don't think I like where this is headed."

"Nor do I. I need your boys to get some close-up reconnaissance photos asap. I doubt they will reveal much, but those are my marching orders. I imagine the higher-ups are trying to decide what to do with her."

"You mean scuttle her?"

"I didn't say that."

"Why not just land a helicopter on the ship's deck and perform a quick inspection? My boys can suit up appropriately and be done before the end of the day."

"You're being too logical, Tony. I was told that the physical inspection was going to be managed by a team out of DC. I guess they don't trust us to do the job properly. We're simply to identify any overt issues and report back."

"I'll have a plane in the air in twenty minutes. The digital images will be sent to you in real time for forwarding to Mr. Harbinger."

"Thanks, Tony, I owe you one."

※

As Mark Adams was busy conveying his orders to Tony Cosgrove, Zhao had moved one step closer to escaping with his deadly bounty.

The lifeboats on the Prometheus were state of the art: no wood, no oars and, thanks to an unbreakable plastic hull and a water-impermeable top, no risk of sinking. These emergency vessels were designed to withstand tropical-force winds and waves exceeding forty feet.

Zhao studied the boat closest to him before climbing aboard. Once ensconced, he pulled a release lever that gently lowered the vessel onto the water below. He closed the hatch and began drifting in the Pacific.

Thanks to four tempered glass portholes, he could watch as the lifeboat slowly parted ways with the Prometheus. When the gap widened to several hundred yards, he reached into his pocket and withdrew what look like a spool of fine thread. Opening a porthole, he held one end of the extraordinarily thin wire while he dropped the spool into the ocean. Once unwound, it formed a sixty-foot-long antenna to which Zhao attached a transmitter no bigger than a deck of cards. The device was set to a fixed frequency. Zhao began his message:

> *Viral cultures obtained, but exposure possible. Boarded lifeboat and set adrift. Winds are easterly. U.S. intervention presumably ordered. Expecting guests. Suggest you arrive soon. Will update this transmission in eight hours.*

Zhao switched off the device and stored it carefully in a water-proof compartment built into the hull of the lifeboat. There was nothing to do now but wait. As he lay quietly listening to the rhythmic sounds of the ocean, the signature hum of a Marine Osprey broke the calm.

Zhao leaned forward to peer out of one of portholes, pressing his forehead flush against the glass. The plane, still a small dot in the cloudless blue sky, was approaching from the north. When it was much closer, the pitch of the motors changed, and it began to slow down.

His heart began to race. He wondered how long it would be before they had a visual on him. The Osprey was close enough for Zhao to make out the propellers being rotated from a vertical to horizontal orientation. This would allow it to hover above the Prometheus. Once the wings were locked in position, the rotary craft proceeded to circle the ship twice.

They're taking surveillance photos, Zhao thought. *But with no carnage visible on deck, it's not going to yield any actionable intelligence,* he concluded. There was one thing, however, that could prove catastrophic. The Osprey's crew could spot the missing lifeboat and initiate a search.

Either God was listening or the crew was singularly focused on their mission, for Zhao and the boat escaped detection. His heart was still thumping in his chest as the Osprey departed heading towards Guam.

Zhao knew it wouldn't be long before the Americans sent more than just a reconnaissance aircraft. He needed rest. He closed his eyes and allowed the gentle rocking motion of the waves to lull him to sleep.

Sleep, however, was not a pleasant respite. Rather, it cast him into a netherworld full of demons and despair. *Are my dreams a harbinger of what's to come?* he wondered when he finally awoke, soaked through with perspiration.

He glanced at his watch. More than six hours had elapsed since he had drifted off to sleep. He looked out the starboard porthole in search of the Prometheus, but the ship was no longer visible on the horizon.

Surely, the People's Liberation Army had received his message and were racing it up the chain of command, he thought, trying to reassure himself. But doubt inevitably crept in, along with insidious fears about what would happen if the Americans reached him first. He tried to remain calm, but it was more than the threat posed by the Americans that had him worried.

The emergence of a growing array of symptoms stripped away his strength. His body was hot to the touch, and what had started as a slight tickle in his throat now felt like blisters every time he swallowed.

Zhao knew that something was moving rapidly through his system, and there was little doubt as to the nature of the pathogen.

After two more hours, he repeated his earlier transmission, adding, "Advise you put on bioprotective suit before entering either vessel."

Overcome by his increasing sense of helplessness, Zhao rummaged through the boat's medical kit, tossing aside the bandages, ointments, and seasickness remedies until he found a small repository of pills. He broke the seal on a plastic bottle, extracted three Ibuprofen, and popped them into his mouth, wincing as he washed them down with a swig of water.

Within an hour, the pain in his throat had subsided to a manageable level, and Zhao was able to doze until morning. He awoke as the brilliant yellow rays of the rising sun reflected off the water and through the boat's east-facing portholes. He shaded his burning eyes from the sun's glare, then twisted his aching body to face west. That's when he saw it.

At first, he thought it was a mirage. A small atoll rose up from the sea directly in front of him. He could make out the outline of a beach, and waves breaking against a coral barrier. With each swell of the surf, the lifeboat seemed to inch closer to land.

But it didn't fill him with much hope. No, it was too late for that. Nothing could overcome the intense despair he felt as he realized his life was slowly slipping away. Overnight, his symptoms had worsened: sore throat, weakness, fatigue, and a fever which he guessed to be around 102 degrees; plus, he was growing more anxious and agitated. He knew he was in the throes of what would soon become a fatal rabies infection.

Through the fog of illness, Zhao could now make out waves breaking on the beach. He judged it to be a few hundred yards away. Patience, he told himself. He would be washed ashore within the hour. And, if the direction of the current changed, he could swim the short distance, despite his condition. At least he would be on firm ground when he died.

Zhao once again removed the small gold locket from his neck, opened the invisible clasp, and stared at the face of his long-dead grandfather. "Help me," he whispered under his breath in Mandarin. "Please, help me."

Nearly twenty-four hours had passed since he slit the throat of Captain Seward, then sent his first transmission to the Chinese before fleeing the Prometheus. His urgent call for help, which should have initiated a massive response by the Chinese military, had failed to elicit even a whimper. And for good reason.

Lieutenant Yin Wang, a clerk in the Second Department of the People's Liberation Army, had transcribed Zhao's messages within minutes of their receipt. After marking them *URGENT,* he forwarded the two messages to Major Song Chen, the senior communications officer assigned to the Area Director.

Wang acted precisely according to protocol and, under normal circumstances, Zhao's messages would have been run up the chain of command immediately. But Major Chen was nowhere to be found, not for the six hours he went AWOL.

It wasn't the first time he'd left the base while on duty. He'd done it many times before, his breaches never discovered. Emboldened, he assumed it would be the same that night, a night he whiled away in the arms of a very attractive and very young woman, one who cost him several weeks wages.

By the time the Major returned to his post, Zhao's messages were buried beneath dozens of additional e-mails. It would be hours before Chen worked through all the messages, discovered his oversight, and placed a call to his boss.

CHAPTER 11

A New Threat Emerges

JONATHAN AND MARY CONNER were in the midst of dressing for dinner when there was a forceful knock on the door to their quarters.

"Do you mind, Darling?" Mary asked as she remained seated, holding her mascara in one hand as she stared into a magnifying mirror.

Mary Conner had been a rising star in one of Washington's premier law firms before falling in love with a junior senator from Virginia, a man whom many believed was destined for the presidency. Not only was she Jonathan Conner's companion, lover, and confidante, she was also someone whose judgment he held in the highest esteem.

"Of course not," Jonathan mumbled as he threaded the tiny white buttons through the narrow slits on the starched collar of his dress shirt. He cinched his Hermes tie until it was tight against his neck, and then walked out to the entry hall. Opening the door, he nodded in response to the sergeant's salute.

"At ease, sergeant."

"Mr. President, Secretary Harbinger is asking to speak with you. I inquired if he had an appointment, and he informed me that it was an emergency."

As the sergeant spoke, Harbinger weaved and bobbed behind him in an effort to garner the president's attention.

Conner scowled, wondering what possible emergency could arise after almost being nuked.

"I'll deal with it, Master Sergeant. You can return to your post." The officer saluted and stepped to the side, allowing the secretary to pass.

"I wasn't expecting you, Charlie." Conner's terse tone strongly suggesting that it was not a welcome surprise. "The First Lady and I are scheduled to have dinner with Commander Hart and Dr. Wilkins in ten minutes, and we'd like to be on time. So, what's so damned important that it wouldn't wait until morning?"

"May we discuss this in private, Mr. President? It will only take a few minutes."

Seeing no other option, Conner directed the secretary to the formal living room. He then excused himself for a moment to tell Mary what was happening. She nodded dutifully, knowing that their evening plans were about to change.

Once he had Conner's full attention, Charlie Harbinger explained the reason for his untimely arrival. "Earlier today, I received a coded communication from Captain Seward. As you will recall, he's . . . ."

"The skipper of the Dark Ark," Conner cut him off, using the common vernacular for the top-secret Prometheus.

"Yes, Sir. It appears that we may have a catastrophic problem on our hands."

"Catastrophic! That's a pretty powerful word to bandy about, Charlie."

"Yes, Mr. President."

"Well, don't keep me in suspense, damn it! What did Seward say?"

"That either an infection had broken out on the ship or the crew has been poisoned by some type of toxin. The symptoms strongly suggested botulinum. Seward didn't know if it was an accidental release or a deliberate act of sabotage, but regardless, everyone onboard appears to be either dead or dying."

"What?" Conner shook his head as if to dispel what felt like a bad dream. "When did you receive this message?" he asked, pointing towards the piece of paper in the secretary's hand.

"At 06:00, Mr. President."

"And you're just now letting me know, Mr. Harbinger, more than twelve hours after the fact? What in the hell were you thinking, Charlie?"

"You've been pretty preoccupied, Mr. President. I was trying to spare you any unnecessary anxiety until we had more information. I asked General Cosgrove to dispatch an Osprey from Andersen. The plane's crew completed a couple of low-altitude flybys capturing hundreds of surveillance photos. Those images went straight to Naval Intelligence for analysis. In hindsight, Sir, I should have brought them to you."

"What you should have done is informed me of what was happening. But we don't have the luxury of time for recriminations now. What did we learn from the images?"

"Unfortunately, they reveal very little, other than the fact that a single lifeboat appears to be missing from the ship."

"If it was a saboteur, how much damage can that person do beyond the casualties he's already created?" Conner asked.

"There could be unfathomable damage done if he facilitates the transfer of material from that ship into enemy hands. Not only are we talking about the most advanced bio-weapons on the planet, including novel organisms that are universally lethal, but a digital repository of knowledge and data that powers every program we have underway in the areas of genomics and synthetic biology."

"Maybe you should walk me through those programs, Charlie. I have a feeling there are things that have not been shared with the presidency."

Harbinger leaned back against the couch cushion. "I'm afraid I can't. There are things that I am not privy to, Mr. President."

"You're the Secretary of the Navy, for God's sake. If you don't have the answers, then who does?"

Harbinger returned a vacant stare, afraid to open his mouth.

"Oh, to hell with it!" Conner said in total exasperation. "I want you back here at 21:00 hours, Mr. Secretary, and I'm going to expect answers to my questions. Crystal clear answers, understood?"

Harbinger slowly nodded. Then he stood up and walked towards the door.

"There's one more thing, Charlie. When you brief me, you will also be briefing Commander Hart and Dr. Wilkins."

"That's not possible, Mr. President. They are not cleared for this project. It's compartmentalized. You know that."

"Well, you know what, Charlie? I just cleared them. And you better not hold anything back. We need to know what's going on aboard that ship, and how it impacts the security of our nation. Am I clear, Mr. Secretary?"

"Yes, Sir."

"I'll see you at 21:00 hours."

When Harbinger had left, Conner returned to the bedroom. There, he found Mary patiently waiting, dressed in a black cocktail dress with a single strand of pearls.

"Uh oh, I know that look, Jonathan. You're about to uninvite me to dinner." She reached behind her neck and loosened the clasp on her necklace, letting out a barely audible sigh.

"I'm sorry, Darling, but something has come up."

"What more could possibly come up? We're deep underground in a bunker as the result of a near nuclear catastrophe, and you're telling me there's something else afoot?"

"I'm afraid so. It doesn't represent an immediate danger, but it's a problem that must be contained. John and Liz could play important roles in ensuring that happens."

"Are you suggesting another bio-event? Is that what you're saying?"

"Now, don't press me for details. I'll have Mario prepare chicken saltimbocca for you and serve you in our dining room. I'm afraid that's the best I can do under the circumstances."

"You're doing your job, but if I can confess something, I'll be glad when this term expires. I'm ready to have a semi-normal life again."

"What's that? I wouldn't recognize normal, but I agree with the sentiment, Sweetheart," Conner said, as he gently touched her face and kissed her cheek. "I'll be back by 21:00 to meet with the secretary, along with John and Liz."

CHAPTER 12

Pass the Potatoes

CONNER GLANCED AT THE SHINY BLACK FACE of his gold Rolex Submariner. It was 19:05. "Let's pick up the pace, Sergeant," he instructed his Marine escort. "I don't want to be any later than absolutely necessary."

Entering the private dining room, Conner smiled in an effort to mask the anxiety gnawing at his gut. He shook the commander's hand and then kissed Liz gently on the cheek.

The room was furnished with Colonial-era pieces and decorated with paintings by such luminary artists as Emanuel Gottlieb Leutz, Benjamin West, and Charles Wilson Peale. The round beveled dining room table was set with Wedgewood china—an elegant blue and white design that commemorated major events in the country's history. The plates were framed by the finest Reed & Barton silver, all illuminated by a simple but elegant chandelier that hung directly above them.

"This room is so lovely!" Liz exclaimed, surprised at its beauty amidst the industrial gray of the shelter.

"Actually, Liz, it's an exact reproduction of a private dining room one hundred feet above where we are sitting now. A room reserved for rare and special events."

"I feel honored, Mr. President."

"On that note, have you been offered a drink?"

"I'm on duty, Mr. President," Hart responded.

"No, Commander, you're not. You have no official standing. Remember, you retired."

"Yes, Sir."

"Gentlemen, while you debate whether my husband can drink alcohol or not, I would love a glass of champagne to toast that we have survived to see another day."

"So ordered, Liz," Conner said with a warm smile. He turned to their server. "Dr. Wilkins will have a glass of Dom Perignon, and the commander and I will each have a Macallan neat. I do have that right, don't I, John?"

"Yes, Sir. Will the First Lady be joining us for dinner?"

It pained Conner not to have his wife by his side. "Mary sends her regrets. I explained to her that we had some things to discuss that involved compartmentalized information. Though it's not adequate consolation, I asked the chef to prepare her favorite meal and deliver it to our quarters."

"Please tell Mrs. Conner that we asked about her," Liz said.

"Of course." When the drinks arrived, Conner lifted his glass and offered a toast. "To the security and well-being of our great nation. May we never again face such a threat."

"Hear, hear!" Liz and John intoned in unison, clinking their glasses with Conner's.

Conner turned to the two officers assigned to protect him. "Gentlemen, I need to speak with the commander and

Dr. Wilkins privately. Would you excuse us, and ask the servers to give us thirty minutes before entering the room?"

"Yes, Sir." The men pivoted and left the room.

Hart sensed a storm cloud brewing as the celebratory air that had existed only a moment ago vanished.

"I'm afraid that, as we've been busy neutralizing one threat, another has arisen. And this one could be every bit as devastating."

"Not the Russians, Sir?"

"No, I think Putin took me at my word and has no interest in provoking an all-out war with the United States."

"What could be as threatening as a nuclear missile targeting the heart of our democracy?" Liz asked the president.

"Intimate knowledge of the fundamental secrets of life, Doctor. Knowledge created by advancements in synthetic and molecular biology, as well as recombinant chemistry. Something you know quite a bit about."

"But I'm sure you would agree, Mr. President, that knowledge, in and of itself, does not represent a threat."

"Correct. There is no threat until such knowledge is employed to develop stunning new bio-weapons, fundamentally alter genomes, or in other ways commit genocide."

"I'm not sure I like where this is headed, Sir," Hart said.

"Where is it headed, Mr. President?" Liz asked.

Conner paused, looked at his guests, then asked quietly, "Are you familiar with a naval vessel referred to as the Dark Ark?" He knew that, if the security surrounding the phantom ship was airtight , then the couple's answer would be an unflinching *no*.

"No, Sir," Hart responded without hesitation. But Liz was not so quick to answer.

"I've heard rumors," she admitted. "Something about a stealth naval vessel containing the genetic codes for all known life forms, including bio-engineered pathogens. Frankly, I assumed it was just one more conspiracy theory spawned by kooks, Mr. President."

"A logical conclusion, Doctor, but incorrect. The information I am about to share with you is limited to a handful of people on a need-to-know basis. The *Dark Ark*, as we indirectly refer to it, is quite real, and it appears to have encountered a serious problem. Before I get into the problem, let me tell you what I know about the program. Charlie Harbinger will be filling in the blanks when we meet with him in a couple of hours.

"The vessel's actual name is the U.S.S. Prometheus. It was commissioned in 2014 to serve as a modern-day Noah's Ark; minus the physical animals of course. Rather, their complete genomes are housed in massive computer storage banks along with the genomes of viruses, bacteria, and even prions. To date, the scientists on the Prometheus have sequenced the genetic code for more than 98% of all living matter. In that sense, the vessel's mission is nearing completion."

"Did their work include sequencing variations in the human genome? And if so, what was the intent of that research?" Liz asked.

"I'm afraid I don't know. I received a briefing some time ago, but I have not been kept current on all its projects."

"What else can you tell us about the ship, Mr. President?"

"When it comes to microorganisms, the Prometheus is more than merely a repository of genetic data; its scientists are bio-engineering modified life forms, including creating novel pathogens. That's why she's parked in the middle of the Pacific, far away from any major population centers."

"Sir, what you have just described has been the sole focus of my work at CIA, just as it was at CDC. How could the Prometheus have operated right under my nose without my awareness or inclusion?" Liz's exasperation was obvious.

"You're in good company, my dear. As I alluded to a moment ago, it appears that there are secrets to which even I am not privy, including the full scope of work underway on the Prometheus. If I may continue?"

She nodded.

"The ship is based upon the Independence class design. I believe you are familiar with it, Commander?"

"Yes, Sir, the spear," Hart responded, referring to the ship's unique shape.

Conner smiled. "I've never heard it described quite that way, but it fits. Its stealth design renders it virtually undetectable to land and sea-based radar. Thanks to its range, the Prometheus can remain at sea for an extended period before returning to dock."

"How is it resupplied, Sir, if I may ask?" Wilkins asked.

"Of course. For starters, there's an on-board greenhouse that provides fresh food for the crew. Genetically engineered meat, chicken, and other sources of protein are manufactured in a state-of-the-art facility. It's not the White House kitchen, but I've been told it's quite tasty."

"What about water?" Hart asked.

"An endless supply of water comes from an on-board desalination system. In short, it is a fully-contained, self-sufficient biosphere with stealth properties that helps it remain concealed. All other materials are delivered by an autonomous drone."

"Who dreamed this thing up?" Hart asked.

"DARPA. Based upon your tours of duty there, I'm a little surprised that it flew under your radar. No pun intended, Commander. But I can assure you that heads would have rolled had an unauthorized briefing occurred."

"Never heard a word, Mr. President."

"What about the crew, Sir? Where are they drawn from?"

"The naval operations and security teams are composed of individuals from Naval Intelligence, as well as JSOP. The scientific team is composed of some of the best and brightest molecular biologists, geneticists, recombinant chemists, and a plethora of other medically-related specialists, all of whom went through exhaustive vetting."

"Apparently it wasn't exhaustive enough," Hart said under his breath. Catching himself, he quickly added, "I'm sorry, Sir, I didn't mean any disrespect."

"No apology necessary. I share your concern, Commander."

"What happens after their tour of duty is up?" Wilkins asked.

"A crew exchange occurs every two years. Many of the scientists sign on for additional tours. The ship has been operational for six years, and only a handful of the original scientists have returned to their prior positions."

"Based upon their work with novel organisms, does the crew pose any direct threat to the nation's security?"

"When the crew disembarks, they are quarantined for thirty days before being released into the general population.

I've been told that's a reasonable holding period, though it doesn't completely eliminate the threat of an outbreak."

"You indicated that something has gone awry, Mr. President."

"Yes, Liz. Secretary Harbinger received a coded message from the ship's captain, Barry Seward, whom we believe to have been the last survivor aboard the Prometheus."

"An outbreak?"

"From what we've gleaned, it appears that a modified pathogen or toxin infected the crew, with devastating results."

"Do we know the nature of the organism?" Wilkins asked.

"Not with any certainty. There was a presumptive finding of botulinum toxin made by one of the scientists, but it has not been definitively confirmed."

"Is the captain symptomatic, Sir?" Hart asked.

"Based upon our loss of communications with him, my guess is that Captain Seward is dead."

There was a discrete knock on the door. Thirty minutes had elapsed, and the staff wanted to know if they should serve dinner.

"By all means," Conner said blandly, as though they had been chatting about the weather. "But once we are served, I would ask that you leave us in privacy until we've finished our dinner."

"Of course, Sir," the head waiter acknowledged with a small bow.

Though the grilled tenderloin with demi-glacé was beautifully prepared, Liz found she had little appetite. Hart, however, grabbed a fork and dove in.

With a chunk of steak still in his mouth, John said, "You've brought us into your confidence for a reason, Mr. President. How can Liz and I be of service?"

"You'll have to forgive my husband's manners, President Conner. As you know, he grew up on a ranch, but I think he was born in a barn."

Hart shrugged his shoulders and gave Liz a look.

Conner laughed, "The last thing I'm concerned with, Doctor, is etiquette. In answer to your question, John, all I ask is that you help me define a strategy for moving forward. You don't have to get your hands dirty; you've more than done your share in that regard. But I could benefit greatly from your and Liz's combined counsel."

Hart looked to his wife for permission to proceed. Liz nodded a silent affirmation.

"Sir, I believe we need to gain access to the ship as rapidly as possible in order to determine precisely what we are dealing with and how to manage it. We will, of course, need a team to help with security and disposition of the bodies, as well as data acquisition and organism collection."

"What about your retirement, Commander?"

"What retirement, Mr. President?"

"How do you feel about that, Liz? Are you in agreement?"

"Yes, Mr. President. As you know, I've spent my professional life studying Category A pathogens. I know my way around a Biolevel-IV lab, so there won't be any learning curve. And, as for John's retirement, truth be told, I think he was beginning to climb the walls."

"Okay, then. As I said earlier, the secretary will be giving us a more thorough briefing following dinner. I chewed his ass out for not being more forthcoming with me about the problem, pardon the expression, Doctor. Harbinger knows that I'm expecting the full story on this vessel, including whether other countries might be aware of its existence and implicated in this incident."

"Are you suggesting that there might have been a foreign agent onboard, Sir?"

"I've asked the DDO, Mr. Kahn, to pore over the crew manifest in order to identify any points of vulnerability that were somehow missed during the vetting process. If it was sabotage, there could be a race to reach the Prometheus and loot its secrets."

"What do you believe in your gut, Sir?"

"I don't believe this was an accident, though I think the timing was coincidental relative to the Iranian nuke. I think we damn well better be the first on-site. We need to unload the data and pathogens, then scuttle the ship.

"How quickly can you assemble a team?" Conner directed the question to both Liz and John.

"We can get on it first thing in the morning with the intent of being ready for deployment within the next thirty-six to forty-eight hours, Mr. President."

"Thirty-six hours is the outer limit, Commander."

Hart looked to Liz for confirmation, which she gave with a nod of her head.

"We understand, Sir. What was the last known location of the Prometheus?"

"I'll leave it up to Secretary Harbinger, who should be awaiting us, to answer that question."

CHAPTER 13

The Mission

CHARLIE HARBINGER, HALF SUBMERGED in an overstuffed chair, was lost in thought as he waited in the hallway outside the president's quarters. When Conner, Hart, and Wilkins arrived, he less than gracefully pushed himself up with a grunt.

"Damn knees," he said, as the pain of bone-on-bone arthritis slowed his movements. Twenty-five years in the Navy had taken its toll.

"I apologize for intruding on your time with the president, but I assume that he explained the situation."

"Yes, Sir," Hart and Wilkins responded in unison.

Conner showed his guests into a small rectangular conference room and remained standing while they took their seats. "Just to be clear, Charlie," he said, looking hard into the eyes of his secretary, "I assured John and Liz that they would hear an unredacted description of the ship's mission and active projects."

"Yes, Sir." With his head still moving up and down in acknowledgment, Harbinger began the briefing.

"Let me begin with a cursory overview of the vessel so you can better visualize what we're dealing with. It's a unique design with a trimaran hull . . ."

"You can skip the specs, Charlie. I've already shared that information with the commander and Dr. Wilkins. I need you to focus on the research being conducted aboard the Prometheus."

"Yes, Sir." Harbinger took in a deep breath. "The Prometheus has a tripartite mission that includes building a genetic repository of every life form known to man."

"Hence the nickname, *Dark Ark*?" said Liz. "But, beyond its stealth capabilities, why the word Dark?"

"Dr. Wilkins, you are well aware of the myriad of applications for such knowledge, some of which are life enhancing, while others are destructive. Whatever you can imagine, it was either being contemplated or actively explored by the scientific team."

"I'd rather not leave it to my imagination, Mr. Secretary. I'm a scientist who thrives on precise facts and knowledge." Her tone was firm.

"Charlie, give the Doctor what she is requesting."

"Yes, Sir. There were numerous classified research projects underway within the ship's Biolevel-IV laboratory. The majority of such research was related to either enhancing the pathogenicity of existing micro-organisms or creating novel forms of life, such as chimera viruses."

"Were they successful in creating novel organisms?"

"To a degree, thanks to the efforts of the lead molecular biologist, Dr. Zhao. He was just completing the initial testing of an airborne form of rabies when this mayhem broke out. According to his report, much of which I didn't understand, Zhao inserted genetic sequences from the SARS virus into the rabies genome producing a viable chimera that was universally lethal in animals."

"Sound plausible, Liz?" Hart asked.

"With CRISPR and other tools, anything is possible," she answered.

Hart feigned a shiver. "I've been terrified of rabies ever since I saw *Old Yeller* as a child," he said, eliciting a shake of the head and chuckle from Conner.

"Your husband is incorrigible, Doctor."

"Agreed, Sir." She mock-scowled at John before continuing her questioning of Harbinger. "According to the ship's captain, the chimera is not what infected the crew, correct?"

"Captain Seward suggested botulinum poisoning, but we don't know what he was basing this on. We know that there was investigational work being done on the H-variant of clostridium botulinum and its associated toxin. My bet is that it was deliberately introduced into the food or water supply. Water would have been the most effective way of doing it."

"That implies someone quite familiar with the ship," said Liz thoughtfully. "You are describing a pretty sophisticated saboteur."

"Agreed," interjected Hart. "The individual would need to know his or her way around the lab, as well as how to infiltrate the desalination unit, which I assume is guarded and monitored."

"Yes, 24/7," Harbinger responded.

Hart's mind was racing. "Liz, help me understand the specific properites of the H-variant of botulinum."

Liz thought for a moment. "Well, to start with it has a much more rapid onset than other variants, with a dose-dependent response that requires less than one hundred nanograms to achieve one hundred percent mortality."

"Can you be more precise about the speed of onset?" Hart pressed.

"As little as twelve hours post-exposure, with death occurring generally within twenty-four to forty-eight hours."

"Mr. Secretary," said Hart, turning to the older man, "if I may, I would suggest an immediate review of the video surveillance logs for a period twenty-four hours prior to the presumed outbreak. If we see a member of the scientific team visit the desalination plant, we will have clear evidence in support of our hypothesis."

"Have someone get on it now," Conner ordered Harbinger, as he pushed a desk-phone across the table so it was within the secretary's reach.

As soon as Harbinger completed the call, Conner continued, "Charlie, you said a tripartite mission. So far I've only counted two objectives: assembling genetic information and using it to create bio-weapons. What's the third?"

"I can't fully answer that, Sir."

"What do you mean, can't? I told you I expected the unvarnished truth."

"Mr. President, that knowledge is held by a small cadre of men whose identities I don't know."

"Are you asking me to believe that there are projects so dark that not even the president of the United States is privy to their existence, but a group of unelected men are?"

"That's one way of putting it, Sir. I do know that it involves manipulation of the human genome with the intent of improving our race."

"Our *race?* What the hell does that mean? There's no American race! We're a melting pot, for God's sake."

"Yes, Mr. President, but there are substantial variations of critical traits within our population. The people behind these experiments, whoever they may be, are intent on raising IQs, bolstering strength and agility, and increasing resistance to disease among a privileged group. I've even heard talk of them developing embryos that have complete resistance to viruses. But that's all I know, Sir."

"You're describing eugenics, Mr. Secretary!" Liz exclaimed in shock.

"Yes, Doctor."

"Where is the Prometheus, Secretary Harbinger?" Hart asked.

"She's adrift approximately 350 miles southwest of Guam near the Caroline Islands. We can provide up-to-the second GPS coordinates when you're ready for them, Commander."

"I'm ready for them now, Sir, and I would appreciate hourly updates. I'll also need full schematics for the ship. Dr. Wilkins will need the protocols associated with the BL-IV lab. Finally, I assume you have some thoughts regarding the most efficient way to board the vessel?"

"Yes, Commander. As you know, the airstrip in Guam can handle a C-5. Your team may be small, but I trust you'll need the cargo space of two planes to transport a couple of Mark V's and your associated gear. Once the boats are delivered, we'll have them ferried by helicopter to a safe zone close to the Prometheus."

"And what are your thoughts regarding the transport of Liz's team, Sir?"

"My Chief of Naval Logistics has advised that we initially land them directly on the ship's rear flight deck, which is designed to accommodate two Sikorsky MH-60R/S Seahawks. The team will, of course, be in full bioprotective suits.

"Until their mission is completed, Dr. Wilkins' team will rely on one of the Mark V's to shuttle them back and forth between the Prometheus and a ship that will serve as their home base."

"Any chance that the Prometheus will have visitors?"

"I think there's a strong chance of that, Commander, since the bounty she houses could literally change the power balance in the world overnight. As you can probably imagine, I'm most concerned about the Chinese."

"What are the ship's defensive capabilities?"

"She was the first ship in our fleet to incorporate Raytheon's SeaRAM Close-in-Weapons-System, designed to detect, evaluate, track, engage, and kill threats to the vessel."

"Can you give us more detail?" Conner asked.

"Yes, Sir. Though not designed as an active combat vessel, the Prometheus possesses formidable firepower. Her twin helicopters each house dual 7.62 mm machine guns, a pod of Hellfire missiles, and a single air-launched torpedo. In addition, the ship is armed with AGM-114L Hellfire missiles, a 57 mm gun, and multiple automatic weapons. Suffice it to say that she can hold her own in a brawl."

"It sounds like the Prometheus wouldn't go down without a fight, but she would go down if sufficiently outgunned," Hart concluded.

"That's why Captain Seward was under strict orders to scuttle the ship if overwhelmed by an adversary," the Secretary said in a hushed tone, "even if it meant the entire crew would ride her down to a watery end."

"I guess he didn't consider the poisoning of her entire crew an attack," Hart mused.

"Possibly, Commander," Harbinger agreed with a nod.

"I'm not interested in the ship's firepower, but I am interested to know how we will manage any remaining survivors. How do we get them into a quarantined environment where we can attempt treatment?" Liz asked the secretary.

"We're working on it, Doctor. Right now, CDC Director Linfield is coordinating with Deputy Director Kahn to ensure you have what you need. But remember, Dr. Wilkins, your overriding priority is to extract all of the Prometheus's knowledge, whether in the form of its data files or living specimens. Then, and only then, are you to address the needs of any potential survivors. Am I clear?"

Hart could see Liz's body stiffen in response to the orders and knew she was about to erupt. "I took a sacred oath, Mr. Secretary, that obligates me to view life as precious, not data files and viral samples."

"I don't give a damn, Doctor, those are your orders. If you cannot follow them, we'll get someone who can."

"Charlie, I don't think we need to be quite so heavy-handed," Conner interjected. He smiled before speaking to Liz. "Dr. Wilkins, I would never ask you to violate your oath. I would, however, ask that you approach the situation in a utilitarian manner, the greatest good for the greatest number. It would be a pity to save a handful of lives if it meant losing millions later."

Liz took a deep breath and exhaled slowly. "Yes, Sir, that seems responsible and appropriate under the circumstances."

"Charlie, I want a hospital vessel deployed to the area immediately. That will kill two birds with one stone, providing Dr. Wilkins' crew with a place to bunk down, plus the enhanced capabilities for decontamination, isolation, and treatment of survivors that the doctor has requested."

"I'll have the USNS Mercy redirected, Mr. President," Harbinger said with the humility of man just smacked down in front of two subordinates.

Conner continued, "Liz, I've asked Mr. Kahn to brief you at 08:00 hours regarding his conversation with Tom Linfield."

"Yes, Sir."

"Commander Hart, your mission is to ensure the safe delivery and extraction of Dr. Wilkins' team, along with the data and bio-samples."

He turned to Secretary Harbinger.

"Before we conclude this meeting, there's one critical topic that we've not addressed, Charlie. It is my understanding that Naval Intelligence has completed its analysis of the surveillance photos of the Prometheus."

"Yes, Mr. President, but the only irregularity was a missing lifeboat."

"And you don't consider that significant, Mr. Secretary?" Hart asked in disbelief. "What if that boat is harboring the saboteur?"

"I think your imagination is in overdrive, Commander Hart."

"Maybe, but we should be doing everything in our power to track down that boat."

"I agree with the commander," Conner weighed in. "Your mission, Commander, now includes locating and interdicting that lifeboat. Is there anything else you require of Mr. Harbinger at this time?"

"No, Sir."

"Then will you and Liz please excuse us for a moment. I need to speak with the secretary in private. You can wait here."

The president and Secretary Harbinger stepped into the hallway.

"You and I have a great deal to discuss, Charlie, including how you could so blatantly violate the chain of command by taking orders from a faceless cabal. Our founders had a word for that: Treason! And I'm quite sure you've had plenty of time to contemplate the consequences of your action."

Harbinger's head hung low, his face reddening as Conner continued,. "But as egregious as the infraction may be, the issue will have to wait until the Prometheus has been secured.

"Look at me!" Conner shouted, now inches from the man's face. Locking eyes with him, Conner said, "I expect you to maintain absolute confidentiality relative to our conversation and the Prometheus. By your own admission, we don't know who is involved in this conspiracy. That creates a huge point of vulnerability for the teams we are sending in. Do not allow our vulnerability to be exploited, Mr. Secretary." Conner ushered Harbinger out the door.

He returned to his chair in the conference room, clasping his hands behind his head. "A dead crew, an unholy chimera virus, eugenics run amuck, and the revelation of a shadow government. Have I left anything out, Commander?"

"A Secretary of the Navy who violated his oath to the Constitution. I'm still shocked that he allowed an elite group to control research into eugenics. And on an American ship!"

"Not *elite*, Commander, *twisted*."

"Point taken, Mr. President."

"I want you and Liz to find out what in the hell they were up to on that ship. Once we have all of the Prometheus's secrets securely in hand, you are to send her to a watery grave. Remember, it needs to be deep enough so that none of our adversaries can get to her."

"What about the bodies of the crew, Sir?" Liz asked.

"Mass burial at sea, Dr. Wilkins. They go down with the ship."

CHAPTER 14

Searching for a Saboteur

"Mr. President, before we adjourn, I'd like to put a call in to General Scott. With your permission, of course," Hart added. "He could be invaluable in helping me put together a crew."

As the head of Joint Special Operations Command, Lt. General Mark Scott oversaw the Naval Special Development Group, including SEAL Team 6. There was a strong bond between Hart and Scott, one forged during SEAL training on Coronado Island. After graduating from the program, each man's talents took him in a different direction, Scott towards senior military leadership and Hart as an unstoppable force on the front lines of international conflicts.

"Let's get him on the phone right now, Commander," Conner said, activating the speakerphone. "Get General Scott for me, please."

A moment later, the startled naval officer was speaking to the president. "To what do I owe this honor, Sir?"

"General, I have Commander Hart and Dr. Elizabeth Wilkins in the room with me. We have a situation that requires your assistance."

"Of course, Mr. President."

"There appears to have been an incident involving a biological agent aboard a naval research vessel called the Prometheus. I have charged Commander Hart with interdiction and Dr. Wilkins with investigation into the matter. I'm relying on Mr. Kahn to provide Dr. Wilkins with whatever support she needs, and I'm relying on you to assist the commander."

"Commander Hart, I thought you had retired."

"I had retired, Sir, but then this matter came up. I'd be grateful to have the resources of JSOC behind me, General."

"Just tell me what you need, Commander."

"I'm not one hundred percent sure yet, Sir. Secretary Harbinger just finished briefing us, but my initial thought is that we will run two teams of five with each team assigned to a Mark V," he said referring to the SEALS' mid-range, high velocity insertion vehicle.

"Team One will be responsible for close support and transportation of Dr. Wilkins' team, while Team Two ensures the ongoing security of the mission. That's as far as I've gotten, General."

"We believe that the Prometheus may have been the victim of a saboteur," Conner added. "If that's true, we may find ourselves butting heads with a foreign power intent on looting the ship."

"That changes the calculus, Mr. President. With your permission, I will speak with the Secretary of Defense regarding air support, including Predators and a squadron of F22's or F-35's."

"Permission granted, General."

"Commander, is there anything else you can think of at the moment?"

"No, Sir."

"How time urgent is the mission, Mr. President? As I understand it, you are talking about a ghost ship."

"It may be a ghost ship, General, but it's laden with secrets. We cannot allow them to fall into enemy hands."

"Any likely candidates, Mr. President?" Scott asked. "It would help to know who we are up against, and the degree to which time will be a factor."

"I spoke to Marvin Kahn a short time ago. CIA has been scouring the ship's manifest trying to ferret out a potential perpetrator. They have narrowed the field to two people onboard: a Chinese defector, who serves as the lead scientist on the Prometheus, and a second generation American whose parents were Muscovites. Right now, CIA is reviewing the video-logs from the Prometheus in the hope that they may conclusively identify the saboteur."

"If I may ask, why would we allow a defector onboard our most sensitive research vessel?" Scott asked.

"It's a damn good question. The man went through a year of intense debriefing without a hiccup. He appeared to possess knowledge of synthetic biology that went far beyond our own. Remember, some of our greatest leaps in the defense of our country have come courtesy of defectors, Werner Von Braun and General Shirō Ishii to name just two. But why am I telling you this? Commander Hart was front and center during the interrogation process. Correct, Commander?"

"Yes, Sir."

"I think it would be helpful to both General Scott and myself if you shared what you know about our potential perpetrator."

"The man you are referring to is Dr. Wei Hai Zhao. His purported defection took place a number of years ago during an international symposium on bio-defense hosted by George Mason University. We knew, at the time, that Zhao was a senior scientist in the Chinese bio-warfare program. Suffice it to say that it was a loosely guarded secret. In retrospect, we may now know why."

"How did he approach us?" Scott asked.

"He waited until after the keynote address by General Peterson from USAMRID, then approached the stage. After introducing himself, he told General Peterson that he was seeking asylum."

"And why didn't we immediately suspect this was all a ruse?"

"For starters, General, we were busy managing the ruckus kicked up by the Chinese government, which accused the United States of the wholesale kidnapping of one of their leading scientists. Threats were made and sanctions imposed as Sino-U.S. relations sank to a new low. Every bit of vitriol expressed by the Chinese government served to solidify the legitimacy of Zhao's apparent defection."

"How was he ultimately cleared?" Scott continued to probe.

"It took months for their protests to die down, during which time we conducted daily debriefings with Zhao at a site in Reston. That's where I first met him."

"Did he simply purge himself of his secrets?"

"No, he doled out what he knew methodically, which gave us time to corroborate many of his claims through other sources. Frankly, General, he appeared to be the most valuable asset we had acquired since the defection of Colonel Kanatzhan Alibekov from the former Soviet Union."

"Was there any internal pushback?"

"Yes," Conner answered. "Marvin Kahn went on record saying that it was foolhardy to give serious consideration to allowing this man aboard the Prometheus. He used every bit of his clout as CIA's Deputy Director of Operations to vociferously argue against employing a 'turned' foreign national."

"So, what happened?"

"Despite his passion and his vehemence, Kahn was overridden by the Director of National Intelligence, Arch Stinson, whose judgment I trust."

"So, you approved his integration into our bio-programs?"

"Yes. I personally signed off on his clearance and subsequent assignment to the Prometheus. As Truman said, 'the buck stops here.' So, if Zhao proves to be our saboteur, I am responsible."

"I think we can drop the investigation into the Muscovite. Based upon what we know about Zhao, we have to assume that it's the Chinese who are headed to the Prometheus," Hart concluded.

"Then things are now a lot more complicated, Mr. President," Scott concluded. "If they reach the ship before we do, there's little we can do to keep them from ransacking it other than to scuttle it. Unless you're willing to risk provoking a third world war."

"All the more reason I suggest you get a team in play within hours, not days, and then pray that we are one step ahead of them."

"General, if we could grab some face time tomorrow morning, it would be invaluable," said Hart. "I can be on a flight to Ft. Bragg first thing in the morning, assuming your schedule accommodates it."

"No need, Commander. I'm already scheduled to fly up to Andrews tomorrow at 07:00 hours. I will plan to meet you at 10:00 hours."

"Thank you, Sir."

After a grueling evening, Hart and Wilkins finally retired to their quarters. Despite suffering from heavy fatigue, neither could sleep.

"Darling, I need you to give me a crash course on this eugenics stuff," Hart said. "The only time I've heard it discussed was in connection with Nazi Germany."

Liz looked at him in surprise. "Come on, you must have learned about it in medical school."

Hart didn't flaunt his academic pedigree, but it was every bit as impeccable as his military training. After receiving his Master's in molecular biology from Georgetown, he enrolled in medical school at Johns Hopkins. He then completed Fellowship training at the United States Army Research Institute of Infectious Diseases. Yet, even then, there were gaps in his knowledge.

"That must have been one of the lectures I skipped," he responded sheepishly.

Actually, Hart had skipped quite a few, to the point of being called before the Dean of Johns Hopkins Medical School and threatened with disciplinary action. Hart was not absent due to disrespect; he just didn't see the purpose of sitting through didactic lectures on arcane topics.

"Okay, Cowboy, here are the high points," Liz's voice took on an academic tone. "The eugenics movement was based on racist ideology that presumed people of Nordic and Aryan descent were biologically superior to other races. The biological explanation was completely bogus suggesting that they were less likely to suffer from 'defective protoplasm,' which rendered a large portion of America's population unfit."

"Defective protoplasm? People actually bought into that shit?"

"Hook, line, and sinker. Their goal was to stop the masses of unfit from *polluting* our national gene pool. That's their words, not mine."

"All in the name of science, I presume."

"Right. In the early 1900s, Charles Davenport emerged as a leader of the eugenics movement."

"Who was this guy?"

"He was a zoologist by training, and he knew how to use scientific precepts to lend an air of pseudo-credibility to the movement."

"But where did his power come from?"

"His propaganda had strong financial backing from such laudatory organizations as the Carnegie Institution and Rockefeller Foundation. It gave Davenport's ideas substantial traction."

"How did they plan to purify the nation? After all, millions of immigrants entered the country in the late 19th and early 20th centuries. That's a lot of 'polluted protoplasm'."

"I appreciate your sense of humor, but not about this matter. This bastard created an office to track down and record those who were deemed *undesirable*. It was a broad label they slapped on the mentally infirm, epileptics, criminals, people of lower IQs, ethnic groups, vagrants, and anyone else discriminated against by the upper echelons of society. But they didn't stop there."

"What are you suggesting, Liz?"

"Thousands of these individuals were forcibly sterilized to prevent them from reproducing."

"Oh, come on, Darling. That sounds like left-wing, liberal bullshit. We don't go around castrating people or performing involuntary vasectomies on them in this country. Never have, never will."

"Oh, you think you know it all, don't you?" she admonished him, putting him firmly in his place. "You have so much to learn, Commander."

"Where were the courts during all of this? If what you say is true, I can't imagine a greater violation of one's personal liberties, other than perhaps death."

"The courts and the American Bar Association tended to side with the eugenicists."

"You're not serious."

"Yes, I am."

"Did these eugenicists articulate a standard for the perfect American?"

"Not only did they describe the ideal American, but they searched out those individuals thought to contribute to the purification and improvement of the race. They even offered them financial inducements for higher levels of reproduction. Eventually it ended abruptly, but not before the hopes, dreams, and lives of a great many Americans were shattered."

"What happened?"

"Ostensibly, the horror created by the Nazis experimentation on concentration camp victims, which was done under the rubric of eugenics, proved to be the death knell for the movement. That, coupled with the defection of the Cold Springs Harbor laboratory, which had once been one of its driving forces."

"What do you mean by "'ostensibly?'"

"Well, based on what we just heard, the eugenics movement never really stopped in America. It just went underground. When you hear today's rhetoric about the 'immigrant threat,' or 'building a wall,' there's a pretty good historical precedent for that type of thinking."

"A thin veneer of civility to keep a profound layer of white supremacy in check?"

"You said it, not me. But I agree. And it's not just the U.S. that has bought into this racist ideology. Look at Hungary. Their birth numbers have been tanking for years, while the number of immigrants entering the country has soared. Now, under far-right leadership, Hungary is creating strong economic incentives for native Hungarians to proliferate. Hell, they're even offering them free minivans if they have three or more kids. And they're unabashed about it, saying that they don't want Hungary to lose its identity as a white, Christian country. It's fucking crazy!"

"I think this is going to get ugly, Darling. Very ugly."

Liz sighed and kissed his cheek. "On that note, good night, John."

CHAPTER 15

Rabid

THE BLOOD DRAINED FROM LI QIANG CHOW'S FACE as he read the transcribed messages from Wei Hai Zhao. Though marked 'URGENT," the communiques just handed to him by his senior communications officer had arrived two days earlier. It was an inexcusable oversight, one that could cost him his rank, if not his life. He knew the delay would effectively negate any time advantage the Chinese had once held over the Americans in reaching the Prometheus. He stared, eye to eye, with Major Song Chen, his fury barely contained.

"You fool," he spat, "do you realize what you may have cost us?"

The soldier stood at attention, his whole body quivering under the weight of Chow's words.

"I'm sorry, Sir."

What sounded like the crack of a bat hitting a ball was actually Chow slapping the man with such force that he was literally knocked off his feet.

"And that's just the beginning of your punishment," Chow growled. "Now get up, you fool, and give me the last known coordinates for the Prometheus."

The soldier, still on his hands and knees, scrambled to his feet and rushed over to a computer console. Scanning the data on the monitor, he read off the ship's last known location.

"Get Commander Huan on the comm," Chow shouted when he'd finished. Huan was the Director of Chinese Naval Operations in the Spratly Islands, the closest access point to the Prometheus.

As he waited, Chow mentally calculated the time that would be required for the Naval Battle Group to reach their destination. The Spratly Islands were 2,100 miles as the crow flies from the presumed location of the Prometheus. However, the Philippines lay smack in the middle of the route, which added another 700 miles to the journey. At a steady thirty knots, if that speed could be sustained, it would take the ships nearly four days to complete the journey.

"General Huan, we are ready to execute *Dragon Fire*," Chow almost shouted into the phone. "Our target is adrift in the Caroline Islands and requires immediate intervention."

"What about the Americans? How much lead time do we have?"

"Very little, General."

"How could that be? We should have at least two days."

"Errors were made, Sir. It'll do no good rehashing them now, not when expediency is the order of the day."

"We may be forced to engage. You do understand that, don't you, Area Director Chow?"

"We both understand the consequences of engaging the Americans, General. So, it will be up to your judgment as to how to move forward."

Twenty-one hundred miles away, Zhao was struggling to focus despite the incessant pounding in his head. Thirty-six hours had elapsed since he departed the Prometheus, and his lifeboat was being carried closer and closer to the beach. When he heard the sound of sand scraping against the bottom of the boat, he struggled to open the hatch but hesitated before stepping down into the waist-high water.

A sudden, inexplicable sense of dread overtook him. He tried to shake it off as he sloshed through the water towards the pink sand. Stepping out of the surf, he fell to his knees, overcome with fatigue. He pressed his fists into his eye sockets in a futile attempt to alleviate the throbbing pain in his head.

He had to hold on, he told himself. Surely help was on the way.

CHAPTER 16

Fielding the Right Players

THE CHIRP OF HART'S DIGITAL WATCH GREW increasingly insistent until it permeated the netherworld of his sleep and summoned him back from his dreams. It was precisely 06:00.

"Can you turn that damn thing off?" Liz groaned.

Hart silenced the alarm, then rolled over, wrapping his arms around Liz and pulling her into a gentle kiss. He waited a minute until she had rejoined the living before throwing back the covers.

"It's time to get going," he told her.

"Just a few more minutes?" she pleaded.

Hart lay back in bed, holding his wife tightly against his chest. He could feel her body rise and fall with each breath. He kissed the back of her neck and nuzzled her hair.

"Thanks," she whispered. "I'm ready to get up now."

As John rose from the bed, Liz admired her husband's sculpted body. Although it was difficult not to overlook the scarring inflicted by his recent brush with a sniper's bullet.

"I need to stop by the condo and get my things before heading out to Andrews," he said as he pulled on a shirt. "Including my uniform."

"The one with a hole in it?"

"Don't be a smartass, Liz."

"Don't worry, I just need to make myself presentable for Mr. Kahn. We'll be be on the road to the Agency by 07:15."

"You couldn't be more presentable. Besides, you don't need to do anything special to win the favor of that son-of-a-bitch."

Since he had returned from Israel, there had been a rift between Hart and his former boss. John chalked it up to two things: his resignation, and a conversation he had had with President Conner regarding the true status of Osama Bin Laden. In Kahn's eyes, the fact that he was very much alive and a prisoner was a secret that should never have been spoken.

Liz let her nightie drop to the floor, ending the conversation. Hart stared at her perfectly formed breasts and taut nipples. Just as he stretched out his hands, Liz sidestepped him. "I thought you said we needed to get going. You can save some of that macho vigor of yours for later."

⚬

Kahn was waiting for her when Liz arrived at the conference room. He glanced down at his watch, then back at her.

"Am I late, Sir?"

"No, Doctor, you are not late." His tone was impatient, devoid of any warmth.

"As you know, Sir, we've been sequestered in a bunker beneath the White House. I had to stop by the condo before coming here."

Kahn's anger seemed to pass. "I'm just eager to address this situation while it is still relatively contained."

"Understood, Sir. I trust you've spoken with Dr. Linfield at CDC and have a draft plan regarding how we will salvage what we can from the Prometheus whilst also containing any type of infectious agent?"

"I spent half the night on a video-teleconference with your former boss and a cadre of other experts, piecing together a straw man strategy for discussion. Dr. Linfield will be joining us as we walk through it. Once we are in synch, we can mobilize as quickly as Commander Hart is ready."

Liz nodded. "Excellent."

"Are you ready, Doctor?" Kahn asked.

"Yes, Mr. Kahn. I'm ready."

He began the process of connecting the secure video uplink with CDC.

"Good morning, Liz," Tom Linfield greeted his former employee with a smile.

"Good morning, Sir."

"We miss you down here. Any chance of getting you out of Washington and back to civilization?"

"Civilization? You are speaking of Atlanta?" Kahn asked in a deadpan tone.

"Best town in the country. But we're not here to debate that, are we, Mr. Kahn?" Linfield shifted his attention back to Liz.

"We've got a slide deck we need to review with you, Liz. It provides an overview of what Mr. Kahn and I believe are the key elements of this mission. Your job is to critique and refine our recommendations until you are comfortable owning them. Understood?"

Liz nodded. "Yes, Sir."

"Good, then let's begin." A slide popped up with the words *Working Hypothesis.*

"We now have what appears to be supportive evidence that a toxin, presumably clostridium botulinum toxin-H, was deliberately introduced into the ship's water supply."

As Linfield pressed the remote a second time, a video cued up on screen. "Have a look at what Mr. Kahn's analysts found when they reviewed the video-feeds from the Prometheus."

There, in stunning clarity, were images of a man standing next to the water desalination system. As the video advanced, the man could be seen surreptitiously removing something from his pocket, then reaching with the same hand into the unit.

"That son of a bitch!" Liz exclaimed.

"Yes, he is," Kahn agreed. "The only problem is our camera angle is from behind. We never see the man's face. However, we've extrapolated his height and weight, and they are a perfect match for Zhao."

Kahn let the news sink in for a moment before instructing Linfield to continue.

"Based upon what we know so far, we assume that the crew are all dead, and there is no active biological threat outside of the contaminated water. The exception could be if the BL-IV has been breached or compromised," Linfield said.

A slide showing photos of equipment appeared. "That's why we won't be taking any chances. You will be supplied with mobile bioprotective suits inclusive of sealed air supplies, portable decontamination equipment, and new prophylactic measures from DARPA, including surfactants. Any questions so far?"

"No, Sir."

"Then I will turn it back to Mr. Kahn to finish the briefing."

"Your primary mission, Doctor, is to back up the massive data repository on-board. Your access point will be within the BL-IV lab. We will provide you with a sign-on, as well as the codes necessary for the two-step authentication process. The transfer rate on the data should be approximately a gig per second, but the files are estimated at more than sixty petabytes. Are you still tracking, Dr. Wilkins?"

"Remind me what a petabyte is, Sir."

"It's 1,024 terabytes. That's enough information to fill 1.5 million CDs. In this case, the files would fill ninety million CDs."

"May I interject?" Linfield asked.

Kahn nodded. "Yes, of course."

"While the data backup is in progress, your team will concentrate on collecting samples from key biological projects underway. I would suggest you focus on chimera viruses and modified pathogens, including filoviruses."

"How will we store and transport the material, Mr. Linfield?"

"You will put it in a vacuum storage device, cooled with liquid nitrogen so that it can be removed safely along with the data drives."

Kahn continued the instructions. "Based upon these objectives, Dr. Linfield and I recommend that your team include the best and brightest individuals familiar with Class A pathogens as well as the products of synthetic biology. This team will be supplemented by one of CIA's most experienced information technologists. We will only get one shot at the data, and then the Prometheus will be scuttled."

"Understood, Sir."

Liz instantly recognized the heavily armed soldier whose photograph appeared in the final slide, even though his face was concealed.

"I trust you can identify this man," Kahn said.

"Of course. That's John," Liz said.

"Yes, and he's responsible for ensuring that your team gets in and out without as much as a scratch. I will be meeting with him later. Commander Hart has overall mission responsibility, Liz, as I'm sure you will agree is appropriate."

"Yes, Sir."

Tom Linfield again took the helm. "We need a dream-team, Liz. The best and brightest people in their fields, people who have the requisite clearance and are ready to commit when they get the call. Tell me, who at CDC, CIA, or USAMRID do you think fits that bill?"

"I'd start with Marta Hopkins, who is my second in command here at the Agency. And since we are dealing with novel organisms, I think it would be wise to have Elijah Obaji onboard. Someone I think you know quite well, Dr. Linfield." Obaji was CDC's best molecular biologist.

"Finally, Sir, I would like to have Graham Nielsen. As you know, he's the best geneticist at CDC, and his talent may be needed on this mission."

"A geneticist?" Kahn asked with a raised eyebrow. "Just exactly what do you think you're going to find on the Prometheus, Dr. Wilkins?"

Liz wanted to speak openly, but a niggling concern tempered her response. "A wealth of genetic information, Mr. Kahn. Beyond that, I hesitate to speculate."

Kahn eyed her intently as if her secrets were hidden in the wrinkles of her clothes.

Liz turned to the video screen. "As for the IT specialist, I'm going to defer to you," she said to Linfield.

Kahn jumped in before Linfield could respond. "We'll send Carl Hodges. He's as good as they get, an MIT data whiz, but you'd never know it based upon his appearance."

"How so?" Liz and Linfield asked, as if reading each other's mind.

Kahn projected an image of a man in baggy pants that barely covered his bottom, a skater shirt, and black tennis shoes. He was making gang signs with his hands. "As I was saying . . ."

"Assuming they all agree to join the team, I would like to brief them no later than 20:00 hours. The commander and I are hoping to depart from Andrews tomorrow at 07:00."

"You know that's an aggressive timetable based on the level of coordination necessary before insertion," Kahn advised.

"And you understand the risks we run if any foreign entity captures the Prometheus in international waters," Liz shot back.

"Do you think the chances of that are high, Dr. Wilkins?"

"If you believe President Conner and the Secretary of the Navy, the chances are very high, Mr. Kahn, but I assume you already know that."

"The Prometheus will go down before we ever allow her capture," Kahn stated firmly.

"Given what you now know, are the people, parameters, and process acceptable to you, Dr. Wilkins?" Kahn asked.

Liz hesitated for a split-second. But there was no way she was going to let her husband go without her. "Yes," she finally said.

"That didn't sound very confident, Doctor."

"That's because I understand what we're up against."

Liz returned to her office, closed the door, and shut her eyes in quiet contemplation. Something was amiss, and she couldn't quite put her finger on it. "Think," she told herself under her breath, as she struggled to recount every word of the meeting. It had to be there. There had to be some reason for her anxiety.

It wasn't Tom Linfield. She could read him like a book, plus everything he said added up. The same could not be said of Marvin Kahn, whose body language failed to align with his words. In fact, the more she thought about her boss, the less she trusted him.

CHAPTER 17

One Bad Apple

Twenty-five miles to the southeast of CIA headquarters, General Mark Scott, a squat fireplug of a man with a bushy gray moustache and a hearty laugh, was welcoming the Commander.

Hart snapped a salute as Scott entered the room.

"At ease, Commander. It's been awhile, John. You're looking good. Retirement really must agree with you."

"Thank you, Sir. I'm not sure Liz would agree with you, though."

"She's a smart woman. Never did understand what she saw in you, Commander." But there was a gleam in his eye and he slapped Hart's back.

"Oh, I forgot. That's probably still tender. Sorry about that, John."

"Actually, I'm all healed up, General, and ready to get back to work."

"We'll get to that in a minute. First, tell me, how is Liz doing? You know you're damned lucky, don't you?"

"Yes, Sir."

"What's the pet name your wife calls you?"

A smile emerged on Hart's face. "She calls me *Cowboy*, General."

"Fitting."

"Well, now that you and I have covered the important stuff, I guess you want to talk about the mission. Did you know about this Dark Ark?"

"No, I guess it really is stealth."

"You never got wind of it at DARPA?"

"No, and the president asked me the same thing. They've kept an airtight lid on this one. Absolutely airtight."

"Trust me, I was just as surprised. For God's sake, at my rank, why would they keep the Prometheus out of my purview?"

"I can't answer that, General, but you're in good company. From what I've gathered, other than the ship's crew and those on a need-to-know basis operationally, there were only five people read in to the details of Prometheus's mission. Liz had heard rumors about it, but she thought they were crazy conspiracy theories."

"Apparently not, Commander."

"No, Sir."

"So, let's talk about what you're going to need. I assume you are chaperoning the scientific and data extraction team, including your wife, while also tracking down the missing lifeboat."

"Yes, Sir."

"And I assume you have orders to ensure that no living thing survives aboard that ship."

"That is correct, General. We will be scuttling the vessel, possibly with a hyperbaric, but I wouldn't rule out underwater demolition. As I mentioned last night, I believe we should deploy a standard two-boat team, each with a five-man crew. One of the boats will create a broad and deep defensive perimeter, while also searching for the lifeboat and presumed saboteur. The other boat will shuttle the scientific team back and forth between the Prometheus and the USNS Mercy, while safeguarding them in the event of any unwelcome guests."

"We're of like mind, Commander. I spent most of last night reviewing bios, and hand-picking men for your consideration. Most of them are from Naval Special Warfare Group Three, as well as a few men from your former SEAL team. Mr. Kahn has asked that we include someone from the Special Activities Group at CIA."

"Did Mr. Kahn say who?"

"Captain Mike Anderson, formerly from SEAL Team 6. I believe you know him."

"Yes, Sir," Hart said without enthusiasm.

"What's the problem, John?" Scott asked, his eyes narrowing.

"It's nothing, Sir."

"Commander, don't bullshit me. If you don't have complete trust in the men serving under you, you could find yourself in a world of hurt. So, I'm going to ask you again. What's the hesitancy?"

"I can't give you a good answer, General."

Scott rubbed his jaw. "You don't need a reason. Let's eliminate him from consideration."

"No, Sir. I won't be guided by my feelings rather than facts. And if Mr. Kahn personally selected him, it might be an affront to the DDO for me to reject Mr. Anderson. Trust me, Sir, I don't need Mr. Kahn on my back, if you know what I mean."

"Kahn is an unmitigated prick. You and I both know that, Commander, so why override what you sense in your gut just to keep that smarmy bastard happy? Furthermore, must I remind you that your intuition has saved your ass on numerous occasions. I think you should be listening to it now."

"I appreciate your concern, but Mike Anderson has had an impeccable career, General. Let's leave him on the team. He can command Boat Two."

"Did I hear you right, Commander? You're making him responsible for the safety of your wife's team?"

"Yes, Sir. I will entrust her care to Mr. Anderson."

Scott held Hart's gaze for a few seconds before moving on.

"Remember, these are preliminary recommendations, Commander. As I said a moment ago, you have to have complete confidence in the men under your command. So consider what I'm about to say as a starting point." The general handed Hart the remaining eight dossiers. "Here's everything you need to know on them including head shots.

"Every man on the list is currently state-side. Most of them are proximate to Naval Air Station North Island in San Diego, so they are available at a moment's notice."

Hart examined the first dossier as Scott began his narration. "The man built like a bull, Commander, is Staff Sergeant Juan Ramirez, SEAL Team 5."

"I know Paco," Hart said with a grin. "He's the best underwater demolition man in the Navy. I'd serve with him anytime."

"Then I trust you know that the man's a beast. He may only be 5'4", but he's as strong as an ox."

"Fortunately, he's on our side and he's good tempered," Hart added. "Who's next?"

"I'm recommending five battle-hardened soldiers: Tommy Lamott, Jason Harding, Roman Sitarski, Bob Bridges, and Ronny Good. Don't worry about the details for now. All you need to remember is they are from SEAL Team 3. You can study their dossiers more closely on the flight over to Guam. If I know you and your memory, Mr. Hart, you'll have all the details uploaded into your brain before you reach Honolulu."

Hart nodded, "I'll do my best, General. Unless I'm wrong, Sir, I've only counted eight men, including Anderson and myself."

"The final two men are our best snipers: Joaquin Alvarez and Sammy Latourno. They will remain aboard the Prometheus as a first line of defense."

"Got it. So, in summary, Boat One will be under my command and crewed by Staff Sergeant Juan Ramirez, Lieutenant Tommy Lamott, Platoon Leader Jason Harding, Roman Sitarksi, and myself. Boat Two will be under the command of Captain Mike Anderson, and supported by Bob Bridges, Ronny Good, sniper Joaquin Alvarez, and sniper Sammy Latourno."

"Correct, Commander."

"Looks like you picked a hell of a crew for me, Sir. I'd be honored to serve with these men. How soon can they be assembled?"

"They've been told to pack their things in anticipation of a potential deployment. I can have them here by 18:00 hours. I suggest we coordinate with the DDO and find out what he and Dr. Wilkins have recommended as next steps. He's expecting our call."

Without waiting for acknowledgment from Hart, Scott reached across the table and activated the speakerphone. He asked the base operator to put him through to Dottie, Marvin Kahn's assistant. She picked it up on the second ring.

"General, Mr. Kahn has been expecting your call. I'm putting you through now."

"Mr. Kahn, I'm joined by Commander Hart."

"Have you and the commander agreed upon a plan?"

"Yes, Sir."

"And is Mr. Anderson part of that plan?" The question caused Scott to glance at Hart.

"Yes, Sir. The Commander has requested that the entire team gather at the Agency at 20:00 hours for a mission briefing. Does that work for you?"

"Yes. Commander Hart, I'd appreciate having a few minutes with you prior to the meeting," Kahn instructed his former report.

"I will be there at 19:00, Mr. Kahn."

It was shortly before 13:00 when Hart called Liz on his drive back to the condo. It was a gorgeous day with the temperature hovering in the high sixties. Hart's windows were down, and he could smell the awakening of spring and new life in the air.

"Looks like things are moving quickly, Darling," he shouted into the phone.

"I can barely hear you, John."

Hart quickly closed the windows. "Sorry about that. I was just soaking in a little bit of spring. How did your meeting go?"

"Fine, I guess."

"What do you mean?"

"I don't know. I think it's just Kahn. He's not the easiest guy to read, or to get along with."

"Tell me about it," Hart agreed. "He's asked me to meet with him privately before our meeting with the team at 20:00."

"Did he say what it's about?" Liz asked.

"Probably his version of clearing the air, which means I supplicate myself before him, self-flagellate, then beg forgiveness for my sins, whatever they may be. By the way, he's got a strange fondness for Mike Anderson. I don't know what that's about."

"With Kahn, who knows, but be nice to him, John. There's nothing to be gained by making Kahn our enemy."

"Sure, Darling, whatever you say."

CHAPTER 18

The Wrath of Kahn

HART CAREENED THROUGH THE UNDERGROUND parking garage at CIA headquarters. Spying an open space near the entrance, he cranked the wheel of his aging black 850ci BMW hard to the right and slid in next to a Ford Taurus before coming to an abrupt stop.

It was 18:50 when he entered the half-empty building and opened up the turnstile with a swipe of his ID badge. He proceeded through security, then headed for the stairs leading to the second floor. He was cutting it close, too close, and did not want to give Kahn additional ammunition for a dressing-down.

As he entered the deputy director's office, Hart was surprised to find Kahn standing in the reception area with his arms crossed, waiting for him.

"I was wondering when you were going to show up, Commander." Kahn's words of contempt stung.

"I thought our appointment was at 19:00, Sir."

"Don't be a smartass, Mr. Hart. I'm in no mood." He turned his back on Hart and walked into his private office. The commander followed a few seconds behind him.

"That was not my intent, Mr. Kahn. I trust you called this meeting with a clear purpose. May I ask what it's about?"

That's all it took for the floodgates to open, releasing Kahn's vitriol.

"It's about your god damned attitude, Commander. I never would have singled you out as quitter."

"Are you referring to my retirement, Mr. Kahn?"

"Of course I am. People in our business don't *retire*." He spat out the word with contempt. "They keep going, irrespective of the danger and the damage they endure, until they physically can't go on."

"In *our* business, Sir?" Hart paused, knowing he was venturing into dangerous territory. He felt a contempt for Kahn that he had never allowed himself to acknowledge before. "Sir, to my knowledge, you've never had to get your hands dirty, kill people up close and personal. Have you, Mr. Kahn?"

"I've sent plenty of men to their death."

"Yes, from the sterile sanctity of your office. You have no clue as to the toll combat takes on your soul. I've watched the last flicker of life drain from a crew member's eyes; I've seen the remains of enemy combatants eviscerated by Hellfire missiles, and I've picked up the mutilated body of a young girl and handed her to her grieving mother. That was my job, and I never complained, Sir."

"I don't need to be lectured by you," Kahn snarled.

"There must be something more, Mr. Kahn, to justify your anger. What is it?" Hart demanded.

"Damned right there's more! You had the audacity to reveal the status of Osama Bin Laden, arguably the Agency's most tightly guarded secret. In so doing, you jeopardized the security and integrity of our nation."

"Mr. Kahn, I wasn't the source of the revelation. It was Prime Minister Rabinovich who informed me that Bin Laden was alive."

"Yes, and you then felt compelled to share that information with the president."

"The last time I checked, Sir, he was the Commander in Chief."

"I don't need your sarcasm, Commander."

"Mr. Kahn, there is nothing that should be out of the president's purview."

"That's where we disagree, Commander. Information is power, and that power that must be carefully balanced within our democracy."

"I don't know how to respond to that, Sir. Tell me what you need to hear from me in order to move on to the business at hand."

"I need to hear, Commander, that once you have completed this mission, you will retire permanently."

"That's my plan, Mr. Kahn. In the interim, I would be grateful if you could do everything in your power to support me on this mission, irrespective of your view on my past transgressions."

"I'll support you for the duration of this mission, but that's as far as it goes, Commander. After that, you're on your own." Kahn stood up abruptly, signifying the meeting was over. "Now, let's get over to the conference room."

Hart followed Kahn out, his mind reeling from the exchange, and wondering how he could have allowed himself to be sucked into such an overt confrontation.

◆

CHAPTER 19

Extra Crispr

THE LONG WALK FROM KAHN'S OFFICE was made in silence, broken only when they entered the conference room and greeted Liz.

"I'm sorry to have delayed your husband, Dr. Wilkins," Kahn said in a clipped voice, his anger still smoldering. "I've asked security to have your attendees congregate in room G2 until you are ready. You can buzz my admin, Dottie, and let her know when it's show-time. I will join you then."

Kahn had just closed the door behind himself when Liz turned to John. "What was that all about? You sure stoked something in that man."

"I wanted to be sure we had Mr. Kahn's full support before moving forward with the mission."

"Looks like you did a hell of a job, Cowboy!"

"He's one mean bastard, Liz, and he's dangerous. Mr. Kahn either fails to understand that our nation is governed by a Constitution or he doesn't give a good God-damn."

"I warned you not to cross him, John."

"Yes, you did. Look, there's nothing I can do about Kahn at the moment, and we're running out of time. I suggest we figure out our respective roles before we meet with our people. Do you have an outline for the briefing?"

Liz handed her husband a thick printout of the presentation she, Tom Linfield, and Marvin Kahn had honed earlier. He quickly perused the plan.

"You should have commanded a battalion, Liz. You've got it buttoned down."

"I wouldn't go that far, but I think we'll leave tonight as prepared as humanly possible. Under the circumstances," she added.

At precisely 20:00, all attendees were shown in to the long, narrow conference room where three rows of chairs were lined up facing the podium at the front. Liz and John stood huddled together, just out of range of the microphone.

"Is this a conference room or a meat locker, Darling?" Hart said under his breath. "It can't be more than sixty degrees in here. I know we want to keep people awake, but I'd prefer them not to be hypothermic."

Liz gave him a look, then walked over and adjusted the digital thermostat. "Sixty-four degrees, to be precise, Commander. Are you ready now?" she asked, already moving towards the podium.

"Good evening." Liz waited for the buzz of conversation to die down before continuing. "For those of you who don't know me, I'm Dr. Elizabeth Wilkins, one of your hosts this evening. I'm joined by my co-presenter and husband, Commander John Hart. I know many of you have been traveling all day and probably had little time for a meal. So, before we get started, please take a moment and get something to eat or drink. You've probably already discovered that light snacks, soft drinks, and coffee are available at the buffet in the back. We'll begin in five minutes."

She didn't need to tell them twice, as a line quickly formed at the buffet. She watched as people introduced themselves to each other, soldiers and scientists searching to find common ground, before returning to their seats. As the chairs filled, Liz adjusted the room lights, turning off the glaring fluorescent bulbs and dimming the overhead cans. She switched on the LCD projector and waited for the title slide to come into sharp focus. Lastly, she picked up the phone and alerted Dottie that the briefing was about to begin.

"Welcome and thank you for joining us on short notice," Liz began. "As I mentioned a moment ago, my name is Liz Wilkins, and I'm part of the bio-preparedness team here at CIA." Gesturing to the man beside her in naval dress uniform, she added, "And I believe everyone is familiar with Commander Hart."

As she spoke, DDO Kahn entered the room, avoiding eye contact as he negotiated his way to a chair in the back of the room.

"We know that many of you have families at home, and your willingness to step forward at this time of crisis is admirable and appreciated. We promise to use your time and talents well." She paused, looking intensely into the eyes of a half dozen attendees. "Expect to be tested in a way you've never been tested before. Even you, gentlemen," she added, directing her stare at the SEALS and special ops staff. "In short, the commander and I will expect nothing less than excellence from each of you every step of this mission. Now, let's begin."

Liz brought up an image of a grayish-black, trimaran ship. "Ladies and gentlemen, I give you the Prometheus, a four-hundred-foot long, stealth research vessel responsible for cutting-edge experiments in genetics and synthetic biology. She houses a Biolevel-IV laboratory, which is normally staffed with a scientific team of twenty individuals."

"What do you mean by *normally staffed*, Doctor?"

The question came from Marta Hopkins, a Swiss-born epidemiologist and rare disease expert, who had been one of Liz's co-workers at CDC.

"We are operating under the presumption that the crew of the Prometheus is dead, Marta."

"All of them?" Hopkins shuddered. It was a noteworthy reaction from a woman who had been on the front lines of numerous outbreaks including Ebola and Marburg, and had always remained unflappable.

"I'm afraid so. We'll discuss it more in a few minutes. First, I want to be certain everyone understands what we will be dealing with onboard the Prometheus: Type A pathogens, toxins, and genetically engineered chimera viruses."

Before Liz could continue, she was interrupted once more by a raised hand.

"Yes, Dr. Obaji, you have a question?"

"Dr. Wilkins, the work on chimeras is still relatively primitive, is it not?"

Originally from Zaire, Elijah Obaji had been a child prodigy who went on to earn degrees from Harvard, Stanford, and Duke. Yet, despite his stunning academic accomplishments, the man remained humble and soft-spoken. Taller than the Commander at 6'6", he was rail-thin, weighing only 170 pounds, but with a backbone made of steel.

"The Prometheus appears to have been in a league of its own, significantly outpacing the advancements occurring in laboratories around the world."

"But how is that possible, Dr. Wilkins? We both know the height of the hurdles its scientists faced."

"The best analogy I can think of is the Manhattan Project, where a core group of scientists made advancements initially thought to be impossible. The Prometheus was staffed by an equally exceptional group of biologists, geneticists, and recombinant chemists. They were armed with cutting-edge tools for genomic manipulation, the most basic of which is CRISPR. From what we have gleaned, the crew of the Prometheus was able to achieve in a few years what would have required decades not long ago."

"Beyond chimeras, what other research was underway relative to the manipulation of genomes?" Obaji asked.

Liz stole a look at Kahn, who was slowly shaking his head.

"We don't yet know the full extent of the research, but our overriding concern is to avoid exposure to pathogenic agents."

It was a non-answer, and Obaji knew it. But he wasn't about to put Wilkins on the spot. "Thank you, Doctor."

Another arm shot up in the back. Liz acknowledged the heavy-set man in military fatigues. "I'll take one more question, then the commander and I need to move on."

In a deep voice accented by a heavy southern drawl, the soldier asked, "If you've got CRISPR, Ma'am, do you have Extra CRISPR, too?"

As the laughter died down, he continued, "Doctor, you're not expecting us jugheads to retain this stuff, are ya?"

"No Sergeant, I'll be quite content if you simply stay as far away from the lab as possible.

"That brings me to my first major point. The holy grail is not the active biological material residing in the lab, but rather the data that resides within the ship's extensive digital archives. That's where you come in, Mr. Hodges."

All eyes turned towards a disheveled man whose mind appeared to be somewhere in another galaxy.

"What was that?" Hodges asked.

Hart shook his head in disbelief. And this was CIA's information superstar?

"You're going to have a short time in which to retrieve petabytes of data, while working in a potentially lethal environment. Do you understand that, Mr. Hodges?"

"No problem," he said nonchalantly, before lowering his gaze.

Irked by Hodges' laissez faire attitude, Liz nonetheless continued. "A final note before I hand things over to the commander. Though data may be the holy grail, we're still going to collect artifacts, meaning biologically active samples from the freezers in the lab. In addition to the chimeras, I want any bioregulators, modified Category A pathogens, or any other demons."

Wilkins handed the remote to Hart. "They're all yours, Commander."

Hart pressed the button and brought up an image of islands ringed by rich blue waters. "I know. It looks like your dream vacation destination, right? The one you've been planning since your honeymoon? Well, I hate to burst your bubble, but this is no picnic we're about to embark on. My first major point is that you not allow yourself to be distracted for as much as a moment. There's an intense amount of work to be done, and little time in which to do it. I expect a laser-sharp focus from each of you."

Hart brought up the next slide, which revealed a ship proximate to the islands. "The Prometheus is currently located approximately 350 miles southwest of Guam in the Caroline Islands. It appears to be adrift, moving slowly in the direction of Palau. We've attempted hourly radio contact, but there's been no response."

"Is there any direct threat to the vessel, Commander?"

The question came from Mike Anderson. It appeared innocent enough to Hart, who responded by bringing up an image of a world map. He pressed the remote again, causing red arrows to radiate outward from Washington, D.C. and the southern coast of China, converging on the Caroline Islands.

"Does this answer your question, Mr. Anderson?"

"Yes, Sir."

"Ladies and gentlemen, tomorrow morning, the race begins. As you've undoubtedly discerned from this slide, we are not the only ones pursuing the Prometheus and her bounty. We have good reason to believe that the Chinese are en route to the vessel with the hope of sacking it before our arrival. That could prove existentially damaging to our nation's security."

Anderson spoke again. "That's a powerful claim, Sir. Would you care to elaborate, Commander? What makes you believe that the Chinese have an inkling of what's happening with the Prometheus?"

"As Dr. Wilkins alluded to, we believe the crew was exposed to a toxic agent or a pathogen, most likely botulinum. Furthermore, we don't believe it was attributable to a lab accident, but that it was a deliberate and methodically planned act of sabotage perpetrated by a foreign agent."

"Has that agent been identified, Commander, or is this speculation?" Anderson pressed.

Before he could answer, Kahn interrupted. "We don't yet have conclusive evidence, Mr. Anderson, but Dr. Wei Hai Zhao is at the top of our list. As many of you know, Zhao defected to the West a number of years ago. At the time, he underwent an exhaustive debriefing by numerous agencies, including this one. There wasn't the slightest hint of subterfuge in any of his interviews. Quite the contrary, he revealed a great deal of highly secretive information about the Chinese bio-warfare division. If my assumptions are correct, that was a carefully constructed artifice designed to win our confidence."

Hart was grateful that Kahn didn't use the question as an opportunity to throw him under the bus, which would have been easy considering Hart's involvement in Zhao's interrogation, a process that, if it had been properly conducted, should have uncovered the true nature of his so-called *defection*.

"You're implying that Dr. Zhao has been functioning as a double-agent since his arrival. To what end, Mr. Kahn?"

"Mr. Anderson, I trust you are familiar with the Chinese. So, I would ask you: Why would they spend years building what they can steal? They've done it with our technology. Hell, they even do it with our movies. Zhao's job appears to have been the theft of our most precious secrets."

Hart continued. "In the interest of time, I'm going to move on to mission objectives, followed by your roles and responsibilities. Before we adjourn tonight, Dr. Wilkins and I need to ensure that we have addressed any remaining questions."

Kahn slipped silently out of the room.

Over the next two hours, boat assignments were reviewed, as were protocols for boarding the Prometheus, decontamination, and security. Timelines were established with an emphasis on urgency. Finally, there was a short discussion regarding the ultimate fate of the ghost ship.

"Any final questions?" Hart asked the group. The tension in the room was now palpable.

"Just one, Sir," Mike Anderson said. "Based upon the bounty, the Chinese may throw a number of assets at this mission; anything from a carrier group to fast-attack boats. I've not heard you mention anything about firepower, so what happens if we find ourselves in a situation with the Chinese?"

"I see you saved the easy questions for last, Mr. Anderson," Hart joked before providing a serious answer. "As you know, we will be relying on two Mark V's for transportation and security. For those of you unfamiliar with the SEALS' fast insertion boat, the Mark V is extremely well armed. On this mission, the boats will carry ship-to-ship ordnance. We will also have a handful of Predator drones armed with Hellfire missiles at our disposal. From what I've learned, the Prometheus can handle her own. I'll be happy to brief you on the specifics, Mr. Anderson, off-line. Finally, a carrier task force is being repositioned as we speak. Within twenty-four hours, the area from the

Caroline Islands south to Palau will be within air-range of our F18's, F22's and F35's." Hart paused.

"But let me make one point abundantly clear: We do not, I repeat, we do *not* want to get into a shooting war with the Chinese. Nor do we want them to overrun our ship. Let's hope we can avoid a confrontation while simultaneously accomplishing our mission."

Elijah Obaji tentatively raised his hand. "I'm sorry, Commander, I know you must be eager to end this briefing, but I can't help but wonder why we would risk such a confrontation over a bio-warfare laboratory and some data files. Today's secrets, even if highly advanced, are tomorrow's old news."

"You are entitled to your opinion, Doctor. I'm following orders handed down by the president. Are there any final questions?" Hart asked.

Not seeing any hands raised, Hart proceeded to adjourn the meeting. "Okay, I think everyone here needs to get some sleep. You are to report to Joint Base Andrews at 05:30 for a 06:00 take-off. You did hear that, Mr. Hodges?"

"Yes, yes." The man smiled sleepily. "I heard that, Commander."

"Dismissed!" Hart bellowed.

"That goofy bastard is going to be a problem," Hart said to Liz once Hodges and everyone else was out of earshot. "You're going to have to keep a tight rein on him, Darling, and kick him in the ass if he's not moving heaven and earth to get his job done."

"I can't believe Mr. Kahn would entrust data collection to him. Presumably, there's more to him than meets the eye."

"There'd better be. Also, I always knew that Elijah Obaji was off-the-charts smart, but he's remarkably insightful as well. He picked up on the fact that there were critical things we omitted from the presentation."

"Without a doubt," Liz responded. "Did you see the look Kahn shot me after Obaji's question? He didn't want me to go near it."

"I bet the Agency is knee-deep in this shit. I can't imagine why you weren't read in to the program."

"Maybe they think I'm a Girl Scout and can't handle the truth."

"Then they've got a big surprise coming."

As Hart and Wilkins left the building, two men remained behind. Marvin Kahn sat in his office, tapping his finger incessantly on top of his desk as he waited for his appointment to arrive. Finally, a man appeared at his door.

"Permission to enter, Sir," Mike Anderson requested.

Kahn raised his hand and motioned him in. "Have a seat, Mr. Anderson. I was beginning to wonder if you were planning to join me."

"I'm sorry, Mr. Kahn, the briefing ran ten minutes over."

Kahn stood and began to pace behind his desk before turning to address him.

"I want to be sure there's no ambiguity in your mind when it comes to the commander, Mr. Anderson."

Anderson stared intently at Kahn. "Ambiguity? What do you mean, Sir?"

"Let me be clear. If the commander does anything to threaten your mission, I don't want you to so much as blink before taking him out."

"Yes, Sir."

"And that includes Mr. Hart uncovering any experiments involving the crew."

"Understood, Mr. Kahn. What about his wife?"

"The same rules apply. But *after* we've secured the data. At that point, Dr. Wilkins is expendable too."

"Shooting a woman! That's not going to look good, Mr. Kahn."

"I couldn't care less about optics, Mr. Anderson. You are being entrusted to secure a project that has spanned generations, a project that could change the fate of our nation. I trust we picked the right man for the job. Someone who appreciates the magnitude of his responsibilities."

"Don't worry, Mr. Kahn." He smiled coldly. "You picked the right man."

CHAPTER 20

Guam

STILL SLUGGISH FROM LACK OF SLEEP, Hart and Wilkins downed the dregs of their coffee and hoped that the caffeine would kick in soon. It was 05:20, and they were fast approaching the junction of 495 and Suitland Parkway, minutes away from Joint Base Andrews.

"You okay?" Hart asked his unusually quiet wife.

"I was just thinking about our lives and wondering if there will ever be a period of time that feels, I don't know, just normal."

"What's normal look like to you, Darling?"

"A time when we might actually be able to relax, watch TV, walk the dog."

"We don't have a dog, Liz."

"I know." She cocked her head and gave him an impish grin. "But we could get one."

"What kind of a dog should we get, Darling?" Hart asked, happy to play along.

"I want a lab, but not just any lab. I want a blond, British lab with a big, square head. And I want to name him Nigel."

"Nigel?"

"Yes, Nigel. I think it's got a ring to it."

"How about a rottweiler?" Hart countered. "We could name him Siegfried."

"A rottweiler? I can't picture you with a rottweiler. Maybe a toy poodle," Liz teased.

"That's not a dog, it's a rodent! I don't like any dog under twenty pounds, and I sure as hell don't like these new designer dogs. What do they call them, shitapoos?"

Liz chuckled.

It was good to hear her laugh, Hart thought. "I'll tell you what, I'll buy you that lab just as soon as we return from this mission. Deal?"

"Deal!"

He tapped the brakes, then downshifted the BMW, eliciting a growl from the monstrous V12 as he merged onto the ramp for Exit 9. From there, it was a quick sprint across Allentown Road until he reached the main gate. Rolling down the window, he handed the guard their IDs.

After studying them for a brief instant, the MP came to attention and saluted the commander. "Colonel Shepherd is expecting you, Sir. If you will give me just a moment, Commander," the MP informed him as he disappeared into the guard shack.

Returning less than a minute later, the sergeant bent down until he was eye-level with Hart, then pointed to a three-story building visible from the gate. "That's Colonel Shepherd's office, Sir."

He handed Hart a credit-card-sized piece of plastic with an embedded microchip. "This card will give you one-time access to the building, Commander."

In the distance, Hart could make out the hulking shape of Air Force One. Next to it, a small fleet of Gulfstream IVs and Vs were lined up. Gassed and ready to go, they awaited any senior governmental officials who needed to be shuttled around the world.

Once parked, Hart popped the trunk, grabbed their duffels, and proceeded to the door. A video camera transmitted their image and activated a voice-prompt instructing Hart to insert the security card he had just been issued. As he complied, a voice instructed the couple to proceed to the third floor using the elevator on their right.

Colonel Matthew Shepherd was waiting for his guests. After an obligatory exchange of salutes, Matt Shepherd embraced his old friend. "Jesus, John, where have they been keeping you? I haven't seen you in these parts in a blue moon!"

"Trust me, Matt, retirement isn't all it's cracked up to be. I sure miss my friends." Hart turned towards his wife. "Say hello to Liz. I think you two met at a dinner we attended at the Ritz in Pentagon City."

Shepherd shifted his attention to Liz. "I couldn't forget Liz," he said with utmost charm. "And, yes, it was at a military ball at the Ritz. Welcome to Joint Base Andrews, Doctor."

"Thank you, Colonel," she said, extending her hand.

"I don't know what you're up to, Commander, but you've created a hell of a lot of havoc around here in the past twenty-four hours." He gestured towards an east-facing window. "Have a look." He pointed at two massive C5s that were sitting on the taxiway just shy of Runway 35.

The C5 was an extraordinary feat of engineering. A plane with a 220-foot wingspan and a height of 65 feet.

Fully loaded, it weighed in at more than 800,000 pounds. Despite its mass, the C5 was capable of flying more than 5,000 nautical miles at an airspeed in excess of 500 mph before refueling.

"The planes and their crews arrived last night from Westover Air Reserve," Shepherd explained, referring to a base located near Springfield, Massachusetts. "We have been prepping for your mission non-stop since 20:00 hours."

From a distance, it looked as though a colony of ants was scurrying around the planes, as the ground crew worked feverishly to finish loading the vehicles, weapons, and equipment required for the mission.

"They'll be done by 05:45, in time for wheels up at 06:00, Commander." The colonel reached down and pressed a buzzer, summoning an Air Force sergeant.

"Would you please escort Commander Hart and Dr. Wilkins to their aircraft. Once they are onboard, you can escort the rest of the team. You will find them waiting in the flight room, Sergeant."

"Yes, Sir."

Shepherd bade his guests goodbye with a warm handshake and firm salute.

Seconds later, Hart and Wilkins were being driven across the tarmac in a Humvee.

As they ascended the stairs leading to the ship's fuselage, the captain greeted his guests. "Welcome Commander, welcome Ma'am. We're honored to be flying with you today. I'm Kevin Taylor."

"Thank you, Captain. The remainder of our team will be here momentarily. While we're waiting, would you mind giving us a quick briefing on the flight plan?"

"My pleasure. You are onboard a C-5M Super Galaxy, our latest and greatest flying workhorse. Our first leg will take us from Andrews to Honolulu. Estimated flying time is nine hours and forty-two minutes. We'll be stopping just long enough to refuel before flying the eight hours to Guam. I'm sorry to report that there won't be any time for sunbathing, Ma'am."

Liz was caught off-guard by Taylor's sexist sense of humor, while Hart fought not to crack a smile.

"According to the flight computer, it'll be a total distance of 8,700 miles with point-to-point travel time slightly under eighteen hours inclusive of our brief stopover in Hawaii. Of course, that doesn't factor in the fourteen-hour time change."

"Are you anticipating any weather en route?" Hart asked.

"Other than a hurricane due south of Hawaii, no, Sir."

Seeing a flash of anxiety on Liz's face, the captain quickly added, "Just kidding, Ma'am. It's part of my standard monologue."

"Right," was all she could manage in response.

Taylor's sardonic sense of humor was a carbon copy of most of the Air Force pilots Hart had met. Aka, a smartass. They must press them out of the same mold, he thought. At least Air Force officers had a sense of humor; he wasn't sure the same could be said for Marines.

Directing his remaining comments to the commander, the Captain added, "We'll reach our cruising altitude of 40,000 feet about twenty minutes after take-off. After that, it should be smooth sailing. We'll try to give you plenty of warning if we're headed for rough air, but I don't anticipate it. Even so, unless you're using the lavatory, it's probably best to stay buckled up."

As soon as the captain had returned to the cockpit, Liz turned to her husband. "I didn't find him funny at all."

"Oh really? I hadn't noticed."

Hart gestured towards two empty seats closest to the cockpit. "Would the little lady please take a seat?" Hart bowed slightly.

"Not funny, John," Liz said as she sat down.

"Permission to come aboard, Sir." Mike Anderson saluted Hart.

"Permission granted. At ease, Mike."

"Yes, Sir," Anderson responded as he led a small procession of scientists and warriors to their seats. Hart and Wilkins acknowledged each person as they passed.

It was 05:55, and Hart could hear the four massive GE turbofan engines beginning to wind up. He turned to his wife. "Buckle up, Darling, we'll be taking off soon."

Hart and Wilkins seemed to close their eyes in synch. It had been an exhausting few day with no respite between the calamitous events that had engulfed them. Hart knew there could be a few sleepless days ahead, and it would serve them both well to get some rest now.

✺

After the C-5 reached its cruising altitude, the captain throttled back the engines, reducing the interior noise from a strained roar to a constant drone. In no time, Hart and Wilkins were lost in sleep.

Halfway to Honolulu, Hart awoke suddenly. He'd been having a nightmare in which he'd been shot and was gasping for air.

"Are you okay?" Liz asked, startled awake by her husband's thrashing.

"I'm fine." He swallowed and took a deep breath. "Just a bad dream. Go back to sleep, Darling. I'm going to spend some time going over the dossiers General Scott provided."

Liz closed her eyes and, almost instantly, fell back to sleep. John watched her for a few seconds before reaching into his duffel and extracting a worn leather portfolio, which held the crew's information. Opening it up, he discovered Scott had written a brief paragraph that sought to condense the voluminous information in each man's service file down to a manageable sound-byte. The first man up was Tommy Lamott. As Hart began to read, he could hear Scott's deep voice resonating in his head.

'Lieutenant Lamott has served as the OIC on innumerable missions. He hails from south Boston, and he has the attitude to prove it. There's very little that Lamott can't do. I would consider him to be your right hand on this mission, particularly in light of your reservations about Anderson. I would trust Lamott with my life.'

It's hard to argue with that endorsement, Hart thought to himself, before moving on to Jason Harding.

'Jason is a platoon leader whom the men respect. He grew up not far from Macon, Georgia, and he has a drawl that will have you hanging on every word. With no wife or children, the Navy is his life. Jason has consistently performed in the top one percent of our core leadership.'

A smile crossed Hart's face as he held up a picture of Roman Sitarski. He bore a striking resemblance to a muscular version of John Belushi.

'Roman is a piece of work,' Scott's summary began. 'Were it not for his impeccable skills as a medic, I'm convinced he would have washed out of the Navy years ago. He does an extraordinary job of keeping people alive until they can reach a hospital, but he sometimes has trouble keeping his mouth shut.'

In his imaginary conversation with Scott, Hart commented, "And yet you are recommending him, Sir."

"I know other impeccable warriors who sometimes have the same problem, Commander," came the imagined response.

The last two members of the team were paper-clipped together along with a single summary: 'Bob Bridges and Ronny Good are both E-6 operators. Bridges will be your ordnance guy and will work hand-in-hand with Staff Sergeant Ramirez to scuttle the Prometheus. Good will be your gunner and navigator.'

After committing much of their content to memory, Hart returned the dossiers to safe storage, then closed his eyes once again and dozed off.

It seemed like only an instant before the captain's voice came over the intercom. "Please take your seats and ensure that your seatbelts are fastened in preparation for landing in Honolulu. We'll be on the ground in about fifteen minutes. Feel free to stretch your legs after we've stopped taxiing, but I have orders for everyone to remain onboard."

Liz opened her eyes to find John staring at her intently. "Is something wrong?" she asked.

"No, Darling." He reached over gently and kissed her cheek. "I was just thinking about how much I love you, and how grateful I am to have you."

Liz smiled. John Hart could be a real prick at times, but she was privy to a side of him reserved for the few, a side that had grown more vulnerable following his close brush with death in Israel.

"When we take off for Guam, I'm going to ask the Captain if I can ride shotgun, assuming you don't mind losing your seat-mate for a few hours. I'll bet Mr. Hodges would keep you company if I asked him."

"Don't even think about it," Liz warned him as she reached into her carry-on and pulled out a dog-eared book by her favorite author, Nelson DeMille. *Plum Island* was a classic thriller involving a former U.S. bio-warfare site located just off the North Fork coast of Long Island. It was right up her alley.

Hart nodded. "You won't miss me."

Liz squeezed his hand once, then opened the book.

The captain was standing in the doorway of the cockpit as Hart approached. "Smooth ride, so far, Commander?"

"I slept like a baby, Captain. How are things looking up ahead?"

"No reports of turbulence. It looks like it's going to be a cakewalk all the way to Guam. Would you like to ride up front? There's plenty of room. We can accommodate Dr. Wilkins as well."

"Liz is nose-down in a book, but I'd enjoy the view."

"We're about five minutes from take-off, so why don't we go ahead and get you situated." Beckoning Hart into the cockpit, he introduced him to the co-pilot and navigator.

"The Commander is going to be riding with us to Guam, so I would appreciate it if you would avoid any jokes about the SEALS. By the way, Commander, is it true that the way SEALS separate the men from the boys is with a crowbar? If so, I guess that also explains why you use powdered soap in the showers. It takes longer to pick up."

"You know, Captain, I was going to join the Air Force, but then I found my balls," Hart retorted as he slapped the man on the back.

"On that note, gentlemen, we are headed for Guam!"

The banter quickly died off as the crew became immersed in their duties and they became airborne. Hart was grateful for the quiet; it allowed him to meditate on the extraordinary beauty of the ocean below. Even at a height of 38,000 feet, the water seemed endless in its expanse, a glistening indigo sea that merged with the cloudless sky ahead.

He had begun to see the world differently following his epiphany. Natural beauty was accentuated, colors more vibrant. Life pulsed all around him. The threat of conflict no longer energized him as it once had. That warrior's spirit seemed to have taken a leave of absence.

Could I still kill, he wondered? The question haunted him. It was not an issue of competence, but of confidence. He knew that he could not afford to blink in this business. Reactions had to be preprogrammed and instantaneous. Any hesitation on his part could prove fatal, not only for himself, but for his compatriots. If they were lucky, they would get in, accomplish their mission, and get out without incident. But luck was a fickle thing, and he'd already tested it too many times.

Halfway to Guam, Hart thanked the crew for the ride upfront and returned to his seat. Liz had plowed through nearly two hundred pages, proof that he had not been missed.

"We should be about four hours out. I think I'll just close my eyes and rest, Darling." With that, he shut out the world.

Mount Lamlam, Guam's highest peak, rose from the ocean like a small spike on an otherwise uninterrupted horizon. The island was much larger than Liz expected, measuring more than two hundred square miles, with a population hovering around 165,000. As America's western-most territory, it carried the unofficial slogan, *Where America's Day Begins.*

Liz kissed her husband's cheek, causing him to turn towards her. Hart brushed her hair back, then gently kissed her forehead. "Everything is going to be just fine."

"Don't forget your promise," Liz said, pointing her finger at his chest.

"No, Ma'am, I won't forget Nigel."

CHAPTER 21

A Game of Chicken

ANDERSEN AIR FORCE BASE was under the command of Brigadier General George Solomon, a man more comfortable in the air than behind a desk. The legendary pilot had led one of the first F-117 sorties to light up Baghdad during Operation Desert Storm. He then went on to fly innumerable missions during the 42-day air assault that followed. In short, the general had big balls and nerves of steel. He was the kind of officer Hart respected.

"Good morning, Sir, and thank you for hosting us," Hart said as he welcomed the silver-haired Solomon into their temporary quarters.

"You're quite welcome, Commander." Then, turning to Liz, he added, "Good morning, Ma'am. I hope the accommodations are acceptable."

"Quite comfortable, General, thank you."

"May I?" He gestured to a wicker chair before taking a seat. "Commander, I'm sorry I wasn't able to welcome you and Dr. Wilkins when your flight arrived last night, but I assumed you would be ready for a good night's sleep."

"Yes, Sir," Hart acknowledged, though he had tossed and turned much of the night after dozing for so long on the plane.

"I have some good news. The weather is picture perfect and forecast to stay that way. You should be able to get a good look at the Prometheus from the helicopter. I know you've studied the early recon photos, but there's nothing like being face-to-face with the target."

Hart rose to his feet. "How soon can we leave?"

Solomon motioned for Hart to sit down. "I appreciate your enthusiasm, Commander, but you can relax. It's going to take a few minutes for the crew to finish prepping the Knighthawk."

"Once you have completed your flyover, I've arranged for you to meet with Chief Master Sergeant Ketchum regarding the deployment of your equipment and transportation. We've got Chinooks lined up to ferry the Mark V's and decontamination equipment to a drop zone proximate to the Prometheus. Upon your instruction, of course."

"Dr. Wilkins, I assume you will be joining the commander this morning."

Before she could respond, Hart spoke for her. "Actually, I'd prefer that Liz remain on base until I have some sense of what we're dealing with."

Liz started to protest, but a sharp look from Hart stopped her cold. It would be one thing to challenge her husband privately, and quite another to object in front of the general.

Solomon looked at his watch. "In that case, Commander, be on the tarmac at 07:30."

"Understood, Sir." Hart stood and saluted as the general made his exit.

"What in the hell was that about?" asked Liz, turning angrily to her husband. "Is it just too dangerous for the little missy? God damn it, John, I've been to hell and back with you. I'm going on that helicopter."

Hart opened his mouth to argue but, realizing it was futile, he shut it again.

"Don't worry," his wife said, relenting a little, "I'll be okay. Remember, it's just a ghost ship."

"It's not the ghosts I'm worried about."

A vehicle was waiting outside of their quarters as Hart and Wilkins exited. In less than five minutes they were aboard the helicopter, strapped in, their heads encased in Gentex HGU-56/P flight helmets equipped with state-of-the-art earphones and microphones.

"You couldn't ask for a prettier morning for a recon flight," said Captain Peterson from the pilot's seat. "Based upon our current fix on the Prometheus, I'm anticipating right at two hours of flight time at an airspeed of 175 knots. So make yourselves comfortable."

"You've got enough gas to get us there and back?" Hart teased.

"That's one of the things I love about this bird. She's got a hell of a range, plus a hover-in-flight refueling system. There will be an HC-130P on-station, a flying gas pump, to cover us. Any more questions, Commander?"

"Does the general plan on using a Knighthawk to ferry the scientific team onto the ship's deck?"

"Yes, Sir. Mr. Ketchum will cover those details with you when we return."

"One more question, Captain Peterson. Beyond the .50 calibers, what type of counter-measures are you packing in the event we have unexpected company?"

"This baby has an FLIR electronic warfare self-defense system that includes Hellfire air-to-surface missiles and mk54 digital torpedoes. There are also 7.62 mm guns mounted port and starboard, Commander. Anything else?"

"No, that should do it."

"Sir, I do have one question for you. How close do you want me to bring this bird to the Prometheus?"

Hart turned to Liz. "You're the expert. How close is too close, Doctor?"

"I don't want to be within a hundred yards of that ship," Liz responded. To which Hart added, "Close enough to get a good look at the empty lifeboat bay, as well as for me to see into the bridge with binoculars."

"Yes, Sir," Peterson responded.

The next ninety minutes crawled by as Hart impatiently awaited his first glimpse of the ship. Finally, the captain turned towards him and pointed due west. "We're five miles out from the Prometheus. She's still hard to make out, thanks to her non-reflective coating, but you'll see her clearly through the binoculars. I'm reducing our forward speed to fifty knots. When we get within five hundred yards, I'll hover and await your instructions."

Hart nodded as he reached for the Steiner 7X50 binoculars. The autofocus locked on to the ghost ship, magnifying it by a factor of seven. After scanning the length of the ship, he handed them to Liz for a look.

As the pilot reduced airspeed, a chirping noise penetrated their headsets.

"What the hell is that, Mr. Peterson?" Hart asked, though he recognized the sound of a radar advance warning system.

"It appears we have visitors, Sir." Glancing at the screen, he added, "It looks like a spotter plane. It's flying low on a vector that will intercept the Prometheus."

"I need a visual on that plane, Captain, so match his altitude and put us on an intercept course with the bogey."

"Yes, Sir."

"What are you doing, John?" Liz asked anxiously.

"I'm going to fly up that guy's asshole, Darling. Remember, you insisted on being part of this flight, so let me do my job."

Liz fell silent.

The pilot increased forward thrust, descended to five hundred feet, and set a new heading that would force one of the aircraft to either deviate or collide mid-air.

"I'll circle back to the ship after we welcome our guest, Commander."

"Understood, Captain. Let's hope he's not armed."

"Pretty small radar signature to be armed with anything other than an automatic rifle, Sir."

Glancing at the radar, the pilot said, "We're forty seconds from intercept, Commander. It's going to be a quick fly-by."

Hart saw a glint of sunlight reflecting off the polished aluminum of a plane. He trained the binoculars on it and, with the turn of a wheel, it came into sharp focus. It was a Shaanxi Y-9 operated by the People's Liberation Army.

There was no deviation in the plane's course, despite the helicopter's provocative action. Hart sensed it was turning into a game of chicken, and he wasn't about to blink.

He shouted an order to the pilot. "Maintain your course, arm the Hellfires, and give me a radar lock on that plane."

Peterson hesitated for an instant, causing Hart to bark even louder, "Do it now!"

"Yes, Sir!" the startled airman replied.

A loud buzz sounded in their earphones, indicating that targeting radar was locked on to the plane. "Should I fire, Commander?" Peterson asked nervously.

"Not unless you want to start WW III," Hart responded flatly. "Take your finger off the trigger, Mr. Peterson."

"We're twenty seconds from intercept and impact, Sir." Peterson's voice had risen an octave.

"When we're five seconds away, break off."

With only eight seconds remaining, the Chinese pilot veered abruptly, affording Hart a clean look at the full length of its fuselage. As the pilot passed within shouting distance, Hart gave him the universal gesture of friendship via his middle finger.

"God-damned Chinese!" he shouted.

"Could you read the markings on the fuselage, Commander?"

"There were none, but I got a good look at the pilot's face, thanks to you, Mr. Peterson."

"What are they doing here, John?" Liz asked anxiously.

"The same thing we are, and it looks like they will be joining us in the very near future. I suggest we take a quick look at the Prometheus, then head back to base. We need to deploy no later than tomorrow morning. I don't want to take a chance on a Chinese vessel coming within shouting distance of the Prometheus."

As they spoke, Peterson returned to where the ghost ship was drifting. He held the bird at an altitude of two hundred feet a mere five hundred yards out from the ship to provide an unobstructed view of its starboard side.

"Do you want me to bring us in closer, Commander?"

"Take us within one hundred and fifty yards, no closer, then hold," Hart ordered as he once again picked up the binoculars and began to scour the ship from stem to stern.

"What are you seeing?" Liz asked.

"I can't see anything through the anti-reflective coating on the windows of the bridge. But there's no question that someone lowered a lifeboat," he said, handing the binoculars to her.

"That changes the nature of this mission, John. If something other than botulinum got loose on the ship, there could be hell to pay. Particularly if the person in that lifeboat is infected. You're just going to have to find that lifeboat, and find it fast."

Hart didn't need to be told; he'd already come to that conclusion after studying the earlier surveillance images.

"We're done here, Captain. Put the pedal to the metal and get us back to the base as fast as this bird will fly."

Hart pulled a small satellite phone from his pack and began to type an encrypted message to the president with a copy to Marvin Kahn at the Agency:

Prometheus located, coordinates to follow. Encountered company en route. Appears the Chinese have an interest in our vessel. No immediate threat, but situation may change in the short term. The Prometheus appears untouched with the exception of a missing lifeboat. Please advise.

The minutes dragged by as Hart waited for orders. Finally, a text came through from DDO Kahn:

Under no circumstance is the Prometheus to fall into enemy hands. Scuttle if a threat is imminent. Advise Dr. Wilkins that her team will have 48 hours once on-site to complete their mission. Your orders, Commander, are to find the lifeboat and eliminate any possibility of a contagious agent spreading, then sink the Prometheus.—MK

He turned the screen so that Liz could read it.

"I don't know if we can complete our work that quickly. The databases onboard the Prometheus measure in petabytes. It can only be downloaded so fast, particularly when we're working in bio-hazard suits. And what did Mr. Kahn mean by 'eliminate any possibility of contagion?'"

"Exactly what he said. There cannot be any form of life capable of transmitting disease aboard the vessel or external to it."

"So, kill any survivors who were fortunate enough to escape death on the Prometheus?" Liz's righteous indignation was unambiguous.

"Stop right there, Liz. In all probability, whoever is on that lifeboat is responsible for the death of the Prometheus' crew."

"You don't know that. It could have been someone from the lab, or a cafeteria worker for that matter. We can mitigate any risk by covering them with a bioprotective suit and then moving them into an isolation unit. After that, they can tell their story and be judged accordingly."

"That's not how it works in the field, Darling," Hart responded. "Out here, justice is doled out from the barrel of an MP-5. If the person is alive, I'm afraid it won't be for long."

Liz stared at her husband for a moment. Then, with a scowl, she turned away from him. The rest of the trip back was spent in silence.

CHAPTER 22

A Body on the Beach

THE RICKETY FISHING TRAWLER PUTTERED through the shallow water, its ancient diesel engine belching smoke as it ran parallel to the beach. From the boat's stern, a man cried out in his native Carolinian and gestured frantically towards a bright orange lifeboat bobbing in the surf. Just beyond it, something lay motionless on the sand.

The boat's captain throttled back the engine and, while his first mate hunted down an old pair of binoculars, he strained to see what was causing all the excitement. But it was just too far to see. At last, the binoculars were found. Grabbing hold of them, the captain focused on the lifeboat. Instantly, he recognized it as U.S. Navy. He then tilted the binoculars to bring the object on the beach into focus.

No doubt about it, it was a human being. But was the person alive, he wondered. He fired up the engine and carefully steered the boat through an opening in the shallow coral reef that ringed the atoll. As he anchored in about eight feet of water, he shouted at the man in the bow, "Go! Find out if the man is alive."

Stripping off his shirt, the man dove off the side of the trawler and began swimming towards the beach.

As he emerged from the surf, he saw what appeared to be a corpse stretched out on the crystalline white sand. The man's skin was crimson and blistered from prolonged exposure to the sun. Uncertain what to do, he hovered over the man, shading his burnt face from the glare. Without warning, the body jerked convulsively, as if it had been electrified.

The fisherman leaped back in fright. "What happened to you?" he shouted, but there was no response. After a moment, he dropped to his knees and began inching closer. When he was directly over the man, the fisherman cocked his head and lowered it until his ear touched the man's mouth. He strained to hear the sounds of breath.

By then, two of his crew mates had arrived in a heavily patched, inflatable dinghy.

"Is he alive?" the first mate asked as they approached.

"Barely."

"Come on, let's get him to the boat. Captain's orders."

The three men lugged the semi-conscious man across the sand and onto the tiny dinghy; then, scrunching their shoulders, they squeezed in next to him. With the yank of a cord, the small outboard engine sputtered into life. The first mate cranked the throttle, and instantly they were skipping across the waves, water spraying over the bow. It only took a minute or so to reach the trawler.

As they carefully hoisted the man onto the boat, the captain rattled off instructions. "Put him in a bunk and see if he'll take some food and water. He doesn't look long for this world, but we must do what we can."

The crew nodded.

"Check the lifeboat," the captain ordered one of his men.

The man nodded and swam over to the bobbing vessel. Climbing aboard, he found it empty except for a jumbled medical kit and what appeared to be a thermos. As he opened the container's lid, a cold, fog-like liquid wafted out. Under it, he could see a dozen or more vials, each labeled with a barcode. Sensing danger, he carefully resealed the container and swam back to the ship, holding the mysterious cargo above his head.

"This is all I found," the man said as he handed the container to the captain. "Be careful, Captain, it has something strange in it."

The captain nodded and stowed it in the wheelhouse.

That night, Zhao faded in and out of consciousness as his rescuers struggled to relieve his suffering. One of the fishermen held a cup of water to Zhao's lips but, despite his throat being badly parched and his body aching from dehydration, he couldn't bring himself to drink. Not even a sip. An inexplicable fear of water overpowered even his most primitive survival instincts.

The rabies chimera virus was ravaging his brain, neuron by neuron, causing a rapid descent into madness. Death would be a welcome relief, as his consciousness finally surrendered to the overwhelming infection.

"We've done all we can," the captain observed. "Return to your bunks and get some sleep. I'll stay at the wheel until morning's light."

"Could we at least radio for help?" implored the fisherman who'd first swam over to help the man.

"It won't do a damn bit of good, but if it makes you feel better, I'll radio Palau."

The captain turned his marine radio to the frequency monitored by the Palau Harbor Patrol. He reported the details of what had transpired, including the missing naval lifeboat, and requested emergency assistance for the man when they finally reached the dock.

"Thank you, Captain," the fisherman said, smiling at his crusty, but soft-hearted boss. Then, feeling he'd done all he could, he made his way to his hammock.

The captain's assessment proved to be correct; Zhao did die in his sleep. Although he did not go quietly. He thrashed wildly, at times his eyes wide open and bulging as if staring at something invisible to the crew. With a final, piercing cry, his body gave up and was delivered from the cruel torment of the virus.

Though they lay in their bunks until the wee hours of the morning, no one slept.

"What if we catch it?" one of the crew whispered to his bunk-mates.

"I heard that," the captain shouted from the helm. "You're not catching anything!" he admonished the man. "Now go to sleep. We've got work to do tomorrow."

But even as he said the words, the same fears plagued the captain. What foolhardy thing had they done by bringing this man aboard? What fate awaited them? What was in the strange container they found aboard the lifeboat? And, finally, why would God punish them for their efforts to save a dying man? None of it made any sense. But, then, a lot of things in life didn't make sense.

Hundreds of miles southwest of their location and more than 20,000 feet above the ocean, the captain's conversation with the port authorities had been intercepted by the crew of a Chinese Y-8 GX8 electronic intelligence warfare aircraft. Having been alerted to Zhao's status, the radio operators recognized the potential significance of the communication and forwarded a recording to the SIGNIT division of the People's Liberation Army on Paracel Islands for analysis.

This time, there would be no failure to rush-deliver the message to its intended recipient. Within minutes, General Huan, the commander of all forces assigned to Dragon Fire, had assembled a virtual meeting of his key leadership.

After sharing the transcripted message, Huan communicated a stern message of his own. "I want the trawler intercepted, and I want the battle group in position and ready to board the Prometheus within forty-eight hours."

As the threat grew and the timetable shrank, the Americans remained blissfully unaware of just how close the Chinese were getting to the Prometheus.

CHAPTER 23

No Survivors

"A PERFECT THREE-POINT LANDING!" Hart said to the captain of the Knighthawk as its two forward and one aft wheel touched the tarmac. "I think you've done that a time or two."

"Yes, Sir, a time or two." He smiled as he cut power to the rotors and slipped off his helmet, prompting Hart and Wilkins to follow suit.

"I appreciate soldiers who know their equipment inside out," Hart said while they waited for the massive blades to come to a stop. "I was at Lejeune a few years back when the Corps was running a live-fire exercise for a bunch of Washington VIPs, including a NATO four-star from Italy. We were sitting in the mess tent, taking a break from the action, when a pilot brought his Chinook in to simulate an evacuation."

"I think I know where you're going with this one, Commander," the pilot laughed.

Liz just sat back and closed her eyes, having heard the story a dozen times before.

"Mr. Peterson, we were up close and personal with that Chinook. All of sudden, our plastic lunch plates started to vibrate and, before we knew it, they were airborne."

"Oh, no!"

"Oh, yes! Pretty soon almost everyone in the tent was wearing their lasagna, but it didn't stop there. Next, the tent poles start to vibrate, then they lifted from their moorings. In an instant, they were flying like javelins through the air. One almost clipped my nose en route to the forehead of the Italian general."

"What happened?"

"It hit him right here," Hart said as he thumped his forehead with his index finger. "They rushed him off to the infirmary, where he got a dozen stitches."

"What about the pilot?"

"That poor bastard. He got transferred the next day to Twentynine Palms," Hart said. He was referring to a dreaded Marine base located in the heart of the Mojave Desert. "The only water out there is Lake Bandini, which is nothing more than a glorified sewage pond for the base."

"That's a hell of a story, Commander."

"I've got plenty of them, Captain. It's what happens when you make a career of the military. You see plenty of SNAFUs."

"Speaking of which, Sir, there's no excuse for my failure to immediately execute your orders. I will note it in my report, and I trust that you will inform Command Headquarters."

"We all hesitate at times, Mr. Peterson. I'm sure there's a lesson to be had, and it's your job to discern it. And, no, as far as HQ is concerned, I plan to tell them that you performed flawlessly."

"Why, Sir?"

"I don't know many helicopter pilots who've played chicken with the People's Liberation Army Air Force. That's something you can take pride in, Mr. Peterson."

"Thank you, Sir. It was good to have you aboard."

Hart put his hand on his shoulder. "I would fly with you anytime."

"I've been told that General Solomon is waiting for you and Dr. Wilkins in his office. There should be an airman here momentarily."

After a quick drive across the tarmac, they knocked before entering Solomon's office. Based on the grimace on his face, Hart sensed a tectonic shift in the general's mood from earlier that morning.

"I just got off the phone with Marvin Kahn," the general said by way of a greeting.

"How is Mr. Kahn?" Hart asked a little too buoyantly.

"He was less than cordial, not that Mr. Kahn is ever charming. He's extremely concerned about the Chinese getting their hands on our hard-won biological secrets. He made it abundantly clear what will happen should that occur."

"Sir, neither you nor I report to Mr. Kahn, no disrespect meant to the DDO."

"He's a mean-spirited SOB, Commander, who can kick up a lot of dust." He smiled sourly. "Oh, and I don't expect to be quoted."

"Well, I do report to him," Liz reminded them. "And while I understand Mr. Kahn's concerns about the data, I don't understand why he isn't more singularly focused on the risk of a pandemic. We're not talking about a minor threat, General. We're talking about a virus that has the potential to wipe out entire populations. Mr. Kahn's data may be precious, but so are the lives that could be in jeopardy if an infected individual comes in contact with others."

"So noted, Doctor. With that said, I've been ordered to light a fire under your team. Chief Master Sergeant Ketchum will be joining us momentarily. With Kahn chewing on my ass, I need to know that we are doing everything possible to expedite this mission."

"We understand, Sir," Hart quickly assured him.

No sooner had the Master Sergeant arrived than Solomon barked an order. "Mr. Ketchum, brief Commander Hart and Dr. Wilkins on the details of the deployment plans, as they stand."

"Yes, Sir." Directing his attention first to Liz, Ketchum began, "Dr. Wilkins, our plan is to have a Knighthawk deliver your team directly to the deck of the Prometheus. That includes your security detail. Before departing Guam, everyone will, of course, need to suit up in personal protective equipment. Once you've landed on the ship's heliport, the security detail will deplane and sweep the ship from stem to stern. Only after Mr. Anderson gives the all clear may you and your colleagues disembark."

"What about Commander Hart's team?" she asked, feeling a little unnerved. She had assumed they would be flying together.

"The Commander's team will be leaving twenty minutes prior to your departure to compensate for the slower airspeed of the Chinook. We'll be using two of them to transport the Commander and his team, as well as two Mark V's, plus all of your decontamination equipment."

"Where is our insertion point, Mr. Ketchum?" Hart asked.

"If I may?" the general interjected, causing Ketchum to yield the floor to his CO.

"Several days ago, Secretary Harbinger informed me that he was ordering the USNS Mercy redirected from the Marshall Islands to where the Prometheus is adrift. The Mercy will serve as the insertion point for your team, Commander. Dr. Wilkins, it will also provide your team with secure sleeping berths, as well as a place for respite between shifts as needed." The general paused.

"Finally, should there be unexpected casualties, we will have a method for decontamination, as well as isolation facilities available on the ship."

"General, you mentioned shifts. How long and how many per day? My team isn't afraid of long hours, but they will be working under the adverse conditions required for bio-containment."

"Right now, we are planning on three, three-hour shifts with ninety minutes of recovery time between each shift. Your primary objective is information collection. Mr. Hodges will be responsible for the data download, but the balance of your team is responsible for sorting through and cataloguing any printed data-files, journals, or logs that seem relevant. Do that *before* you touch anything else."

"General, I don't feel your priorities are correct," said Liz.

"Doctor, how you feel is irrelevant," Solomon said, not wishing to be questioned further. "We are all operating under orders—immutable orders."

After shooting Liz a look that communicated, 'Are you crazy?,' Hart jumped in. "General, I'm sure you understand that, as physicians, Dr. Wilkins and I took a sacred oath to *do no harm*, which arguably means, in this case, stopping the spread of a deadly pathogen."

"As I said, Commander, immutable orders."

"Understood, General Solomon." Hart pivoted to Ketchum. "How will the scientific team get from the Prometheus to the Mercy?"

"The Knighthawk will remain on-station and be at Dr. Wilkins' disposal. Additionally, Mr. Anderson will have full discretion over the use of one of the Mark V's for transportation."

"Has the Mercy arrived?"

"I have been told that it will be on-station at 05:00 tomorrow."

"Mr. Ketchum, would you please provide a few more details about the deployment of our assets?"

"The Chinooks will deliver the Mark V's proximate to the Mercy. The first boat will be moored adjacent to the hospital ship, where it will remain for Mr. Anderson's use as just noted."

"And my boat?" Hart inquired.

"We'll set her down a few hundred yards from the Mercy and hover while your men repel down a line onto your Mark V. I assume everyone on your team remembers how to repel, Commander?" Ketchum asked with a grin.

"Yes, Mr. Ketchum, I believe they do. If not, they're going to get pretty damn wet."

"The Chinooks are scheduled to be wheels up at 05:00 hours, followed by the Knighthawk at 05:20. Dr. Wilkins, the first shift aboard the Prometheus is slated to run from 07:30 to 10:30."

Hart quickly calculated travel time to the Prometheus before raising a concern. "That means Mr. Anderson has to complete his sweep in about twenty minutes. I'm not sure that's adequate time to secure the ship."

"It's going to have to be, Commander," Solomon countered.

"If I may continue?" Ketchum asked. "The second shift will run from 12:00 to 15:00, and the final shift will run 16:30 to 19:30. We will repeat the schedule until our mission is accomplished, mindful that Mr. Kahn has given us only two days in which to complete it."

Before there could be any further objections, Solomon stood. "If that's all, I know you have a great deal to do and little time in which to do it." The meeting was adjourned.

Hart rose to his feet and saluted. "We'll be ready, General." He turned, taking Liz by the arm, and exited command headquarters.

"What the fuck are you doing?" Liz muttered as soon as they were out of earshot.

"Less than twenty-four hours on a naval base and look who's swearing like a sailor!" Hart laughed.

"It's not funny, John. Our first priority should be find-ing the lifeboat and its occupant, not securing the data. We've been through this drill. We've seen the destruction wrought by a novel organism. Hell, we came damned close to succumbing to it. Surely my boss understands that."

"Remember, we don't know that there has been any outbreak, and we cannot set our priorities based upon presumptions. Furthermore, it's not our job to question

Mr. Kahn's priorities, which I have to trust were developed in tandem with the president. Our job is to execute our orders, and that's exactly what we will do." Hart's tone was firm.

"With that said, as soon as Anderson clears you to board the Prometheus, my team will depart, ostensibly to establish a security perimeter, but also to locate the missing lifeboat."

"How is that any different than the priorities I was recommending to Solomon?"

"I'm not in the general's face countermanding a direct order, Darling. You often tell me that I'm about as a subtle as a bull in a china shop. Well, if that's true, then we are well matched."

Before Liz could respond, Hart went on, "Let's hope it hasn't drifted far, and we can accomplish both objectives without appearing to violate orders. Meanwhile, you'll have half of the security detachment—a team of five battle-hardened warriors under Mike Anderson's command—keeping you company. I think that should bring you some level of comfort."

"Five men versus the Chinese Navy? That's what I would call *cold comfort*, John."

"Understood. All the more reason why we need to wrap this one up in two days, before we have visitors."

"What if there are survivors aboard the Prometheus, John? It will take time to transfer them to the hospital ship. They will have to be placed in bio-hazard suits and go through decontamination, which is tough enough with a healthy individual. It's even harder with people who are dying."

"Unfortunately, I think the chances of that happening are pretty remote. For now, I would keep a razor-sharp focus on procuring the data, followed by the biological samples."

"How can you be so cavalier about people's lives?" She looked at him as though she didn't recognize her own husband.

"I'm not being cavalier. I'm being realistic. I don't think you will be transferring anyone to the hospital ship."

"Why not?"

"Because everyone aboard that ship is dead. The hospital ship isn't on a mission of mercy, no pun intended. It's there to provide cover if the Chinese show up."

"What are you talking about?"

"General Solomon omitted a final reason why Harbinger and the president ordered the Mercy to be on-station."

"And what would that be?" Liz asked, clearly not tracking.

"Try to imagine how bad it would look if the Chinese attacked a rescue mission in progress. They might get away with boarding the Prometheus based upon the claim that it was an abandoned ship in international waters, but there would be no justification for storming the Mercy."

Hart could sense something welling up in Liz. She wasn't interested in how things appeared. She was focused on saving lives.

"I don't think I'm cut out for this!" Liz blurted.

"I disagree. You're one of the toughest human beings I've ever met. How many people have ridden out a nuclear blast?" He paused. "Or survived a biological attack involving hemorrhagic smallpox? I'll put you up against any SEAL anytime, Darling. You may not have the bulging biceps, but you've got the balls."

"It's not about machismo. It's about human decency, John. I'm feeling set up knowing that my values are incongruent with Solomon's orders."

"Trust your instincts and your values, Darling. You will make the right decision at the right time, regardless of Solomon's priorities."

"That sounds a bit like insubordination."

"No, it's reacting in real time to the situation. We are the boots on the ground, not Solomon. Come on. We've got a lot of work to do."

CHAPTER 24

The Smell of Decomposition

THE RISING SUN HAD PIERCED the early morning's darkness and ushered in a brilliant new day. Two shapes were now visible on the horizon, with one standing out prominently thanks to its iconic white paint and red cross.

The pilot's voice crackled through Liz's headphones. "That's the Mercy, Ma'am—all nine hundred feet of her. If you look very closely, you can see the Prometheus to her right."

"I'm having trouble making her out, Captain," Liz responded. "Oh! Oh, yes. I see a dark silhouette. I assume that's her."

"Yes, Ma'am. Let's take a quick look at the Mercy. That will give your team a minute to finish getting fully outfitted in their bioprotective gear."

As they passed a few hundred feet over the hospital ship, Liz could see the two Mark V's bobbing gently in the water just next to her. A man stood in the aft portion of one of the boats waving his arms. Liz recognized her husband and, although she knew he couldn't see her, she waved back.

"You ready, Ma'am?" the pliot asked her.

"We're ready, Captain."

As the Prometheus loomed large. Liz wondered if anything had survived other than the deadly organisms contained in the BL-IV lab. And, if anybody was still alive, how she could circumvent orders and get them back to the Mercy without running afoul of Anderson.

A sudden maneuver by the pilot jerked her back to the moment. Her stomach lurched in protest. He had just executed a tight arc and was now allowing the 17,000-pound Knighthawk to drop like a stone towards the helipad. At the last instant, he slowed its descent, and they landed without so much as a bump.

"Show off," Anderson shouted to the pilot, as he prepared to deplane.

While he waited for the rotors to wind down, Anderson tapped Liz on the shoulder and spoke into his mike. "Sorry about that landing, Dr. Wilkins. These Navy boys tend to show off when there are women as previously discussed."

"This lady wasn't impressed. Next time, I'll lean forward and puke all over the cockpit. I trust you heard that, Captain?"

"Yes, Ma'am," the pilot answered sounding a little sheepish.

"I want your team to remain in place until I give you the all-clear," Anderson said. "Is that understood, Dr. Wilkins?"

"Understood, Mr. Anderson."

A crewman opened the gantry, and the security detail filed out.

Anderson was followed closely by Joaquin Alvarez and Sammy Latourno, two of the deadliest shots on the planet.

Based on the close quarters found on the Prometheus, the men were carrying short-barreled, fully-suppressed Uzi's with extended clips. With a firing rate of nine hundred rounds per minute, it was point and shoot.

Within minutes, they saw the bodies, many of which were already in an active state of decomposition. Anderson wondered if it was his imagination or whether he could truly smell the stench of putrefying flesh through the bioprotective suits.

They moved slowly towards the bridge. As they entered, Anderson noticed that the door to the communications room was open, a clear breach of protocol on the top-secret vessel. He approached cautiously, flanked on either side by Alvarez and Latourno.

Crouching low, he stepped directly in front of the door, his gun leveled. But there was no need. The decaying remains of the ship's captain lay on the floor amidst a pool of congealed blood. Anderson reached down with his gloved hand and turned the man's face towards him. A deep slash pierced his flesh from ear to ear.

"Well, that answers the question regarding a saboteur," he muttered to himself. Standing back up, he turned to his men. "Let's take a look below." He gestured towards a wide metal stairwell that he knew led to the scientific team's quarters.

After descending the stairwell, they proceeded down a long hallway lined with doors. Anderson saw that each door bore the name of a crew member. Suddenly, Anderson stopped. He reached for a doorknob with his left hand while clutching a 9 mm Beretta in his right. Slowly, he turned it, but it was locked.

Anderson took a step back before thrusting his boot hard into the door. In a shower of splinters, the frame exploded and the door flew in. Entering the room, he discovered the body of a woman curled up in a fetal position on the bed. Her bedclothes and sheets were soaked with feces, and her eyes and mouth were open, as if her last breath had been an anguished cry for help.

Room by room, they searched. Death was everywhere. Whatever had killed the crew of the Prometheus had been efficient. Not a single survivor was found on the first level. They proceeded to a lower level where the ship's operational crew bunked, but all they discovered was more death. They moved on, deeper and deeper into the bowels of the ship until, finally, they entered the decontamination area.

"Did you hear that?" Anderson asked his two men.

"No, Sir," answered Alvarez, "I didn't hear anything. But that .50 caliber sniper's rifle hasn't exactly improved my hearing."

Anderson cupped his hand to his ear. "There!" he exclaimed. "There it is again."

But, no matter how thoroughly they searched, they could find nobody alive.

"It's a bloody ghost ship," muttered Latourno.

Anderson nodded. He couldn't help but agree. "To hell with it," he eventually said. He turned to his men. "Let's get top-side and bring Dr. Wilkins' team aboard. The sooner we're finished here, the happier I'll be. Then we can send this floating coffin to a permanent resting place."

As Anderson extended his hand to help Liz off the helicopter, she greeted him with a barrage of questions.

"What did you find, Mr. Anderson? How many survivors do we have, and is there any indication of what happened?"

"Slow down, Doctor. It appears that there are no survivors. As for what happened, we have a captain whose neck was slit and a lot of decomposing bodies. You're the one who's going to have to determine the crew's cause of death."

Anderson led the team to the lab. As they approached it, he heard it again. A faint moan. He walked in the direction of the sound, entering a bunkroom. On the top bunk, a man lay stone still with his eyes staring at the ceiling. Anderson saw that his body was partially decomposed. Below him, there was another man. But this one was very much alive, huddled under a blanket and groaning in agony.

Liz, following closely behind Anderson, instinctively dropped to her knees and peeled back the blanket. The man seemed to struggle to focus on her. He tried to lift his hand and touch her suit, before closing his eyes and dropping his arm.

Liz stood up, her hands on her hips, and approached Anderson. "We've got to get this man to the Mercy immediately!"

Anderson pointed at the airlock leading into the BL-IV lab. "Dr. Wilkins, you are needed in the lab, now! We will handle this situation."

"Not until I have your assurance that you will help this man."

"We will take care of it, Doctor. Now I suggest you get moving. I'm going to inform Commander Hart that the situation is under control and your team is ready to begin the collection process."

Liz reluctantly moved out of the bunk room and towards the BL-IV lab. Before entering the airlock, she turned one last time towards the bunkroom. The door was closed.

As Liz's team of scientists entered the lab, they began a visual assessment. There were no bodies in the room, suggesting that the scientific team had extricated themselves before succumbing to a yet-to-be-identified agent. There was, however, one thing that immediately attracted Liz's attention.

Glass shards from a broken test tube lay on the floor. Liz saw that the bottom of the tube was still intact, held together by a sticky label. Snatching up a test tube holder, she very gently picked it up and examined it. On the label there was a number; it was a code, representing whatever noxious life form had been in it. Marta Hopkins called her attention to another piece of glass that had been placed on a lab table. An almost invisible trace of dried blood tinted its razor edge.

Liz recoiled at the implications of the blood. "Are you thinking what I'm thinking?" she asked Hopkins.

"I'm thinking someone may have cut himself while trying to clean up the mess. I don't know what was in that tube, but I'll bet it's fulminating in that person's bloodstream as we speak."

Liz turned to Carl Hodges. "I need the record corresponding to this ID number brought up on the database."

"It's going to take a minute, Doctor. The network was powered down, which would be standard protocol when there is some form of major event like a security breach. There are multiple layers of encryption. I'll let you know as soon as I have access to the server."

As he was speaking, a wave of anxiety gripped hold of Liz. Images of the smallpox pandemic, which had claimed 85,000 American lives, flooded her mind. She struggled to inhale, to exhale, to breath at all, but her lungs wouldn't cooperate.

Just as wholesale panic was about to set in, she was jarred out of her self-absorption by a loud concussion reverberating off the walls of the lab.

"I'll be back," she told her team, her anxiety replaced in an instant by anger. She re-entered the airlock and proceeded through decontamination, stopping just short of the crew's quarters.

She watched as the door from the bunkroom opened, a surprised Anderson looking out at her.

"What are you doing here, Doctor? You are supposed to be in the lab. Didn't I make that clear?"

Liz struggled to peer around the hulking frame of the SEAL. The man in the lower bunk was no longer groaning. A small red circle was visible in the middle of his forehead.

"What in the hell did you do?" she screamed as she raised her fists and began to swing wildly at Anderson.

"What I was ordered to do, Ma'am," he said grasping her wrists and holding her at bay.

"What are you talking about? We could have tried to save that man's life!"

"How much time and effort would that have taken, Doctor? Time that needs to be focused on your primary objective of getting the data and specimens off this ship."

"Who gave you the order to kill this man?"

"No one ordered me to kill him."

"You just told me you were under orders."

"I was told to do whatever was necessary to meet our first objective, Ma'am. Now, I suggest you get back in the lab and focus on the job at hand."

Liz wanted to rip his throat out. Never in her life had she felt such overwhelming rage. But there was nothing she could do. Not now anway.

"This isn't over, Mr. Anderson," she thundered. Then she turned sharply on her heel and stormed back through the airlock.

Elijah Obaji was awaiting her return. "Hodges gained access to the system," he told her, "and I have the record that corresponds to the coded test tube."

Despite her cumbersome bio-suit, Liz raced over to the computer monitor and scanned the data on the screen. Midway through the record, she stopped reading and sighed heavily.

"What is it?" Marta Hopkins asked.

"A chimera. It appears that they managed to combine the genetic attributes of SARS with a particularly virulent strain of rabies, producing an airborne pathogen designed to attack the nervous system."

"Jesus Christ!" Carl Hodges exclaimed. "If that's not some unholy shit!"

"I've got to get this information to John," Liz called over her shoulder, as she moved swiftly to exit the lab. As she emerged from the decon unit, Anderson was waiting for her.

"I thought I had been clear, Dr. Wilkins," Anderson said menacingly, as he blocked the corridor.

"Get out of my way," she seethed.

He didn't move.

"I need to radio Commander Hart."

"What for?"

"It appears there was an accident in the lab. Whoever is aboard that lifeboat may be infected with a deadly form of airborne rabies. Now get the fuck out my way, Mr. Anderson."

"Go back to your lab, Doctor. I'll radio the Commander."

🧬

Anderson reached Hart, who was twenty miles due south of the Prometheus, on the sat phone. "Commander, we've cleared the ship."

"Any issues, Mike?"

"Yes, Sir. This was no accident, Commander. The Captain's neck was slit from ear to ear."

"What about the rest of the crew?"

"Based upon initial inspection, the docs believe everyone onboard was exposed to some type of toxin. The bodies don't have the appearance of having harbored an infectious agent."

"Any survivors?"

"We had to accelerate one man's death."

"Understood."

"Sir, Dr. Wilkins is very upset. She was insistent that we transfer the sole survivor to the Mercy."

"She'll get over it. What else, Mike?"

"Dr. Wilkins indicated that there may have been a lab accident involving an airborne form of rabies. She said it may have infected the perpetrator. And, Sir, I don't think she's going to let this one go."

"I'll deal with it, Mike. Tell Dr. Wilkins that I will contact her later. Hart out."

Terminating the call, Hart placed an encrypted satellite call to Marvin Kahn's office.

"Good morning, Dottie. I need to speak with Mr. Kahn, please."

"He's been expecting your call." That was code for get ready for an ass-reaming.

"What in the hell is going on down there, Commander?" Kahn growled. "I was expecting a status report hours ago. Or perhaps I didn't make it abundantly clear that time is of the essence."

"We are working as fast as we can, Mr. Kahn. So far . . ."

But before Hart could continue, Kahn interrupted. "Work faster, Commander. If you don't hurry, the Chinese are going to be on-site before we can remove everything from that ship and scuttle it."

"Sir, what about the bodies? I know you said they were to go down with the ship, but the families are going to want closure. They are going to expect funerals."

"That's not going to happen. Nothing is going to jeopardize your primary mission."

"But, Sir, we've encountered a major problem."

"Are you not listening to me, Commander?"

"Sir, are you saying that not even the escape of a chimera virus capable of wholesale destruction should impact my orders?"

"What are you talking about? I think you'd better start from the beginning and tell me everything you've learned thus far, Commander."

Hart recounted everything he knew from the moment Mike Anderson's group set foot on the Prometheus, including the evidence that it was a deliberate act of sabotage, and the perpetrator might be infected with a lethal chimera virus.

"Your primary mission has not changed, Commander."

"I understand, Sir. To that end, Mike Anderson is providing security for the scientific detail as they upload all of the ship's data and securely remove critical viral and bacterial cultures. Sergeant Anderson and I will be in constant communication while I begin the search for our perpetrator."

"And what happens when the Chinese Navy shows up, Commander? Based upon what we now know, they've got far too much invested to stand off and watch us sink that ship. A couple of .50 caliber machine guns are not going to cut it against an aircraft carrier, a naval destroyer, and a guided missile frigate, all of which appear to be headed in your direction."

"Let's pray that the Chinese are at least twenty-four hours from our location," Hart responded, "and that our people work fast."

"I'm not interested in praying, Commander. I'm interested in doing whatever is necessary to ensure a successful mission, which is why I sent you there in the first place." And without another word, Kahn ended the call.

"Take us back to the Mercy, Mr. Lamott, and push it," Hart ordered. He pulled Staff Sergeant Ramirez aside.

"Things are moving faster than I anticipated, Paco. We need to have charges in place in the event the Prometheus needs to be scuttled. We can't rely on an airstrike using a hyperbaric. Mr. Lamott has set a course back to the Mercy. I want you in a wet-suit ready to dive as soon as we dock. That gives you about thirty minutes. Ten minutes to suit up and twenty minutes to prepare the charges. I'm assuming you'll be in the water for ten to fifteen minutes."

"Understood, Commander, but you've got a boatload of people on the Prometheus. I don't like setting charges until we've cleared the area."

"I appreciate your concern, Paco, but the only people who are going down with the Prometheus are already dead."

"If I may ask, Sir, who is authorized to activate the electronic detonators on the charges?"

"Two people: me and Mr. Kahn. Set a twelve-digit password for each of us."

Paco nodded. "Will do, Commander."

As Ramirez walked towards the bridge, Hart felt the vibration of his sat phone. It was Christopher Hamil, the captain of the Mercy, calling.

"Commander Hart, we just received a priority message from Secretary Harbinger's office. National Geospatial Intelligence Agency has a satellite fix on the lifeboat. It washed up on the beach of an atoll about thirty-five miles south of here. They scanned the atoll using infra-red imaging but found nothing."

Hart completed the thought. "So, either the occupant is dead and not giving off a heat signature, or someone took him off that beach."

"That would be a safe bet, Commander. I'm sending you the coordinates of the atoll."

"Thank you, Captain."

As promised, Paco was ready in less than thirty minutes, at which point the crew ferried him the short distance to the Prometheus. Ramirez hefted two MILA computer-controlled underwater mines onto his back before dropping into the water. After inspecting the ship's hull, he used the mine's strong magnets to attach them to two of the ship's key points of vulnerability. He surfaced long enough to arm himself with an additional two charges, then repeated the process. Once finished, he climbed back aboard the Mark V.

"Done, Commander, and I can assure you that there's sufficient explosive force in those charges to tear that boat in two. Her compartments will flood instantly," Ramirez promised.

"Good work," Hart said, resting his hand on Ramirez's shoulder; then he turned to Tommy Lamott. "Set a course for the atoll and fire this baby up!" Within seconds, the 5,000-horsepower turbine engine was rocketing the boat southward at a bone-jarring velocity.

CHAPTER 25

Some Help from a Friend

"JUST A MOMENT, COMMANDER, and I'll put you through," advised an aide to Sue Goodman, Deputy Director of the NGIA at Fort Belvoir.

"Commander Hart, it's a pleasure!"

"Thanks for taking my call, Sue, and my apologies for the noise."

"You sound like you're in a wind tunnel, John."

"Nope, just hanging out a few feet from a 5,000-horse-power turbine engine on full throttle. Can you hear me okay?"

"I'll make do. I assume you're calling about Prometheus's missing lifeboat that showed up on one of our satellite feeds."

"Your powers of deduction amaze me."

"You are so full of it, Commander. How long has it been since I saved your ass by identifying the source of the smallpox pandemic? You, Sir, owe me one hell of a debt of gratitude."

"Yep, you're better at locating things than a blind pig finding a truffle."

"Oh, you went too far with that one, Mister!"

After they were done trading insults, Goodman and Hart chuckled, as only close friends can do.

"What's your current location, Commander?"

"We're closing in on the coordinates where your folks spotted the lifeboat. Actually, I can see it dead ahead. Any ideas on how we find its former occupant?"

"Look for a corpse floating off-shore." Goodman's biting wit remained very much in play. "In all seriousness, he or she is either dead or not on that atoll. That much I can tell you with complete certainty."

"Is it possible to piece together images of that beach from the past twenty-four hours?" Hart asked. "Maybe we'll get lucky and spot something."

"I'll get back to you, Commander," Goodman said, embarrassed that the thought hadn't occurred to her.

After Goodman had hung up the phone, she summoned her staff. "I want a thorough review of all available satellite feeds of the area proximate to where the lifeboat was located. If any other boat came within spitting distance of that beach, I want to know about it. You've got an hour, not a minute more. Get on it!" she barked.

Thousands of miles away, they approached the bright orange boat. "That's close enough, Mr. Lamott," Hart called out to the helm.

"Do you want me to anchor, Commander?" Tommy called back.

"No, let her drift. We're not going to be here long, and I don't want to be downwind from that thing."

Without the requisite personal protective equipment, Hart was not going to let anyone board the vessel. It would have to wait. While he contemplated his next move, Hart's sat phone vibrated.

"Commander, looks like we hit pay dirt," Sue Goodman began, "and a hell of a lot faster than I thought possible."

"Don't tell me you found a boat that meets our criteria. Not already."

"Well, I've reviewed the images and, on one of them, there's a fishing trawler. It approached the beach and it looks as if the crew transported a body back to their vessel. I'd give ten-to-one odds that's our target."

"How old are the images?" Hart asked.

"Ten hours."

"That's a pretty big lead, Sue."

"Agreed, but we can provide you with a vector to intercept the trawler. She's only moving at about 12 to 15 knots, so you should be able to overtake her."

"Is the trawler heading towards a major port?"

"Yes. Palau. And, by the way, it looks like they removed some kind of container from the lifeboat."

"Viral samples," Hart said without hesitation. He knew what would happen if that trawler docked in a busy port.

"Tell me we're not going through that drill, again, Commander," Goodman said anxiously. She still remembered the anguish of the previous pandemic, a pandemic that had lasted for over a year.

"Not if I can help it," Hart responded.

"One more critical piece of information, Commander. We ran the man's image through facial recognition software.

The resolution wasn't very high, and his face was swollen and blistered from sunburn, but we still managed to get a hit with a 95% confidence level."

"Was it Wei Hai Zhao?" Hart asked.

"Bingo!"

CHAPTER 26

The House on Forsythe

THE MODEST BRICK RANCH on Forsythe Street seemed lifeless to its neighbors. Were it not for a few nights each month, when a half-dozen cars filled the driveway and spilled out onto the curb, they would have assumed it was abandoned.

But on those nights, the lights remained on until the wee hours of the morning. By dusk, all the visitors were gone.

It was the kind of mystery that Mary Adams couldn't resist. She was an inquisitive sort—some would say nosey—who had moved in next door a little less than a year ago. For months, she had walked up to the front door and knocked, but no one ever answered. Undeterred in her resolve to meet her elusive neighbor, she began perusing tax records online.

It didn't take her long to discover that the house belonged to one Patrick Henry, the original owner. Since the home had been built in 1952, Mr. Henry was either very old or had been very young when the house was deeded. She resolved to pay a surprise visit the next time there was a late-night gathering.

It was 1:20 a.m. on an unusually cold Sunday night, when Mary ventured out of her house and began peering into her neighbor's windows. Careful not to be detected, she watched the home for at least fifteen minutes, observing six well-dressed gentlemen inside. Only then did she move slowly towards the front porch.

Before she could press the button, the door opened and a gray-haired man in his sixties greeted her. "Why my dear, what are you doing out at this hour of the morning?"

"I'm your neighbor," she said hesitantly.

"Oh, you must be Ms. Adams." Extending his hand, he continued, "I'm Tom Henry. It's nice to finally meet you. Would you like to come in and join us for a glass of wine?"

Hesitant at first, her curiosity got the better of her. "Well, I'll stick my head in for a minute, but I'll take a rain check on the wine," she said, as she stepped through the foyer into the comfortably furnished home. The five other men in the room all acknowledged her with a nod of their head and a smile before returning to their conversations. They were all of a similar age, dressed conservatively in dark suits with white shirts and red-striped ties. They all communicated an air of privilege.

"You'll have to forgive them. We only get together once or twice a month for conversation and a late-night card game. It's a chance to reminisce on old times."

"Old times?"

"Yes, we're all Yalies. Before that, it was Phillips Exeter. You can probably imagine, there's a lot of history between us. I hope we weren't being too noisy, you know, keeping you up."

"I'm a bit embarrassed, Mr. Henry. I've stopped by at least a dozen times, but never found anyone home. I thought the house was abandoned until I checked the tax records. It said the home was owned by Patrick Henry, but surely that is not you."

"No, that's my father, my 95-year-old father, to be precise. He hasn't lived here in years. He's in a skilled nursing facility. I keep an eye on the house for him. In exchange, he doesn't mind if we use it as a gathering place, as long as we leave it in one piece. You know us wild Baby Boomers, party, party, party!"

This elicited a laugh from Mary.

"Well, now that you know who I am and understand the situation, you're welcome any time. Are you sure you won't stay for a glass of wine?"

Still feeling embarrassed, Mary was eager to return to the sanctity of her house. "I'll take a rain check, Mr. Henry."

"Please call me Tom, and I'll look forward to having that glass of wine with you, Mary," he said with a wink.

She blushed as she walked hurriedly past him and out the door.

"What in the hell was that about?" George Sinclair asked as Marvin Kahn closed the door and turned the deadbolt.

"A very nosey neighbor who doesn't understand the grave danger she's putting herself in."

"What if she had recognized you?" Sinclair continued. "What if she recognized any of us?"

"But she didn't," Kahn asserted.

"That's not the point, Mr. Kahn. You know we cannot afford mistakes, including having outsiders checking on us."

"I'll take care of it," Kahn assured them. "Right now, she thinks I have an interest in her. That will make getting rid of the woman a little easier. But gentlemen, we have far more significant issues to deal with this night than Ms. Adams. I suggest we refresh our cocktails, then retreat to the meeting room."

Kahn led the way down a flight of stairs to a finished basement. It looked like an average man-cave, complete with a small bar, pool table, and posters of old black and white movies. Kahn stepped behind the bar and pushed firmly against one of the shelves. It yielded to the pressure, revealing a small, dimly-lit corridor. The five men followed behind him as he proceeded down the corridor until it dead-ended at a heavy metal door. He approached a panel adjacent to the door, removed his glasses, and stared into a camera. It took less than a second for the device to analyze every blood vessel within his iris and confirm his identity. Then an electronic bolt retracted, and the men filed in one by one.

"I believe you have a matter of vital importance to share with us, Mr. Kahn, regarding the Prometheus," Sinclair said when they were all comfortably seated. "We're quite eager to hear what is happening with our ship, and what you intend to do about it."

Kahn cleared his throat and fidgeted with his tie, tics that were rarely apparent unless he was under duress. Taking a sip of scotch, he explained what had transpired to-date, including the apparent sabotage aboard the ship. He concluded with his concerns regarding the Chinese Navy.

The men were shaking their heads and grumbling, until Harold Arnold gave voice to what the group was thinking. "This is not good news, Mr. Kahn, not good news at all. How long have we been working to purify the race by developing a genetic standard for what constitutes an American?" Without waiting for an answer, he continued, "Our work has been built upon the shoulders of generations of men who came before us, men whose life's work was to ensure the domination of white America long after everyone in this room has turned to dust."

"I'm well aware of that, Mr. Arnold."

"And wasn't it you, Mr. Kahn, who convinced this group that our eugenics project should be moved to the Prometheus? If I remember correctly, you insisted that it would be safer there than at a land-based facility."

"I told you, Mr. Arnold, that the pace of our research would be greatly accelerated if we leveraged the cadre of assembled scientists aboard the Prometheus, along with their tools. Furthermore, it was my belief that our work could be easily cloaked amidst the more expansive genetic research being conducted onboard."

"Correct me if I am wrong, Sir, but did you not specifically state that there was no safer place on earth for our secrets than aboard the Prometheus?"

Kahn could see four heads nodding in agreement.

"That is correct, Mr. Arnold. As I speak, we are investigating how our security broke down."

"I don't give a rat's ass about your investigation, Mr. Kahn. You've put all of our work in jeopardy. Not only might we lose years of scientific progress, but our collective knowledge may fall into the hands of our greatest adversary. The Chinese have always considered themselves superior to everyone else. Well, in a few generations, that claim may finally be valid, thanks to your negligence. Do you understand the significance of what I'm saying, Mr. Kahn?" Arnold's voice rose in pitch and intensity.

"Yes, Mr. Arnold, I understand the magnitude of the problem."

"And what do you plan to do it about it? And don't bother telling me about the investigation."

"Right now, there is a team onboard the Prometheus downloading all of the ship's data. I have given them forty-eight hours in which to accomplish this objective. They will be finished well before the Chinese can arrive on site."

"Who is in charge of the team?" Arnold asked.

"Commander John Hart is responsible for the security of the team. His wife, Dr. Elizabeth Wilkins, is leading the scientific mission. They have been ordered to scuttle the ship rather than allow the data and other materials, including bio-weapons, to fall into the hands of the enemy."

"What assurance do you have that this order will be followed by Hart if his wife is onboard the Prometheus when the Chinese arrive in force?"

"Commander Hart is running two separate security details. One is assigned to form a broad security perimeter around the area, the other to ensure the direct safety of Wilkins' team. Mr. Anderson, whom you have met, is heading the latter."

"I trust that Mr. Anderson will not flinch if he is asked to act in this country's best interest," said Mr. Arnold.

"That is correct. He will execute the orders of this group without question or hesitation."

"Is there anything else you wish to share with us, Mr. Kahn? You know how I hate surprises."

"There is one last thing, Mr. Arnold. It appears that the saboteur, Wei Hai Zhao, escaped from the Prometheus on a lifeboat. We believe he is infected with a highly transmissible and universally fatal virus. Satellite surveillance suggests that he may have been picked up by a fishing trawler headed for port in Palau. If so, he could spread the infection widely. We may have another global pandemic on our hands."

"And you offer this as an afterthought, Mr. Kahn? Something that endangers not merely our work, but our lives?"

"I thought your primary focus was on the security of the data, Mr. Arnold," Kahn pushed back.

"What is being done to address the problem?"

"Commander Hart has orders to interdict the fishing vessel and neutralize any threat."

"If I were you, Mr. Kahn, I would pray that both Commander Hart and Mr. Anderson succeed with their missions. I expect to be kept informed of any changes in status." He smiled coldly. "If that's not too much to ask?"

Kahn swallowed the lump in his throat. "No, Sir. Of course not."

CHAPTER 27

Amniocentesis

Liz was surprised to hear the familiar hiss of air as the pressure within the airlock was equalized to that of the lab. She wasn't expecting anyone, and a quick glance around the room confirmed that all of her crew was present. As she watched, the circular lock on the stainless steel door rotated clockwise, and Mike Anderson stepped across the threshold into the lab.

"What are you doing here?" she demanded.

Anderson didn't respond.

Not one to be intimidated, Liz pushed harder. "I asked you a question, Mister. What the hell are you doing in my lab?"

"I gave your message to the commander, Doctor, as you requested."

"I hope you also communicated my disdain, Mr. Anderson."

"I believe that you can do a better job of that than me, Dr. Wilkins, and you will have plenty of opportunity, once we wrap up this operation."

"What did my husband say?"

"The Commander indicated that he would talk with you later."

"You came all the way here just to tell me that?"

Anderson did not respond and simply stared at her. Liz finally turned her back on him and had started to walk away.

"The commander is in the process of intercepting a trawler," he called after her. "We believe it may have rescued the inhabitant of the lifeboat. The saboteur."

Liz turned back. "Is that all, Mr. Anderson?" she asked him stonily. Although shaken by the news, she was unwilling to betray any sign of emotion to this cretin.

"Yes, Ma'am."

"Then you must excuse me; I have work to do."

She waited for Anderson to leave before walking over to Carl Hodges. He was half-reclining in a chair, his bio-protective boots propped up on the work table. Hodges seemed to have all the time in the world as he twirled a pencil in one hand and poked sporadically at the keyboard with the other.

"Tell me you are on schedule, Mr. Hodges," Liz said.

"You are on schedule," the man mimicked her.

"I'm not in the mood to suffer fools, Mr. Hodges," she said as she abruptly slapped his feet to the floor.

"I'll bet you learned that trick from your husband," an unfazed Hodges responded.

Liz stepped forward and bent down, putting her face squarely in front of his. With her unblinking eyes riveted on Hodges, she roared, "We've got less than two days to complete this mission or there is going to be hell to pay. Am I getting through to you, Carl?"

The color drained from his face as he responded, "Yes, Dr. Wilkins, I'm working as fast I can."

"Be damned sure of that, Mr. Hodges," she cautioned him, before moving on to the other side of the lab. There, Marta Hopkins was deep in conversation with Elijah Obaji.

"I hope I'm not interrupting," Liz began.

"No, we were just about to ask you to join us," Marta said with a smile. "Elijah and I were discussing how to move from a presumptive diagnosis of botulinum poisoning to a definitive determination of the cause of death among the crew. Not that it will change the outcome."

"No, it won't, but it may impact how we mitigate vulnerabilities in our security in the future," Liz began. "I know we don't have necropsy capabilities, but we need to obtain some tissue samples from several of the deceased. I'm confident that will provide everything you need for clarity."

"We're on it, Dr. Wilkins," Obaji responded.

Wilkins walked back towards Hodges, who winced in anticipation of being chastised again. "There is some information I need immediately, Carl."

"Yes, Ma'am. What is it?"

"I need to know who was the principal investigator on the rabies chimera virus, and also the PI on the botulinum-H toxin."

Relieved not to incur her wrath for a second time, Hodges exhaled and began feverishly typing on the keyboard. Screen after screen appeared and disappeared until he finally stopped.

"I can tell you right now, Dr. Wilkins. The principal investigator for both botulinum-H and the chimera rabies virus was Dr. Wei Hai Zhao."

Liz nodded as her brain connected the dots. She informed Marta and Elijah that she would return within the hour. Then she headed topside to get a clear signal for the sat phone. She placed a call to Marvin Kahn.

"I hope you're making some progress, Doctor, while your husband is out gallivanting around."

"Sir, the commander is trying to stop a potential pandemic. As for the identity of the perpetrator, I think we can now be one hundred percent sure as to his identity."

"Beyond the video of the desalination unit, and what NGIA revealed, what new evidence gives you the confidence to make such an unequivocal assertion?"

"Zhao was the PI on the rabies chimera project. He was also the PI in the botulinum-H research, which is the toxin we believe was used to kill the crew. My team is working to confirm that hypothesis, but we're somewhat hamstrung by a lack of forensic capabilities. For now, I think you should assume that our working hypotheses are valid until proven otherwise, Mr. Kahn, and take whatever action you deem appropriate."

"Thank you, Dr. Wilkins. When you have confirmation, let me know."

"Yes, Sir. And, Mr. Kahn, it appears that approximately a dozen vials of pathogenic agents are missing from the laboratory. I thought you should know that, as well."

"Thank you, Dr. Wilkins. I assume the missing vials are what is contained in the vacuum bottle observed by the NGIA—the object that was removed from the lifeboat by whomever rescued Zhao."

As soon as he finished talking with Liz, Kahn placed a call to the office of the Secretary of the Navy. "Charlie, it's Marvin Kahn. I need a favor, and I need it stat."

"Of course. What is it?"

"Could you have someone pull the full dossier on Dr. Wei Hai Zhao? And one more thing, Charlie. We need to keep this confidential, just the two of us until I have some proof behind our working hypothesis."

"The only person I would feel obligated to share the information with is President Conner, and only if it has a direct bearing on a question he asks."

"Thank you, Charlie."

Liz returned to the lab and headed directly over to Marta Hopkins.

"Have you obtained the tissue samples yet?"

"Yes, four of them," Hopkins said as she gestured towards a binocular microscope. "They are fixed in formalin, stained, and ready for your review."

Liz adjusted the fine focus knob until the image was sharp. As she did, Hopkins provided commentary. "Looks like you were dead on the money, Liz. There's clear evidence that something caused broad synaptic disruption. It could have been a nerve agent, like a Novichok-V, but if it were, the bodies would have a different appearance. Plus, one of Anderson's men swept the ship for any residual chemical contamination with an M4A1-JCAD detector. If there had been any type of airborne nerve agent, it would have signaled an alert."

"I need more, Marta. I need unequivocal proof of poisoning."

Hopkins nodded. "Follow me," she said, leading her boss over to a separate area of the lab that held animals for experimentation. Three laboratory mice lay on their sides in a cage. They were all dead.

"On a hunch, I inoculated them with water from the ship's potable water supply. Within minutes, they showed classic signs of botulinum intoxication. I think you have all the proof you need, Liz."

"Good work, Marta." Liz turned her attention to Elijah Obaji, who appeared to be deep in thought.

"Elijah, have you made a first pass through the collection of bio-material yet?"

"Yes, Doctor, and I feel as if I've descended into hell. This material should not exist on earth. It can serve little purpose other than to create massive death."

"I appreciate the editorial, Elijah, but we've got a job to do and little time in which to do it. Tell me what you've found, and how far along you are in the process for safe containment and transfer of the bio-active material."

"Yes, Doctor. I found a cornucopia of Category A and B pathogens, from Ebola and Marburg to the more benign glanders, tularemia, and plague. I also found some bioregulators and toxins whose molecular structure is contained in the database."

"Anything else?"

"Yes, the chimeras. This lab's research into synthetic biology is far more advanced than what I've seen in any other lab, including CDC. You know about the Rabies/SARS virus. It is but one among many such hybrids. But it's not merely the modification of the genome of pathogens that concerns me, Dr. Wilkins. The scientists were actively working on the modification of the human genome."

"Whoa! Stop right there. What exactly are you talking about, Elijah?"

"In a word, Dr. Wilkins, *eugenics*."

So it was true, Liz thought. The movement had not ended with the Nazis.

"No one in their right mind would resurrect that pseu-do-science, not even the most ardent racist!" she exclaimed, not wanting to betray what she had previously been told.

She took a deep breath and tried to calm herself before continuing. "I'm sorry, Elijah for the visceral reaction. Let's try again. What evidence do you have to substantiate your claim?"

"Human embryonic research. It appears to have focused on three primary traits: intelligence, resistance to disease, and athletic prowess. The scientists were replicating what Dr. Mengele sought to accomplish, only now they finally had the tools and knowledge to be successful. It's a first step in creating a master race."

"Did they artificially support the embryos used in the research?"

"It appears that they were grown to the point when they could be implanted and prove viable."

"Are you suggesting that such an ungodly event occurred?"

"Have you examined the dead crew members, Dr. Wilkins?"

"Only a handful of men."

"I suggest you focus on some of the younger women. Based on my cursory observation of the corpses, there is a surprisingly high rate of pregnancy. I would guess that most were in their second trimester."

Liz paused, disgusted by what she was about to order. "I'm not sticking my neck out without clear evidence that human experimentation was being done on this vessel. I want a fetal genetic analysis performed on at least five of the pregnant women. I'm sure they were doing regular amniocentesis, so the necessary medical supplies should be in the sick bay."

Obaji nodded, though the thought of doing amnios on deceased fetuses in the womb sickened him.

"Agreed, Dr. Wilkins. The Prometheus has the most advanced equipment in the world. I should be able to run the genetic analyses within hours."

"How about eight hours? That's what I want you to shoot for, Elijah."

"Understood, Dr. Wilkins, but what about preparing the bio-material for safe transport? That will take time."

"I'll handle it," Liz assured him. "I'm returning topside. If anyone needs me, tell them to call me on the comm line. And Elijah, this is on the QT. If you're right, the question then becomes, who ordered it?"

※

With each step, Liz rehearsed her words, knowing that she had to be efficient in conveying critical information to her husband while avoiding discovery by Anderson.

She was relieved to see that the body of the captain had been removed by Anderson's team, but disheartened to find her nemesis staring out of the ship's vast windows towards the horizon, presumably keeping watch for intruders.

"How are things going in the lab, Ma'am?"

"We're moving forward as rapidly as possible, Mr. Anderson."

"Any surprises, Dr. Wilkins?"

Liz paused; her hesitancy was not lost on Anderson.

"No, just a lot of deadly organisms and mountains of data."

"You're sure about that, Ma'am? Just your garden variety hemorrhagic fevers and such?"

She was taken back by the man's pretense of knowledge. He wouldn't know a hemorrhagic fever from herpes.

"As I said, I have nothing to report, Mr. Anderson. I need some privacy. Where would you suggest I go?"

Anderson's eyes darted from side to side as he contemplated a flip response, but he chose restraint. "Use the bridge, Ma'am. I need to get some air anyway."

"Thank you. I only need about twenty minutes."

As soon as he stepped out and pulled the door securely closed, Liz extracted the sat phone from her pocket and dialed John.

"Are you okay?" he asked without saying hello.

"I think so."

"Didn't Mike tell you that I'd call later?"

"Yes, but this won't wait."

"Listen, Darling, I don't want to get into a long argument about my men's tactics. There's not time right now."

"Nor do I, John, but you can damn well bet that we're going to have that conversation."

"Understood. Then why did you call?"

Her tone softened. "We found some disturbing things in the lab, things we are trying to confirm with certainty."

"Are you talking about novel life forms, like the chimera virus that we may be hunting down?"

"That's the tip of the iceberg."

"So, what is it?" Hart asked impatiently.

"It appears that they were actively manipulating the human genome and then implanting modified fetuses into female crew members."

"What? NO! That's not possible."

"That was my immediate reaction until I saw the first round of evidence. If the second round is confirmatory, the evidence will be undisputable."

"What exactly are you doing?"

"DNA analysis of the embryonic fluid via amniocentesis. There are a disproportionate number of pregnant females on this ship, most of whom appear to be in the early stages of their second trimester."

"Who knows about this, Liz? Have you shared it with Kahn?"

"No, only Marta and Elijah."

"Throw a blanket over it. I don't want anyone outside of your scientific team to get a whiff of this, including Mr. Kahn. And I would include Mike and his crew in those orders."

"You don't trust your own men, Commander?" Liz was surprised.

"Let's just say that this part of the mission is on a need-to-know basis, and they don't need to know."

"It might explain why the Chinese are after our data-bases. Rather than an arms race, perhaps we're competing to see who can be the first to create the master race."

"I suggest you get back to the lab and instruct your team on silence. Be certain that their work is not visible to the security detail. And, for God's sake, give me a heads-up if any uninvited guests show up at the party."

Liz walked briskly down the stairs towards the lab, stopping as she rounded a corner and discovered Anderson peering into a cabin. "What are you doing, Mr. Anderson?" Her tone was curt.

A startled Marta Hopkins looked up, saw Anderson, and pushed past the hulking man to get to Liz.

"I had no idea he was watching me!" she exclaimed.

"Just curious," he said with forced nonchalance. "What were you doing in there?"

Before Marta could respond, Liz came to her aid. "She's trying to get a precise time of death based upon the state of the placental blood. Now that you know that, Mr. Anderson, you can leave my crew alone." As she spoke the words, her husband's warning echoed in her mind.

Anderson smirked, then sauntered away, his body language making it clear that he was not under her command.

"Are you okay?" Liz asked the shaken Hopkins.

"I'm fine, but that guy gives me the creeps."

"Listen to me carefully, Marta. No one outside of our team is to know what we've discovered. Do you understand?"

Martha nodded. "Of course."

Anderson went to the far side of the ship where he could have a private conversation without interruption. He dialed a number on his sat phone and waited for the connection.

"I told you never to call me," the male voice said in a scathing tone.

"You did, Sir, but there's been a development."

"What kind of development? The Chinese?"

"No, Sir. Marta Hopkins, part of Dr. Wilkins' team, is collecting samples from dead bodies."

"And that's why you called me? Let her knock herself out." His tone could not have been more patronizing.

"Sir, I'm no doctor, but it looked like she was collecting amniotic fluid from the pregnant women's bodies. I thought you should know."

A long period of silence followed, prompting Anderson to finally ask, "Are you there, Sir?"

"I want you to listen to me very carefully, Mr. Anderson. If Dr. Wilkins' team verifies the nature and status of our genetic experiments, I need to know immediately. Do you understand?"

"Yes, Sir."

"If a decision is made to scuttle the ship, you will receive a two-minute warning via a short text on your sat phone. It will simply read *ASN*."

"*Abandon ship now*, Sir?"

"Correct. The charges Mr. Ramirez set are going to blow that ship sky-high. So, as soon as you receive that message, get the hell out of harm's way as fast as possible. Take the Mark V."

"What about Dr. Wilkins and her team?"

"It will be my little present to her son-of-a-bitch husband. Hopefully, he will bear witness to her death and be unable to do a damn thing to prevent it."

"And how will I explain what happened, Sir?"

"You ordered everyone to evacuate the Prometheus via the Knighthawk, and were subsequently horrified to learn that your orders had not been followed."

CHAPTER 28

Tidying Up Loose Ends

THE SAPPHIRE-BLUE OCEAN WAS AS FLAT AND CALM as a mountain lake. Its tranquility stood in sharp contrast to what lay ahead for Hart and his crew. The idea of killing people to prevent the possible spread of disease weighed heavily on the commander's shoulders. He thought back to his conversation with Liz, in which he told her to trust her instincts and not to blindly follow orders. It was easy for him to dole out such advice, but an entirely different matter to follow it himself.

"Mr. Lamott, what's the computer showing?"

"Based on our current course and speed, the nav is showing us an hour out from Koror Island. We will intercept the trawler in just over thirty minutes, Commander."

Koror Island was the economic hub of the Republic of Palau and home to more than 20,000 islanders.

"Are you saying that we'll no longer be in international waters?"

"That is correct, Sir. We will be two miles inside of Palau's territorial waters. Should I notify their Marine Law Enforcement division?"

"No, I'm hoping to fly under the radar on this one. Let's pray that neither of their two patrol boats are in the area."

"Understood, Sir."

Hart remained in the bridge, scanning the horizon for vessels. He knew the closer they came to port, the more likely they were to have company. As the minutes ticked by, he glanced over Lamott's shoulder at the navigational computer.

When they were ten minutes from the intercept point, Hart could make out the trawler dead ahead. They were approaching it broadside.

"I want you to swing this baby around so that we greet them head-on, Mr. Lamott." He turned to Sitarski and Ramirez. "Be ready, gentlemen. I want the M60 locked and loaded. Mr. Harding, I need you in the bow."

Tommy Lamott turned the ship clockwise, placing the Mark V just as Hart had directed. Hart tuned the radio to a commercial frequency and tried to hail the fishing boat. After three unsuccessful attempts, he replaced the microphone and directed his attention to his gunners.

"We're going to park smack dab in their path. You're not going to have much time until they're right on top of us. So, on my command, I want you to open up with a burst from the M60. Fire just over their head. I want them to hear the bullets whizzing past."

"And if they don't slow down, Commander?" Sitarski asked.

"Then you'll strafe her deck and wheelhouse."

"Sir, we've got company."

"From Palau?"

"No, Sir. From the north. It's still more than twenty miles out, but it's moving fast. Thirty knots."

"Keep an eye on it and let me know if it alters course or speed."

The man nodded.

"Cut the engines!" Hart ordered. The Mark V stopped dead in the water, like a shark waiting for its prey. Hart lifted binoculars to his face and saw the trawler bearing down on them. "Sixty seconds, Gentlemen."

On his order, a deafening burst of bullets sprayed from the machine gun, bringing the trawler to an abrupt halt less than a hundred yards from the Mark V. "Let's hope they speak English," said Hart as he picked up a bullhorn.

"Captain of the trawler, shut down your engine and identify yourself."

A short, dark-skinned man emerged from the wheelhouse and walked cautiously towards the bow of the ship.

"I am the captain," the man said defiantly.

"Why did you ignore our commands to stop?" Hart shouted, though he knew damn well that he was the provocateur.

"What do you want? Surely not our fish."

"We are looking for a man that we believe you picked up. He is quite ill. We need to know if he is aboard your vessel."

The captain hesitated as he considered his response.

"Captain, we'll board your vessel if necessary." Hart threatened. "I need to know now if the man is on your trawler."

"The man you are asking about is dead. We are taking his body to the port to turn it over to the authorities."

"How did this man come to be aboard your ship, Captain?"

"We found him lying on a beach near to where a lifeboat was stranded. It was an atoll many miles to the north. We didn't think he would make it to Palau, and he didn't."

"How many men on your boat, Captain?"

"Four, including myself, plus one corpse."

"And where is the man's body now?"

"In a berth below deck."

As Hart interrogated the trawler's captain, Lamott continued to monitor the small blip on his radar. Based on its current speed, the approaching boat would arrive in thirty-five minutes.

"I want you to listen to my instructions closely. You are not to restart your engine or use your radio until I give you further instructions. We are pulling back but keeping you within range of our guns. Do you understand my orders, Captain?"

"Yes," the man said.

"Good. Then await my instructions." Hart turned towards Lamott. "I want at least five hundred yards separating us, Mr. Lamott. Sitarksi and Ramirez, hold your positions. Mr. Harding, keep your eyes open for that other boat. And let me know if that trawler moves an inch."

Hart pulled out his sat phone, ensured that he had a strong signal, then dialed Marvin Kahn.

"Where in the hell are you, Commander?" Kahn barked.

"We are within Koror's territorial waters, and five hundred yards from the trawler, Sir."

"Why didn't you intercept that damn boat while you were still in international waters?"

"Sir, we've had the Mark V at full-throttle since being given an intercept heading by NGIA. This was the best we could do, Mr. Kahn."

"What is the status of the trawler?"

"Her engines are shut down, and I believe the captain will maintain radio silence until further instructed. In addition to fish, they are transporting the corpse of a man who we are confident is Zhao."

"What gives you that confidence, Commander?"

"They described where and how they found the man, Mr. Kahn. It jives with what I learned from Sue Goodman. There is no doubt in my mind that we have located the saboteur, or what is left of him. There's one other thing, Mr. Kahn. We appear to have uninvited guests closing in on our position. How would you like us to proceed, Sir?" Hart asked.

As they were speaking, one of the trawler's crew quietly slipped from sight. He eased his body into the water and began to glide silently away, the trawler effectively blocking any view of him from Hart. When he no longer feared detection, the man began swimming in earnest towards a small island.

As Hart was awaiting instructions from Kahn, he heard the familiar buzz of a Predator drone in the distance.

Kahn's voice broke through. "We've had a drone parked over Palau in anticipation of your arrival. On my command, it will unload a Hellfire missile targeted at the trawler. I suggest you create a bit more space. Five hundred yards is cutting it too close."

Hart gave Lamott instructions to back off an additional five hundred yards from the trawler until after the detonations, then returned to his call.

"Done, Sir. We're a safe distance from the trawler, but there has to be another option, Mr. Kahn. The men aboard that vessel have done nothing wrong. Quite the contrary, they tried to save a man's life."

"That's very touching, Commander, but I don't have time for sentimentality, and neither do you. We have to assume that those men have been exposed to the chimera virus that killed Zhao."

"But we don't know what killed Zhao. Why not keep the crew confined to the trawler—a floating isolation unit, if you will, and see if they manifest symptoms over the next few days?

"And there's another reason, Mr. Kahn, to keep the vessel intact. It likely houses the container Zhao used to store the pilfered viruses. We don't know what might happen if those viruses escape, but I think we're taking a hell of a risk sinking that trawler."

"I told you, Commander, there's no time. By questioning my orders, you are raising doubt in my mind as to whether you are fit for duty. Are you fit, Mr. Hart?"

"Yes, Sir." But as the words rolled off his tongue, Hart's gut lurched at the idea of slaughtering innocent men.

"Good. After the missile has done its job, I want a body count. I trust you'll find the remains of four plus one, probably in innumerable pieces. And if anyone miraculously survives, don't get any ideas about saving them. I want them taken out instantly with the M60. And Commander, do not engage with whoever is pursuing you."

"Understood, Sir."

🧬

Half a world away, Lieutenant Cory Tyler sat in an air-conditioned trailer staring at what looked like a video game. Every few seconds, he would make a minute adjustment with a joystick, slightly altering the drone's approach to his target. The decrepit fishing boat sat motionless, a proverbial sitting duck, Tyler thought, as he armed the drone's missile. He wondered what crime the crew had committed to be sentenced to death. But his job was not to judge, merely to execute. Without another thought, he put the drone on a glide path that would ensure successful delivery of its payload.

The buzzing sound intensified as the Predator dropped from an altitude of five thousand feet to just under fifteen hundred. As it approached the Mark V, an AGM-114N laser-guided thermobaric, blast fragmentation missile dropped from the belly of the drone, emitting a fiery streak as it rushed at Mach 1.3 towards the trawler.

The explosion was immense. Even at a thousand yards distance, Hart was knocked off his feet by the scorching blast wave that rocketed across the ocean at supersonic speed. As the smoke slowly dissipated, it was clear that the drone pilot had scored a direct hit. Little remained of the boat or its occupants.

Cory Tyler turned to his trailer-mate and exchanged high-fives. It had been a few weeks since his last kill, and it felt good to be back in the action. A moment later, the base commander paid an unexpected visit to offer his congratulations, saying simply, "It was a high-value target, despite its appearance."

Hart issued a series of orders. "Tommy, bring us within fifty yards and make a slow circle around the trawler. Jason, get ready to start counting, and make damn sure the body count adds up to five. Count limbs if you have to. Roman and Paco, I want your hands on the M60's. Anything moves, finish the job."

The water was awash with blood, and body parts could be seen bobbing in the waves kicked up by the blast. Hart knew it wouldn't take long for the sharks to move in.

The crew began surveying the carnage. After a few minutes, each had done his best to arrive at a count.

"Four, Sir," Harding shouted.

"What about you, Tommy?"

"Four, Sir."

"That's what I've got—four, Commander," Sitarski reported.

Ramirez nodded in agreement.

"We've got a problem, Gentlemen."

What was left of the trawler was rapidly filling with water, and Hart knew she was about to go down for the count. With her would go any hope of finding the missing body.

"Give me a depth reading, Tommy," he shouted at the bridge.

"Eight hundred feet, Commander."

"That eliminates diving. Keep looking." But their efforts proved futile. The body count would remain at four.

"Let's get the hell out of here," Hart finally ordered. "Set a course back to the Prometheus, and do your best to avoid contact with whoever is pursuing us."

Lamott looked one last time at the radar before pressing down on the thrust.

"Commander, whoever was on our tail has turned. It looks like they've abruptly changed course. It's now headed due north at thirty knots per hour."

"Fucking Chinese," Hart muttered.

"What was that, Sir?"

"It's the Chinese, Mr. Lamott. They must have intercepted a radio message from the trawler regarding our saboteur and sought to intervene. Zhao was a hell of a big loose end—one they needed to disappear."

"I guess we took care of that for them, Mr. Hart. What are you going to tell Mr. Kahn about the missing body?" Lamott asked.

"The truth," Hart answered without hesitation.

Lamott throttled up the Mark V's turbine engine, adjusting the trim so the bow fell smoothly into plane. With ocean on all sides, Hart had an unobstructed view across the water. He kept glancing at an island to his right, a thought percolating in his head.

"You don't think anyone could have jumped ship and swam to that island, do you, Tommy?"

"That's not much more than a mile, Commander. If he was a strong swimmer, he could have made it in a little over twenty minutes."

"How long has it been since we interdicted the trawler?"

Lamott glanced at his chronograph. "It's been thirty-seven minutes, Commander."

"Take me to that island, Tommy. Looks like there's a small beach, and my bet is we'll find fresh tracks. There's a damned good chance that man's infected."

CHAPTER 29

Footprints in the Sand

JASON HARDING WAS STILL RIDING SHOTGUN in the ship's bow when he spied a massive bloom of multi-colored coral dead ahead.

"Reverse!" he shouted at Lamott, but the helmsman was already on it, having kept an eagle eye on the ship's depth-finder. He reversed thrust and backed off a safe distance from the reef.

"This is as close as I dare take her, Sir," Lamott informed Hart.

"Drop anchor," he shouted, already stripping to his skivvies as he prepared for a swim. "Listen up, Tommy. While I'm gone, I want you to find out everything you can about this island. I want to know who's on it and if they are friendly. I don't want any unpleasant surprises like we had on that one mission."

Lamott smiled. "You mean those crazy bastards that pelted us with arrows off the coast of India? The sons-of-bitches missed hitting my leg by an inch."

"As I recall, we were just off shore in the Andaman archipelago when we apparently infringed on the Sentinelese turf."

"Correct, Commander. That's when you dissuaded them with a rifle-launched grenade placed smack in the middle of their canoes."

Hart's grin widened. "It didn't seriously injure any of them, but it sure as hell scared the shit out of them!"

"That it did, Sir! I'm pleased to report that there are no Sentinelese on this island."

Reassured by Lamott's comments, Hart dove off the side of the ship into the crystal-clear water. Beneath him swam a stunning array of brilliantly colored fish, including red-toothed triggerfish with dark purple bodies and blue-green fins, silvery striped chevron barracudas, and a plethora of gray reef sharks.

Hart stretched out his left arm and began a rapid freestyle stroke. His mind flashed back to SEAL training and the marathon swims he'd endured in the surf off Coronado beach, where the water temperature dipped as low as 55 degrees. By comparison, this water felt like a bathtub. A hundred-yard sprint in the mirror-still water would barely elevate his heart rate.

A short while later, he pulled himself out of the lightly breaking waves onto the sand and scanned the half-moon beach. One thing was immediately apparent. He had company.

Fresh tracks emerged from the sea and led in an easterly direction towards the island's interior. He followed them a short distance until the sand gave way to head-high beach grass. As he approached the thicket, he could make out a faint trail of broken stalks where the man had woven his way through the brush. He began to forge a trail through the seagrass, its sharp edges raising welts on his bare skin.

It was beginning to get late, the sun hovering over the horizon in a mess of reds and yellow. Hart knew the chance of him finding the man after dark was remote. Better to turn back, he decided.

As Hart broke off the search, he didn't realize he had come within fifty yards of discovering the missing sailor. As the commander headed back to the beach, the terrified man from the trawler scurried out of his hiding place and ran until his lungs burned. Climbing a hill, he could see the Mark V through a clearing in the island's thick vegetation. Small specks moved about on the boat's deck. He just prayed they would pull anchor and leave him alone.

Returning to the boat, Hart grabbed a chamois and dried off. "You were right, Tommy. He's here and he won't be hard to find. Now tell me, what have you learned about this island?"

Lamott began his report. "It's called Sonsorol Island, Commander. It measures roughly two miles north to south and one and a half miles east to west."

"I appreciate the geography lesson, Tommy, but what about the people?"

"There's one village, Commander, with a population of forty-five. At last count anyway. The indigenous people were described as *civilized and god-fearing.*"

"And the terrain?"

"Based upon the condition of your legs, you must have discovered the dense vegetation that covers the island."

Hart looked down at the small droplets of blood covering his skin. "What else, Tommy?"

Lamott pointed to a craggy peak. "That crater sits at 2,200 feet above sea-level. As you know, Commander, we're smack dab in the Ring of Fire."

Hart nodded. The soldier was referring to a geothermically active band of ocean dotted with volcanoes. "In summation, Mr. Lamott?"

"It may be a small island, but there are going to be plenty of places to hide."

"Any possibility of unexpected guests?"

"Yes, Sir. Apparently one of the resorts on a nearby island runs adventure rides here."

"What the hell does that mean?"

"They've cut trails through the island's interior and brought in lots of off-road sports buggies."

"That's all I need. To cross paths with drunken men in oversized Hawaiian shirts, driving vehicles they don't know how to control. Let's hope that doesn't happen. Mr. Lamott, Mr. Harding, grab your gear. We're camping on the beach. Mr. Sitarski and Mr. Ramirez, you're going to babysit the boat, and I expect you to radio immediately if there are any problems."

"Understood, Sir."

"Mr. Ramirez, keep your eyes open for a patrol out of Palau. That trawler spewed enough smoke to be seen for miles. They may be looking for survivors."

"And if they spot us, Commander?"

"Be nice to them. Indicate we were in international waters on a naval exercise when we received the distress call. By the time we arrived, the trawler was fully submerged. That should keep them happy for a while."

Hart grabbed his fatigues and dressed. He slung a suppressed MP-5 over his shoulder and headed for the dinghy. Lamott and Harding followed close behind.

"We don't have much light left. I want to take one more quick pass, and then we'll bed down. We can canvass the island in the morning."

"Yes, Sir."

While the three men prepared to go ashore, the sailor from the trawler had already moved deeper into the island's interior. Like a roly-poly bug trying to avoid a predator, the man had curled up in a fetal position, then covered himself with the decaying leaves of coconut palms. After witnessing the horrific destruction of his boat, he knew what would happen if he was discovered. But what he didn't know was why. What horrible crime had he and his ship-mates committed to incur the wrath of the United States Navy?

As dusk settled, he thanked God for the protective cover of darkness. But his prayers proved premature, as he soon heard the sound of men trampling through the dry underbush. He guessed it was the Americans from the ship. He stood and shook off the palm leaves. He needed to put more distance between himself and these murderers. If he didn't, they'd kill him too.

With this in mind, he began to trudge up the mountain. After two hours, he reached the peak and began a slow descent to the valley below. A full moon provided enough light to avoid a catastrophic fall, but not enough to reveal anything more than his thin silhouette. Convinced that he finally had an ample lead, the man lay down and fell into a troubled sleep. His body was beginning to ache. The man didn't know it, but it was the first sign that the virus was beginning to take hold.

A dream carried him away. He was back on the deck of the trawler, a boat that had been his home for the past four years. He shouted to his shipmates, but no one answered. He began a frantic search, but it proved fruitless. He was the only man aboard, and the boat was about to strike a massive reef. Just as his anxiety was reaching a crescendo, a sharp pain in his right leg brought him back from the depths of sleep.

He opened his eyes to discover a half-naked man hovering over him, poking him in the calf with a sharp stick. He scampered out of the man's reach, struggling to his feet. For a moment, he thought it was an apparition; a phantom with a long, gray beard who had seemingly materialized out of the ether. Then the man spoke.

"What are you doing here?" he asked in his native Chamarro. Receiving no reply, he repeated the question in English.

The sailor hesitated.

"Do you understand me?" the man asked.

"Yes," the man replied, his head pounding.

"I asked you what you are doing here."

"I swam ashore after our boat sank."

"Ah, we heard an explosion and then saw a cloud of dark smoke," the man said, pointing to the south. "Was that your boat?"

"Yes."

"What happened?"

"The engine blew. The captain ordered us to abandon ship, but then the fuel tank ignited. I was the only one to get off alive."

It was a subtle but necessary lie, he told himself, not knowing how the man would respond to the truth.

"You are lucky to be alive," the man said, sizing him up. "God is showing his favor on you."

But was he, the man wondered? His head now throbbing and his throat was raw.

Smiling for the first time and gesturing with his stick to the sailor's leg, he added, "I didn't mean to frighten you, but we've learned to be leery of strangers. It's my job to protect the village. You can call me Atu."

"Atu," the man repeated. "And I am Jaylen."

"Our village is near." He gestured with his head. "My people will feed you. You can stay until the ferry from Palau arrives in three days."

The two men began walking towards the village. But, after only a short while, the sailor dropped to his knees. "Go on," he told Atu. "I'm sick and I don't want to infect your people."

The village elder reached down and pressed his hand against Jaylen's forehead. It was feverishly hot. Without a word, Atu lifted the man onto his shoulder and continued his trek down into the verdant valley.

The village consisted of a dozen thatched huts arranged in a semi-circle. At its center was a massive stone fire-pit in which a pile of wood and brush smoldered.

"What's that?" asked Jaylen.

"It's where we cook our meals." Atu laughed." Don't worry, we're not cannibals."

A short, round woman with waist-length braids emerged from one of the huts.

"This is my wife. She will care for you until you regain your strength."

Carrying Jaylen into the hut, he rested him gently on a straw bed. Then he told his wife what Jaylen had told him. "Look after him," he said after he'd recounted the story.

"But what can I do?" she protested. "He looks so ill!"

"You will do what you can and leave the rest to God."

CHAPTER 30

Genocide

Hart, Lamott, and Harding sat meditatively facing the east, in anticipation of the first morning light. As they looked out over the water, clouds were transformed into ribbons of rose and blue, ready to herald the sunrise. Within minutes, there was a blinding flash as an orb rose from the sea and began its rapid ascent towards the heavens. As it moved swiftly above the horizon, the last remnants of color were slowly stripped away, replaced by a brilliant golden hue.

Hart had witnessed innumerable sunrises, but none more glorious than the one that morning. He bowed his head and offered a silent prayer to God for the beauty of His creation, ending with a lament for his complicity in murdering the fishermen. As he whispered amen, he heard Lamott and Harding rise to their feet behind him.

"Pretty magnificent, wouldn't you agree, Commander?" Lamott observed.

"Magnificent, indeed, Tommy."

After a final glance to the east, Hart rose and turned to his men. "Let's get moving. If our missing sailor is on the island and he's symptomatic, we're going to have a hell of a mess on our hands."

Harding tugged at the laces on his boots until they were snug. Then, as he slung a rifle over his shoulder, Lamott unsheathed a machete. "Ready to blaze a trail, Commander," he said.

They set off into the thick undergrowth. But, thankfully, the man they were chasing was not light of foot. "He couldn't have made our job any easier if he'd drawn us a map," Hart remarked as the sunlight illuminated the broken branches and flattened grass demarking the man's trail through the brush.

The men ascended a short but steep volcanic slope. They were weighed down by forty pounds of gear, but they kept up a fast pace. Halfway up, Hart stopped long enough for everyone to catch their breath, then they continued the upward trek. As they reached the apex of the trail, a clearing became visible about two miles below. Hart could make out a small number of huts and what appeared to be a fire. Several dozen people were sitting around it.

"Let's take a break before we head down," Hart ordered. "Hydrate, check your weapons, and be on the alert."

After a five-minute rest, Hart stood up and hefted his pack back onto his shoulders. "Ready?" he asked.

The other two men nodded.

Hart led the way as they descended into the valley. After a hundred yards, the commander signaled them to stop. He pointed to a flat grassy area that appeared beaten down.

"Looks like someone slept here last night."

"Let's see if it's still warm," said Lamott, walking over to it, but Hart grabbed his arm.

"Don't touch it!" he warned the SEAL. 'I don't want you to get infected."

Lamott nodded. 'Sorry, Sir, I didn' think."

"Over here!" Harding gestured to a section of moist ground where two sets of footprints gave way to one.

"Those prints are deep, Mr. Harding," Hart said, looking at the singular trail that continued downhill. "My bet is that someone carried our man out of here on his back."

"Looks that way," the other man agreed.

"Let's move!" said Hart.

Within minutes, the men were on the outskirts of the village. They approached, guns strapped across their backs and arms stretched wide to indicate they were not a threat.

Atu stepped out of a hut. With his hands folded together as if in prayer, he approached the soldiers. When he was only a yard away from them, he stopped. Then he bowed.

The men bowed back.

"We mean you no harm," Hart said, hoping the man understood him, "but we need your help."

"Do you always carry guns when you are in need of help?" the man replied in perfect English.

It was a damn good question, Hart thought.

"We never know what we are going to encounter, and we have learned to be prepared, even when we come in peace."

"What is it that you seek?"

"A man whom we believe may be quite ill. He was aboard a fishing boat that sank. Somehow, this man managed to survive. We believe he swam to this island and may be seeking refuge. If you have seen him, please tell us now."

"Wait here." Atu returned to his hut, where he kneeled at Jaylen's bedside. The sailor's forehead was soaking wet with perspiration, and his breathing was labored as his lungs wheezed in a mournful plea for air.

"He's deteriorated so fast," his wife said. "There's nothing more I can do."

"There are three men with guns looking for you," Atu told the delirious man. He was doubtful that Jaylen would understand, but he felt he had to try.

Surprisingly, the man stopped thrashing and momentarily regained coherence. In a barely audible voice, he said, "I worried that I would bring my problems to your doorstep. Tell them I am here, and they can do with me as they please, but they must not punish your village."

"I don't understand," Atu said. "Why would the soldiers seek to punish anyone?"

"I do not know."

"Are you certain that this is what you want?"

"Yes," Jaylen said with finality, his voice trailing off as he closed his eyes. He knew his fate sealed.

Atu placed his hand atop the sailor's shoulder in a final gesture of compassion before walking out.

"The man you seek is in my hut being cared for by my wife. He is quite ill. I expect him to die at any moment. He asks that you do with him as you must, but spare our village. I pray that you will honor his request."

It was Hart's worst nightmare. Everyone in the village ran the risk of having been exposed, creating dozens of vectors for the highly infectious virus. And though the villagers rarely came into contact with others, the risk of the chimera virus escaping was unacceptably high.

"And now I must ask your patience as I confer with others," Hart responded. "We will return within the hour.

Please do not move this man or allow anyone else to come into contact with him."

The three men retreated to the ridge where they would have unobstructed satellite reception. The Commander's first call was to Sitarski and Ramirez.

"We were getting worried, Commander," Ramirez said. "Were you able to locate the target?"

"We found our man, but not before he was taken in by the villagers. Though we did not see him, we've been told that he's in the process of dying."

"How many people do you think he may have infected, Sir?"

"We have to assume the entire village. I'm going to report in and request further instruction."

"Before you do, Sir, you should know that another problem has surfaced."

"What are you talking about, Mr. Ramirez?"

"The Chinese Navy, Commander. They have a carrier group parked in international waters not far from the Prometheus."

"No shit! What's the status of Dr. Wilkins' team?"

"From what I could gather, they're in the final stages of downloading data and securing biological samples for transport to the Mercy."

"Let me know immediately if there is any change in their status or the posture of the Chinese." Hart then called Marvin Kahn.

"I hope you have good news," Kahn said ominously.

"No, Sir, I'm afraid I don't. We found the missing fisherman, but not before he was taken in by local villagers. We understand the man is near death and has undoubtedly exposed numerous people within the village.

"Mr. Kahn, I need you to advise me on next steps."

"You know perfectly well what to do, Commander. But since you asked, let me spell it out for you. Kill them all! Is that clear enough?"

The inhumanity of Kahn's orders shook Hart to the core. He thought about the helicopter pilot who had blinked when ordered to play chicken with a Chinese plane. Now Hart was the one blinking at a direct order.

Hart wondered if he should call President Conner. Conner could override Kahn. But the commander also knew he would be putting the president in an untenable position.

"Sir, I've been searching for ways to contain these people, not slaughter them. We could quarantine the island and place anyone who is ill in isolation. We'd then have to wait and hope that the contagion burned out quickly. Even if we spare one life, that's a huge victory when compared to a total kill."

"Are you not listening, Commander? I said kill them all."

Before Kahn could hang up, Hart interjected, "There's one more thing, Sir."

"And what would that be, Mr. Hart?"

"The Chinese Navy, Mr. Kahn. They are anchored in international waters within easy striking distance of the Prometheus."

"Don't you think I know that, Commander? I suggest you tidy up and get your ass back to protect the Prometheus." Kahn hung up.

CHAPTER 31

Flying Sharks

SURFACE RADAR DETECTED THE BATTLE GROUP long before the caravan of ships became visible to the naked eye. A spotter plane from Guam confirmed their identities: a Soviet-built aircraft carrier called the Liaoning, two guided-missile destroyers—the CNS Jinan and CNS Yinchuan, and the guided-missile frigate, the CNS Yantai.

It was an extraordinary show of force, and it sent a clear message that the Chinese meant business. As Mike Anderson trained his binoculars on the carrier, four Shenyang J15 fighters were catapulted off its flight deck. The Flying Sharks, as J-15's are better known, flew south before making a 180 turn and heading directly towards the Prometheus. Switching to afterburners, the planes were pushing Mach 2 as they nearly strafed the top deck of the research vessel.

"Sons of bitches!" Mike Anderson screamed as he instinctively hit the deck, his voice muted by the deafening sonic boom that followed.

"What the fuck?" Ronny Good muttered as he ducked for cover in response to the fast-moving shadows.

"That was a warning, Mr. Good," Anderson bellowed. "I want our missiles hot. If those bastards head our way again, light 'em up with targeting radar."

"Yes, Sir. Should we transport the research team back to the Mercy?"

"Not until their job is finished. The data drives are our overwhelming priority, Mr. Good. Don't forget that."

Liz Wilkins emerged from the lower deck and made a beeline for Anderson. "What the hell was that?"

"That, Doctor, was the Chinese informing us of who is in charge."

"Are they going to bomb this ship?" Liz's voice shook, her initial bravado now tempered by fear.

"The last thing they want is for the Prometheus to go down. They're trying to get us to abandon ship, but that's not going to happen, not on my watch. How long before your team has completed the data backups?"

"Six to eight hours, maybe more."

"I believe your timetable just got compressed. I suggest you return to the lab and do whatever is required to light a fire under your colleagues. Their lives may depend on it. I will inform Mr. Kahn that the situation is escalating."

Liz turned without responding and hurried toward the lab. Before reaching the entrance, she ducked into a cabin and called her husband. He answered on the second ring.

"I was just getting ready to call you," Hart said, his voice subdued.

"Is everything okay, John?"

"I was going to ask you the same thing."

"No, it's not okay. Four Chinese fighter jets. just did a fly-by over the deck of the Prometheus. Anderson is rattled, and I don't need to tell you that I am too. Anderson told me that we don't have much time left to complete our work."

"How much time did he give you?"

"He wasn't specific, but he suggested it was up to Kahn."

"He's right, and Kahn's decision will be based upon actions of the Chinese. Kahn is not going to let the U.S. get drawn into a shooting war, but he's also not going to allow a foreign superpower to reap the benefits of years of U.S. research. Your team needs to move heaven and earth to get the job done, Liz."

"And what about your team, John? Did you find the saboteur?"

"He's dead. So are three of the four fishermen who came to his aid when they discovered the lifeboat."

"And the fourth?"

"That man jumped ship and swam to an island, where he was taken in by the villagers. The man is near death, and I think he exposed several dozen people to the virus."

"What's been your level of contact? For God's sake, tell me you kept a safe distance!"

"What's a safe distance, Liz? I was within five feet of the village elder who carried the man on his back. Does that put me at risk?"

"There's a lot we do not know about this virus, including its infectivity," she said. "You need to be in quarantine. If any of your crew has not been exposed, keep them at a distance, even it means leaving them for a time on the island."

"Understood. Do we know the presumed mortality rate for the virus?"

Liz debated what to reveal. "All we have is data from lab animals. It's really not relevant."

"Don't bullshit me, Darling. Tell me what we're dealing with."

"Based on the data, I would assume one hundred percent mortality." Her voice trailed off as she made the pronouncement.

Hart responded quickly, causing Liz to wonder if he'd truly heard and processed what she had just told him. "I've got forty-five people in the village, all of whom will probably be symptomatic in short order, Liz. Kahn's given me an explicit order to neutralize the threat of contagion."

"You're talking about murdering forty-five innocent people?" She recoiled in horror.

"Those are my orders."

"Defy your fucking orders, John! We can quarantine the village; it's not that difficult! If the virus claims lives, that's beyond our control. But a bullet to the head! That's not who we are as Americans."

"If I defy a direct order, I can be court-martialed. You understand that, right?"

"You report to the president, remember?"

"Yes, but the president has delegated tremendous authority to Kahn. Defying him is a dangerous line to walk."

"Even if they drum you out of the SEALS, your integrity, your very decency remains intact."

"They'd do more than drum me out. Kahn would do everything in his power to ensure that I spent the rest of my life in Leavenworth military prison."

"Right now, I'm more concerned about your potential exposure than anything else. I'm going back into the lab to see if we missed anything relating to prophylactic treatment of the disease."

"I'll pray you find it. Hart out."

CHAPTER 32

Insubordination

Forty-five minutes had passed, and Hart knew he needed to return to the village. But, first, he had to call Kahn. He pulled out his sat phone and dialed the Deputy Director.

Kahn looked at the caller ID before answering. Seeing it was Hart, he skipped any greeting. "I trust you've come to your senses, Commander, and are executing my orders."

"No, Sir, Mr. Kahn. I cannot comply with your orders," Hart informed the DDO.

The silence that followed was deafening. Finally, Kahn said, "I'm going to give you ten seconds to reconsider, Commander. After that, I'm relieving you of your command under UCMJ-article 91 for insubordination."

But Hart remained resolute. He would not be complicit in more murders.

"Commander Hart, you are formally relieved of your command. I will inform Mr. Anderson that he is now responsible for all deployed personnel on the mission. You are to surrender your weapon to Mr. Anderson upon your return to the Mercy. Do you understand these orders, Commander?"

"Do you understand that my crew and I will need to be quarantined, Mr. Kahn. In all likelihood, we are already dead men walking."

"I don't give a good God-damn about your health, Commander. You were dead to me the minute you refused a direct order." Kahn disconnected the call.

Tommy Lamott turned towards his boss. "I only heard half of that conversation, Commander, but it sure as shit didn't sound good. Forgive my language."

"Mr. Kahn just relieved me of my command for defying a direct order. You will, in all likelihood, face similar charges if you don't place me under arrest."

"Fuck that!" Lamott exclaimed.

"Yeah, fuck that!" Harding agreed.

"You're sure?"

"Couldn't be more sure, Commander," Lamott said.

"That goes for me, too, Commander," Harding added.

"Then we need to get back to that village and evacuate the people. My bet is that Kahn is already in the process of ordering a drone strike. The villagers need to be dispersed and hidden under the palm canopies. I'll give Ramirez and Sitarski a heads-up that they're staying on the island. I want them off the boat before we come aboard. There's no reason why they should risk infection.

"I'm going to instruct them to inform Anderson and Kahn that we forced them off the boat at gunpoint so they bear no complicity in whatever follows. It won't hurt them to spend a day or two on the beach awaiting an evacuation ride, as long as they don't contact the villagers."

Lamott looked over at Harding, who was taking in the conversation. "Understood, but are you saying we're going to end up like the man in the hut, Commander? I'd rather take a bullet through the chest."

"Trust me, that's no fun either. Look, we've been in worse situations, Gentlemen. Cool heads need to prevail. Dr. Wilkins' team is working on a way to help us."

When they returned, Atu was waiting for them.

"You're in grave danger. Your people need to get far away from the village as quickly as possible. Tell them to hide under the cover of plants and trees," Hart instructed.

"Why? And where do you suggest we go?" The elder seemed confused by the suggestion to abandon their home.

"Because there are men who will seek to destroy your village. Disappear into the jungle. And don't contact anyone. Finally, leave the sick man behind. He will only slow you down and expose others to whatever he's got."

"There's no need. The man has passed away."

Dead within seventy-two hours of exposure, thought Hart. They didn't have much time.

"Please do as I say," he implored. Hart raised his hand as he bade the man goodbye. He, Lamott, and Harding headed for the boat.

Had it not been for tangles of tree roots and jagged rocks, the men would have sprinted down the trail. Even so, their pace was hurried. As they approached the beach, Hart heard the distinctive sound of a Predator drone and began to scan the skies.

"Hear that?" Harding asked his commander.

As two drones appeared in the sky above them, Hart advised, "We'd already be dead if we were the intended target. They're headed for the village. Kahn must have triangulated our position from my sat phone call.

"Let's take cover in the high grass. We'll hold our position until the drones complete their mission."

As he spoke, the Predators were on a final approach trajectory to the village. After the drones had disappeared below the tree line, Hart saw four brilliant streaks of light emerge from under their wings, followed almost instantly by violent explosions that echoed off the volcanic cliffs. Plumes of dark black smoke arose in the distance.

"I hope they got out in time," Hart said quietly.

"And that whoever is controlling those things thinks we're dead," Lamott added.

"Let's go!" the commander ordered.

CHAPTER 33

Subterfuge

HART STOPPED JUST SHORT OF THE WATER'S EDGE, cupped his hands like a megaphone, and shouted at the two men on the Mark V anchored just off shore. "Mr. Ramirez, Mr. Sitarski, I need your attention!"

The men rushed to the starboard side of the boat. "Is there a problem, Commander?" Ramirez barked.

Hart summarized what had transpired since he, Lamott, and Harding left for the island's interior, culminating with his call to Kahn. "Not only are we insubordinate, but likely infected with a bio-agent. You're not to come within fifty feet of the three of us."

"That's going to be a bit tricky on the boat, Sir," Ramirez responded.

"That's why you are going to disembark after grabbing a couple days' worth of provisions. You can camp out on the beach until a rescue boat arrives. We'll be commandeering the Mark V."

"Sir, since when do SEALS leave SEALS behind?" Sitarski called back. "We're not here to cut and run. We're with you, Commander, through thick and thin."

"Roman, according to Dr. Wilkins, the virus we were exposed to is universally fatal. I'm not willing to put your life, and the life of Mr. Ramirez, at risk."

"How many times have you put your life on the line, Mr. Hart? I'd venture too many to count."

"Requesting permission to remain aboard, Commander," Sitarski shouted across the water.

"That goes for me too," Ramirez echoed.

Hart looked over at Lamott and Harding, who were both silently nodding their heads.

He knew he would be signing their death warrants if he agreed. But he also knew the determination and commitment that ran through his men's veins.

"Permission granted, but keep your distance from us, and grab a couple of surgical masks out of the boat's medical kit. No reason to tempt fate any more than necessary."

Minutes later, the Mark V was on a heading north towards the Prometheus, a return trip that would take hours.

Hart summoned Sitarski, careful to remain downwind from him. "I want you to contact Mr. Kahn. Tell him that I ordered you and Mr. Ramirez to leave Lamott, Harding, and me on the island, then return to the Mercy. Make sure he understands that you have not been exposed, and that you remained on the boat while the three of us searched for the missing sailor."

"Why not just tell him the truth, Commander?"

"Because he will threaten you with prosecution for insubordination if you don't arrest me on the spot."

"We can handle that, Sir."

"There's another, more pressing reason. I'm concerned that Mr. Kahn may be operating under a separate agenda, and that he has sufficient motivation to arrange for us to mysteriously disappear in the vast Pacific."

"You're not suggesting that Deputy Director Kahn would order us terminated, are you?"

"That's precisely what I'm suggesting, Mr. Sitarski."

"But why, Sir? What could he possibly stand to gain by our deaths?"

"Not by our deaths, per se, Mr. Sitarski. He's simply trying to protect a very dark secret that's buried in the data being extracted from the Prometheus. He doesn't want the Chinese to have it, nor does he want us to get it."

"It's still not making sense to me, Commander. The CIA and the SEALS are all on the same team."

"You're going to have to trust me on this one, Mr. Sitarski. Now, if you don't have any more questions, place the call using my sat phone."

But before the soldier could pick up the phone, Hart bellowed, "Wait! Wipe down that phone with an alcohol swab before you touch it."

Still reeling from the conversation, Sitarski did as instructed. Then he dialed the number.

"Mr. Kahn, my name is Lieutenant Roman Sitarski and I am calling at the request of Commander Hart."

"Where the hell is Mr. Hart? Put him on the line."

"I can't do that, Sir."

"Why not! Don't tell me I've got another insubordinate soldier on my hands."

"No, Sir. We left the commander along with Mr. Lamott and Mr. Harding on the beach."

"Under whose orders, Sailor?"

"The commander's, Sir. He told us that the three of them had been exposed to the virus. As we left, he was returning to the village to assess the situation."

"You are not to have any further contact with Commander Hart, do you understand?"

"No, Sir. I don't understand. Why would you order us not to speak with the commander?"

"Do you know who I am?" Kahn shouted in disbelief. "It's not your job to ask questions, Sailor. Just execute my orders."

"What exactly are your orders, Mr. Kahn?"

"Return to the Mercy. Dock the boat and await further instructions. Kahn out."

Sitarski looked to the commander, hoping for some indication that he had put on a convincing show.

"Good job, Mr. Sitarski. He's pissed off, but hopefully you just bought us some precious time."

Hart glanced at the satellite phone. He wanted desperately to call Liz, but he knew that a call could tip off Anderson. If Anderson was suspicious, he would report the contact to Kahn. It wouldn't take Kahn more than a second to conclude that he was not on the beach, but rather on the Mark V with Sitarski, meaning the lieutenant had lied to him.

An hour into their return voyage, the phone started to ring. Hart could see it was Liz trying to reach him. With a heavy heart, he let the calls go unanswered.

※

"Pick up the god-damn phone, John!" Liz muttered to herself. But no one picked up the call. She shoved the phone into a pocket as she struggled to fend off an impending sense of dread.

"Having trouble reaching the commander?" Anderson emerged from behind a door, a twisted smile on his face.

"Were you eavesdropping on me?" Liz thundered.

The soldier took a step closer to her, close enough to send a chill down her spine.

"Have you forgotten, Doctor, that I'm in command of this ship? I'll do whatever I damn well please." He leaned towards her, close enough that she could smell his unwashed body. He raised a hand as if planning to touch her. But then he stopped and, with a smirk, he turned and walked away.

Marta Hopkins, having witnessed the encounter, rushed to her friend's aid. "What the fuck did he want?"

"I don't know. Maybe just to assert his power."

"Men like that are dangerous, Liz. Promise me you won't let him get you alone. And promise me that you will make Commander Hart aware of his strange behavior."

She squeezed Marta's hand. "I promise, my dear friend, I promise."

❧

Anderson entered the bridge. Then, after checking it was empty, he locked the door. He then called the Agency. "Mr. Kahn, I'm sorry to disturb you, but I thought you'd want to know that our good doctor has been trying repeatedly to reach her husband on the sat phone. Apparently, no one's home."

Kahn put two and two together, concluding that Hart was, indeed, still on the island. "I do appreciate good news,

Mr. Anderson," he said, uncharacteristically cheerful. "How long before you scuttle the Prometheus?"

"I'm afraid that not all the news is good. It seems that our data whiz, Mr. Hodges, is having trouble backing up the final server. Until he breaks the encryption algorithm, I've been informed that we are on hold."

"Damn it, that's totally unacceptable," Kahn fired back, his mood shifting like a fast-moving storm.

"Yes, Sir. I know that. I'm working on a solution."

"Tell them to pull the hard drives out of their docking stations and take them to the Mercy encrypted."

"I already recommended that to Mr. Hodges, Sir. He explained that there's a fail-safe mechanism built into each drive that renders the data unusable if standard protocols are violated. In other words, the disks will be wiped clean before we can remove them from their housings."

"God damn it! Then how long?" Kahn's impatience was palpable.

"It could be another day, Mr. Kahn."

"Have you asked the Chinese if they are willing to wait a day before launching an attack?" Kahn asked sarcastically.

"They've suspended their aerial harassment, Mr. Kahn."

"And you are interpreting that as a positive sign, Mr. Anderson?"

"Yes, Sir."

"I suggest you prepare for a Chinese expeditionary force arriving at your doorstep." And with that, Kahn hung up.

CHAPTER 34

Setting a Trap

"SHUT THAT DAMN THING OFF!" Hart yelled to Sitarski, who was carrying the sat phone. Each call was a powerful reminder that Liz was in peril and there was not a damn thing he could do about it. He turned towards Lamott. "Tommy, let's take a walk. There's something I need to discuss with you."

The two men isolated themselves in the rear of the boat where their voices could not be heard.

"How well do you know Sitarski and Harding?"

"I've been on missions with both men, Commander. They are as good as you get, but you didn't ask me about Ramirez."

"That's because I don't need to. I trust Paco with my life, just as I trust you. Regarding Sitarski and Harding, is there any chance they might have been co-opted by a rogue agent? Even a one percent chance?"

"Rogue agent? What are you talking about, Commander? Or maybe I should be asking: Who are you talking about, Sir?"

"Mike Anderson." Hart's eyes bore into Lamott's unblinking eyes.

"Mr. Anderson, gone rogue? That's a little hard to swallow, Sir."

"I've had my doubts about Mr. Anderson for a long time, but they remained unconfirmed until this mission."

"Yes, Sir. I can't comment on Mr. Anderson, but I'd wager my life on Sitarski's and Harding's loyalty."

"That's exactly what you've just done, Mr. Lamott. Now instruct Mr. Harding to reduce speed to 15 knots, maintaining the course on auto-pilot. Then assemble the men for a short briefing."

"Gentlemen, if my suspicions are correct, we've got a hell of a situation on our hands. We're still hours out from the Prometheus. Directly ahead of us is the Chinese Navy. As if that's not enough of a threat, I have reason to believe that Mr. Anderson is running a separate operation under the direction of Mr. Kahn."

"A separate operation, Sir?" Sitarski asked.

"There were numerous experiments being conducted on the Prometheus, some so dark that only a handful of men were read in to them."

"Are you speaking of the virus, Commander?" Harding questioned.

"No, I'm speaking about eugenics—a project to birth the 'perfect' race. Imagine an entire nation that is highly resistant to disease, whose average IQ is twenty points higher than most; a lily white, Norwegian/Aryan-like populace designed to dominate the world."

"That sounds like the fricking shit that the Nazis did under Mengele, if you'll excuse my language, Commander."

"It's okay, Mr. Ramirez. It is 'fricking shit,' and I'd bet my life that the people running the program are not the only ones pursuing this twisted dream."

"What do you mean, Sir?"

"Why do you think the Chinese are here, Mr. Lamott? It sure as hell isn't for our bio-warfare secrets—they are every bit as advanced as we are in that arena. No, my bet is that our saboteur has been spying for the People's Liberation Army since the day he 'defected' to this country. When we assigned him to the Prometheus, we handed him the keys to our most closely guarded secrets, secrets he then shared with his handlers within the People's Liberation Army."

"And now they're trying to steal the remaining secrets—is that what you're saying, Commander?" Lamott asked.

"Yes. They are ensuring that they have the mother-lode of our data so that there are no gaps in their intelligence. The operation is straight out of the People's Republic playbook; why spend decades trying to mirror our accomplishments when you can steal our intellectual property and achieve parity in months rather than years? I'm sure there is nothing they would love more than to get their hands on our data and advance their own pursuit of a master race—one that isn't white."

"If you're correct, then why haven't they invaded the Prometheus, Sir?"

"They don't want to provoke an international incident that could escalate overnight into a war, not if they can avoid it. The Chinese are smart—I'm sure they've concluded that Prometheus is set to blow if there is any indication of an imminent threat. A scuttled research ship sitting hundreds of feet beneath the surface won't have much value to them.

Even if salvaged, the data will be irretrievably damaged. So it's devolved into a game of chicken."

"What is your plan, Commander?" Lamott asked.

"Assuming we can avoid any interference from the Chinese, we need to proceed to the Mercy as instructed by Mr. Kahn. I don't want anything to set off alarm bells with either Mr. Anderson or Mr. Kahn." Hart paused to make sure everyone was still following him.

"Mr. Lamott, Mr. Harding, and I will remain onboard and out of sight, while Mr. Sitarski and Mr. Ramirez await Mr. Anderson and the scientific team. I'm sure Kahn will arrange a greeting."

"But Commander, we have now been exposed to the virus, just as have you. We may put everyone we come in contact with at risk," Ramirez objected.

"We'll have to hope that, if you actually are infected, you're still in the latency period before the virus becomes infectious. It's a risk we'll have to run."

"Mr. Lamott, Mr. Harding, and I will plan a little surprise for Mr. Anderson when he returns from the Prometheus. He will be greeted by the barrel of an MP-5 leveled at his head."

"You think he'll be alone, Commander?"

"I'm assuming that he will instruct Alvarez and Latourno to stand guard over the ship. That leaves Bridges and Good. Anderson is a cocky SOB, so he'll probably determine that there's no need for two back-ups. I'm betting that he leaves Bridges behind to babysit the snipers and brings Good with him. Remember, we don't know if Good has turned bad, so let's be sure we take him alive."

"What about the scientific team, Mr. Hart?"

"If Anderson follows protocol, the scientific team will be instructed to proceed through decontamination and then to their berths. That's when we will ensure that our conspirator is neutralized."

"And then?" Lamott asked.

"Jesus, Tommy, that's as far as I've gotten. Let's start by praying we get past the Chinese without incident."

CHAPTER 35

Killing a Snake

THE LIAONING LOOKED LIKE a low-hanging black cloud on the horizon. Dusk was settling in as the Mark V sped towards the Chinese Naval Group. Flanking it on either side were destroyers, with the guided missile carrier bringing up the rear. Hart picked up the binoculars, hoping to get a clear view of the armada while there was still light.

Dwarfed by the immense warships, the Mark V was like a fly on the ass of a bull; an annoyance to be brushed off with little more than the swish of a tail. Hart knew it wouldn't take much effort for the Chinese to blow them out of the water. A torpedo or ship-to-ship missile would leave nothing more than an oil slick where the Mark V had once been.

His stomach tightened in anticipation. The crew went silent.

"Steady as she goes, Mr. Lamott," he instructed the helm, as he scanned the water for an incoming fish. But there were no acts of aggression as the Mark V passed within five hundred yards of the Liaoning.

"Why didn't they try to stop us, Commander?" Tommy Lamott asked. "We might dodge a torpedo, but a missile would be tough to avoid."

"Their CO knows that if he take us out, he risks incurring the full wrath of the United States Navy. You know damn well the president would order the sinking of the Liaoning, and I don't think China wants to trade their carrier for a Mark V. Plus, they're not itching for a fight. The Prometheus holds the Holy Grail, and that's their one and only concern."

Within minutes, the carrier group was behind them, causing a collective sigh of relief. But it was short-lived, as the navigation system alerted them that the Mercy and Prometheus lay dead ahead.

"Take the helm and slow her down to thirty knots," Hart instructed Ramirez. "Mr. Sitarski, radio Captain Hamil requesting permission to dock. Mr. Harding, Mr. Lamott, it's time for us to vanish." He pointed to a heavy tarp on the starboard side of the boat.

Hart issued one final order. "When Mr. Anderson arrives, we will be the welcoming committee. I want the two of you backing us up, so be ready to take him out without a moment's hesitation. Is that clear?"

"Yes, Sir," Ramirez answered.

Sitarski nodded.

Hart pulled down the tarp. "Gentlemen, assuming Anderson adheres to orders, he'll leave the Prometheus with the scientific team at 21:00 hours. That's about thirty minutes from now. If he puts up a fight, I want short, suppressed bursts at close range. Nothing that might alert the men aboard the Prometheus that something is awry."

The trap was baited, and now all they could do was wait. Though the time was short, it passed agonizingly slowly as the men remained under the tarp in near total darkness.

"Commander, I thought you had put all of this crazy shit behind you and started a new life with the doctor."

"Tommy, you're not the only one who thought that."

"So, what happened, Sir, if you don't mind me asking."

"First, Washington came within seconds of being nuked. And while riding out the storm with President Conner, I got sucked into this. When you take an oath to defend the country, it appears that there's no expiration date."

"So, you're back in for good, Commander?" Harding asked.

"I wouldn't go that far, Jason. Hopefully just long enough to complete this mission and eliminate any threat associated with the Prometheus." As he spoke, Hart wondered if it was all moot, and the virus would claim his life long before any bullet or bomb could.

As if reading his thoughts, Lamott asked, "Do we have a chance, Commander? Whatever that bug is that we were exposed to, it doesn't seem to take prisoners. Maybe I should be writing a goodbye letter to my wife and kids."

"Let's take this one step at a time, Tommy. We've been facing multiple threats. We squeaked by one—the Chinese—and now we're poised to eliminate our second threat—an internal one. After that, we can focus on whether we're infected. If I know Liz, she's tearing out her hair looking for any possible intervention that might help us. Let's trust her to do her job."

"Yes, Sir."

"Jason, what about you? What are you going to do when we get out of this mess?"

"I'm going back to San Antonio for some R&R and a Texas-sized bowl of chili. I can almost taste the jalapenos, Commander."

Hart laughed. "Stop it, you're making my stomach growl." But he didn't really want it to stop. Such banter was an essential part of reducing stress right before the shit hit the fan. He stoked the conversation to keep it alive until they heard the distinct blip of a message coming through on the radio.

"Commander Hart, come in."

Sitarski responded, "This is Lieutenant Sitarski, please identify yourself."

"Lieutenant, this is Mike Anderson. Put the commander on the comm."

"What the fuck?" Sitarski whispered to Ramirez before keying the mike.

Paco put his hand over Sitarski's to slow him down. "He's just testing us." He removed his hand.

"We left the commander behind on an island, Mr. Anderson, along with Lamott and Harding. They were all exposed to the virus, Sir."

There was a long pause, as if Anderson was trying to ascertain the validity of what Sitarski had told him. Finally, he uttered a terse response. "Understood, Mr. Sitarski."

"We're on our way back, Sir. ETA is less than two minutes. We will await your further orders."

Moments after Sitarski and Ramirez had docked the Mark V adjacent to the Mercy, Hart could hear the waves slapping against the bow of Anderson's boat as it closed in on the hospital ship. As the engine throttled down, he heard the sounds of Ramirez and Sitarski grabbing tie lines from Anderson's boat and securing it in its slip. Once docked, the unloading process began. Good was first off, who extended a hand to Liz Wilkins as she disembarked. Mike Anderson followed closely on her heels.

"Where's my husband?" Liz demanded of Ramirez.

"We had to leave him on a beach, Ma'am, along with Mr. Harding and Mr. Lamott. They'll be okay; they have several days of rations."

"Why in the hell did you do that?" Liz shouted angrily.

"Because the commander ordered it. He was exposed to the virus."

Frozen in place, Liz's eyes closed slowly as she took in the magnitude of the message.

"You've got to keep moving, Doctor," Anderson ordered, giving Liz a nudge.

"Keep your fucking hands off of me." She scowled at him, as she stepped beyond his reach.

Once all of the scientists were off the boat, Anderson ordered, "Take them to decon, Mr. Good, while I catch up with Mr. Sitarski and Mr. Ramirez."

Good turned to Wilkins, Hopkins, Obaji, Nielsen, and Hodges. "You know the drill, ladies and gentlemen, let's get moving."

Anderson watched the quick exodus, discreetly pulling back the slide of his MP-5 and chambering a round. He set the weapon to full-auto before turning towards Ramirez and Sitarski on the Mark V.

"Permission to come aboard," he said almost mockingly.

"Permission granted, Mr. Anderson," Sitarski replied.

Hart could hear the sound of Anderson's boots landing on the hard deck of the Mark V. In a whisper, he instructed Lamott and Harding, "On my mark, Gentlemen."

"I want to know exactly what happened out there," Anderson demanded.

"It's just as we told you, Sir. The commander, Lamott, and Harding went in search of the missing sailor. They found him in a hut surrounded by villagers. By that time, they realized they'd been exposed to whatever the man was carrying. So, rather than risk infecting us, the commander ordered us to leave them behind."

"You stranded three SEALS who may now be dying from an infection? Do I have that right, Mr. Sitarski?" His tone was scathing.

Before Sitarski could answer, Hart whispered "Go!" to Lamott and Harding, as he threw back the tarp and leveled his gun on Anderson's chest.

"Drop your weapon now!" he shouted.

Anderson saw three MP-5's pointed at him and three red laser beams directed at his chest. He slowly set the MP-5 on the deck.

"Shove it out of reach, NOW!" Hart ordered.

"You don't have any idea what you're interfering with, Commander, or how many people have sacrificed their lives to advance this mission."

"Do you know what is being done aboard that ship? I hope not, Mike. I pray that you are not so depraved that you would allow yourself to be brainwashed into supporting such a mission."

"I honor my superiors and follow their orders without question, Commander, as should you. And I support the preservation and enhancement of the white race." He spat out the words.

Hart rushed towards Anderson and, with lightning speed, swept the butt of his rifle across the other man's face, shattering his jaw and dropping him to the deck.

"Bind his hands and feet," Hart ordered.

But before Lamott could comply, Anderson reached for his .45 caliber sidearm. It was cocked and halfway out of the holster when a short burst of bullets from Harding's suppressed MP-5 tore through Anderson's chest. As he lay dying, Hart bent down to the fallen soldier.

"What made you turn, Mike?"

"Fuck you, Commander," were his last words.

Hearing the commotion, Good raced back to the dock with a group of confused scientists trailing behind him. He saw Anderson sprawled amidst a pool of blood with gaping wounds in his chest. He instinctively brought his weapon forward.

"Don't do it, Ronny," Hart advised. "This man was a traitor. Lower your weapon, now!" he ordered.

"You're going to have to give me more than that, Commander," Good bellowed, now in a crouched position with his weapon pointed at Hart.

"Anderson was working for Kahn." Before he could finish, Good cut him off.

"You are the one working for Mr. Kahn, Commander."

"I was, Ronny, until I discovered that Mr. Kahn has a separate and rogue agenda. He may appear to report to our president, but it's a total sham."

"You are talking nonsense, Sir," he said anxiously, his finger still on the trigger.

"I don't blame you for thinking that, but you're going to have to trust me, Ronny. Anderson had one mission, which was to get the data off that ship and into Kahn's hands. Then he was to sink her. He didn't give a rat's ass who went down with her."

"What about the virus, Mr. Hart? Mr. Anderson told us there might have been an accidental release in the lab, and the saboteur might be infected. Are you suggesting that was nothing but a smokescreen?" Good asked incredulously.

"No, I wish it was. That was one of the few bits of truth Mr. Anderson shared with you. We've seen firsthand what the virus does to people. And I suggest you not get any closer. Three of us were exposed. Now, for God's sake, Mr. Good, lower your weapon. There's been enough carnage tonight."

Good haltingly lowered his gun. As he did, Hart ordered his crew to stand down. It was then that he saw Liz.

She started to run across the deck towards him, dodging Good, but stopped abruptly as Hart's arm shot out in a clear motion designed to halt her in her tracks. "Don't come a step closer, Liz. You know we've been exposed, and I'm not about to take you down with us."

Tears flooded her eyes. "I've got to examine you. I've got to find out if you're infected."

"You're going to do it from a distance, Darling. Mr. Ramirez, take the Doctor and her colleagues to decontamination."

"Yes, Commander."

"Liz, I'll meet you once I've cleared decontamination and I'm in a bio-hazard suit."

She stifled a cry before nodding in acquiescence and turning away. She had been poring through every research note she could find related to the chimera virus since learning of her husband's possible exposure. The prospects for a reprieve seemed bleak. But there was one fragile thread of hope, one she would soon share with her husband.

CHAPTER 36

A Deadly Vaccine

RAMIREZ AND GOOD WERE THE FIRST TO GO through decon. They were soon followed by the remaining members of Hart's crew. It took only a moment for their suits to be stripped clean of any uninvited micro-organisms that had tagged along for the ride.

After they had been thoroughly cleansed, Hart addressed his squad. "Sergeant Ramirez, I want you to accompany me. Mr. Sitarski, I want you and the rest of the men to go to the bridge and inform the captain what has transpired. Insist that he not communicate anything more than that you and Ramirez returned safely and were aboard the Mercy when the scientific team from the Prometheus and its escorts arrived."

"What if he refuses to cooperate, Commander?" Harding asked.

"Persuade him, Jason. Tell the captain that Mr. Ramirez and I will meet with him shortly."

Hart called Liz's sat phone. "I've got you on speaker, Liz. Mr. Ramirez and I just cleared decon and need directions to your cabin."

Ramirez listened intently to Liz's directions before pointing at a stairway to the right. "The doctor is this way, Commander."

Liz was waiting at the door and opened it at the first knock. She rushed to embrace her husband, her eyes clenched tightly as she squeezed Hart's cocooned body. As she pulled away, emotions enveloped her, tears welled up before spilling out in a torrent.

"Come on, Darling," Hart wiped her wet cheeks, "it's going to be alright."

She stared back at him. They both knew everything was far from alright.

"Would you mind giving us a moment, Sergeant?" Hart asked.

Ramirez nodded, stepping into the corridor and pulling the door closed behind him.

"Tell me you've found some type of intervention," Hart said.

She hesitated before responding, "We don't even know at this point if you're infected."

"Take a look at me, Liz. I'm diaphoretic, and my throat and head are beginning to hurt like hell. If that doesn't sound like the prodrome of a viral infection, I don't know what does."

"It could just be the flu, John."

"Damn it, Liz," he snapped. "We don't have time for this! What are you holding back?"

She sighed. "They were working on a vaccine, but we don't know . . ."

"That's great news!" Hart interrupted her.

"No, John, it's not. They had tested it initially on mice, and then on rhesus monkeys."

"And?"

"It killed fifty percent of the lab animals."

"And the remaining fifty percent?"

"The animals cleared the virus, but a number of them were left with irreversible brain damage."

"Could they distinguish, even anecdotally, which animals would be most negatively affected?"

As Liz attempted to disassociate from her emotions, her tone gradually changed from that of a grieving wife to that of a dispassionate researcher. "Their studies were not yet that advanced. However, anecdotal observations suggest that the more symptomatic the animal was at time of vaccination, the more likely it was to either expire or be neurologically impaired by the vaccine."

"Let me get this straight. There's a vaccine with a fifty percent chance of curing us if administered shortly before we descend into a living hell. We might even escape with our brains intact."

"Yes, and it has an equally good chance of killing you outright. Hell, John, we don't even know what the dose would be for a human being."

"Do you know if there are any stockpiles of the vaccine?"

Liz held out her right fist and slowly unfolded her fingers. In her palm were five vials of vaccine. Setting them carefully down on a table, she opened a drawer and pulled out a piece of folded cloth. As she unfolded it, Hart saw five syringes.

"I'm not going to administer the vaccine until I know that all of you are symptomatic."

"That's going to be a bit of a problem, Darling, since three of us were exposed at least twenty-four hours before

Mr. Sitarski and Mr. Ramirez. I'm afraid we're all going to have to be your guinea pigs."

As Liz was shaking her head in opposition, Hart continued. "Before you inoculate us, I need to know that you have secured undeniable proof of the research being conducted on the Prometheus. Kahn will do everything in his power to silence our voices, starting by calling us crazy conspiracy theorists with vivid imaginations. If that's not enough, he will go to any length to protect his precious secret."

Liz nodded. "We've assembled detailed genetic profiles for the mothers and babies, much of it based upon amniotic fluid obtained from corpses. But there's more, John. This work has been going on for decades, and there's a data trail to prove it. There's irrefutable evidence of genetic manipulation designed to create a new generation imbued with characteristics someone deemed advantageous to survival."

"How much of a jump-start would a Chinese eugenics program gain by becoming privy to this data?"

"We'd be giving them the keys to the kingdom," she answered flatly.

"Where is this research?" Hart asked.

"I printed out our lab results from the amniocentesis, and I've made digital copies of key documents. As for the detailed history behind this research, Hodges believes it comprises much of the remaining data on the encrypted server."

"If he can't get into the data, how in the hell can he know what's on the server?"

"Because of references we've come across in other documents. Even without the contents of the final server, we can spell out our story with irrefutable supporting evidence."

"Where is this information, Liz?"

"I left it concealed in the laboratory. Anderson and his men wouldn't step foot in there, even in full bioprotective gear. They knew that something horrific was released in the lab. That's why I assumed it would be the safest place onboard the Prometheus."

Hart stretched out his arm and did his best to squeeze her hand through the layers of bioprotective material. "Good thinking, Darling. If you're ready, I think it's time we ask Mr. Ramirez to join us."

"First, I want you to promise me one thing."

"Of course."

"Promise me that you will follow my lead regarding the vaccine, including when or if to administer it."

"You're going to give us the vaccine, Liz."

"No, Commander, that's not what I need to hear. I need to hear that you will defer to my judgment, no matter how much that goes against the grain of that SEAL brain of yours."

Hart studied his wife's face and realized that she was determined that he agree. "Under one condition, Doctor."

"And what's that, Commander?"

"For a moment, you suspend your promise "to do no harm" and replace it with "the greatest good for the greatest number.""

Liz nodded. "Agreed."

With the issue resolved, Hart opened the cabin door and beckoned the sergeant back in.

Hart and Wilkins summarized their conversation for Ramirez, concluding with the need to retrieve vitally important information from the Prometheus.

"What do you need me to do, Commander?" Ramirez asked.

"I need you to escort the doctor and Mr. Hodges back to the Prometheus."

"We're not due back until the morning," Liz interjected. "Don't you think that might arouse considerable suspicion, John?"

"Sir, if I may," Ramirez interrupted. "The men guarding the ship will want to know why we are returning, and why anyone other than Mr. Good or Mr. Anderson is acting as chaperone."

"You will tell them that Mr. Anderson is pressing Dr. Wilkins and Mr. Hodges to complete their work, and they need access to the lab if they are to comply with his orders."

"That explains the return, Sir, but not why Anderson and Good are not accompanying us," Ramirez said.

"You, Paco, offered to take Good's place. And Mr. Anderson has retired for the evening with instructions not to be disturbed. Tell them that he appeared ill. Very ill. That will blow their fricking minds. They won't be able to focus on anything other than who is next in line to fall victim to the virus."

※

The return visit to the Prometheus happened exactly as Hart had scripted. In short order, Wilkins and Hodges were in the lab, while Ramirez waited for them on the boat.

"Why don't you come up and talk to us, Juan?" one of the men yelled down from the top deck.

"Are you crazy, man? I don't want to be exposed to that shit any more than necessary. I'll be just fine waiting right here."

"Suit yourself," the SEAL said as he flung a cigarette butt off the railing into the sea below.

As he moved towards the interior of the ship, he passed Wilkins and Hodges. "Done already, Doctor?"

"Yes. I think Mr. Anderson will be very pleased." Liz forced a smile. "We'll see you in the morning," she said, as she prepared to leave the Prometheus.

Her heart didn't stop racing until her feet hit the deck of the Mark V and they set course for the short return trip to the Mercy.

Not only had they retrieved the proof that Liz had promised to deliver to Hart, but Hodges had succeeded in finally unlocking the server. The massive amount of data would have required hours to upload to a portable device, so he instead mapped the data transfer to a hyper-secure cloud.

As the Mark V pulled alongside the Mercy, Hart was waiting for them. Liz was the first speak. "We've got it, John, well, not all of it. Some of it is still uploading to the cloud."

Wilkins expected Hart to be elated. Instead, he turned to Hodges. "Why would you run that risk, Mr. Hodges? If someone enters the lab, they'll see the files uploading and know something is amiss."

"There are only two men guarding the ship, Commander, and they are both deathly afraid of becoming infected."

"What do you have in the way of physical evidence?" Hart asked Liz.

"Everything we need to make the case, just as I promised." She opened the secure satchel and pulled out a stack of reports and images two inches thick.

Hart helped her out of the boat, with the men following on her heels.

Ramirez spoke. "What's next, Commander?"

"We bring President Conner up to speed, share the supporting evidence for our allegations, and then await his instructions, which will likely be to scuttle the ship."

"While you do that, I'm going to check on the other men," Liz informed them. "We're probably approaching the point where I have to make a decision regarding vaccination."

"You mean *we* have to make a decision."

"That's not what we agreed to, Commander. I'll make the medical call and you and your comrades will fall in line. Are we clear?"

"Quite clear." With that, Hart and Ramirez headed for the captain's private quarters.

CHAPTER 37

A Threat to Democracy

THERE WAS A SUDDEN KNOCK on Captain Hamil's cabin door. When he opened it, he was startled to find two men cloaked in bio-hazard suits standing there. Peering through the visors, he saw it was Hart and Ramirez.

"Your men told me what transpired, Commander," he said. "What are you expecting me to do at this late hour?"

"May we come in, Sir?"

Reluctantly, Hamil beckoned them in, offering them the comfort of two rather wobbly stools. "Now tell me what's so urgent, and why all of this secrecy? And while you're at it, Commander, tell me what makes you believe you can trust me?"

"I have no choice but to trust you, Captain. As for all the secrecy, allow me to explain." Hart began to methodically outline what had been uncovered.

"You're talking about a massive conspiracy that threatens our very democracy, Commander Hart. And, as if that's not enough, you're suggesting that radical experiments were being performed, experiments that outstrip our scientific ability. You're talking about the creation of a so-called 'master race.'"

"That's the gist of it, Captain, however crazy it may sound. As for the science, we have the capabilities aboard the Prometheus to modify the human genome in previously unimaginable ways. I need to get this material in front of President Conner as quickly as humanly possible."

"You risk looking like a fool. I trust you know that, Commander."

"If I'm right, this is a disease that threatens to kill the very heart of our democracy, Captain. So I'll put my reputation on the line in a heartbeat. President Conner needs to know what we've uncovered."

The captain thought for a moment. "Okay, I'll buy it. For now anyway." He stood up. "I'll meet you in the comm room in five minutes, Gentlemen. Now please excuse me while I get dressed."

When they'd left the cabin, Ramirez turned to the commander. "Can you trust him?"

"What choice do I have, Paco?" Hart responded, as they made their way to the comm room. At the door, he grabbed Ramirez's shoulder. "Your job is to not let anyone get within fifty feet of this room until I've completed my conversation with the president and erased all traces of the call."

"Understood, Commander."

Shortly after, the captain arrived. After excusing the on-duty communications officer, he then ushered Hart into the comm room. Ramirez stayed outside, on guard.

"Let me see if I can remember how to use this damn thing," the captain said, a perturbed look on his face. He pulled a pair of reading glasses from his pocket.

Hart scanned the equipment in front of him. "If you wish, I can do it. I'm quite familiar with this technology."

The captain eagerly stepped aside, allowing Hart to initiate a call to Conner on a proprietary line.

Four rings, five rings. Finally on the sixth ring the president answered, "Conner."

"It's John Hart, Mr. President. I'm sorry to disturb you."

The captain seemed to understand Hart's need for privacy, and he quietly left the room.

"Commander," the president began, "I've been receiving regular updates from Mr. Kahn. Are you okay?"

"I'm fine, Mr. President. Are you alone, Sir?"

"Yes."

"Are you certain that this phone is secure, Mr. President?"

"Of course it's secure. If it makes you feel better, Mr. Kahn informed me that even the Israelis wouldn't be capable of hacking it, and you know they can hack just about anything."

"Mr. Kahn?"

"Yes, he delivered it to me the same day your mission launched, right after he gave me a detailed daily briefing."

"Does the First Lady have a secure phone, Sir, and has it also been changed out by Mr. Kahn?"

As Hart and Conner spoke, every word was being captured by a senior intelligence officer at NSA. When the call terminated, the audio file would be sent directly to Marvin Kahn.

"Yes, Mary has a phone, and it hasn't been changed. She's had the same one since I took office."

"Please give me the number, and I'll call you right back on that line."

As soon as they were reconnected, Hart began, "Your phone is not secure, Sir, and I'm concerned that it won't take long for NSA to patch into this number. I need to speak quickly regarding a matter of national security."

"What the hell are you talking about, Commander? And why all the cloak and dagger stuff? Have you lost trust in the very intelligence community that you work for?"

"Sir, Liz's team unearthed a black program being run aboard the Prometheus. From what we've been able to ascertain, only a handful of people may know of this work, work that has been carefully shielded from you and numerous administrations that predate you.

"These experiments represent the continuation of work that began a century ago, draconian experiments that failed based upon the limitations of the technology available at the time."

"You're not talking about bio-warfare, Commander. You're talking about eugenics."

"That's correct, Sir. The effort to create a master race."

"My God, so Harbinger was right? So now we're playing God?"

"Sir, I reacted the same way when I first learned of the program, but I believe you will find the evidence to be beyond question. Mr. President, it's the eugenics data that the Chinese are after—not the bio-warfare agents. That would simply be the icing on the cake."

"Commander, do you realize what will happen to you if your claims are not validated? You'll be drummed out of Washington, a distinguished career ending in disgrace." He paused to let the words sink in. "It won't matter a good God damn that you brought this country back from the brink. You will have put the United States of America on par with Nazi Germany. People will call for your head!"

"Actually, we were in the eugenics business long before Hitler, Mr. President. I think you know of our checkered past; experiments designed to remove so-called *unwanted characteristics* from the Anglo-Saxon gene pool."

"Are you referring to the work funded by a number of laudatory institutions in the 1920s?"

"Yes, the Rockefeller Foundation, the Carnegie Institution, and even the American Bar Association were complicit, along with dozens more."

"I need you to get back here immediately. Bring Dr. Wilkins and the data with you. You will be briefing both houses of Congress and a number of invited guests. They need to hear this first-hand and see your evidence."

"Sir, we can assume that Mr. Kahn will know shortly that I contacted you. He will surmise that my intent was to unveil the truth behind the Prometheus. He will then ensure that neither Liz nor I ever make it back to Washington, and that any evidence disappears with us. Furthermore, if Mr. Kahn doesn't have me killed, the virus I likely harbor will do the job for him."

"So what do you suggest, Commander?"

"Let me scan and transmit everything we've uncovered, as well as provide your designee with sign-on credentials to a secure cloud that contains the complete history of the eugenics project. If I'm silenced, the data can still speak for itself."

"I'll make the necessary arrangements with people I trust."

"Sir, remember that you've trusted Mr. Kahn for years. The people involved in this conspiracy are operating under the deepest level of cover imaginable."

"Thank you for the forewarning, Commander, but it's a risk we must take. I still want you in Washington. How do you propose we get you and Liz back without running afoul of this so-called conspiracy?"

"First, Sir, we must address my possible exposure to the chimera virus. If I am infected, I won't survive the trip back. My only hope lies in an experimental vaccine that may kill me or leave me in a vegetative state. Not what I would call a bright future, Sir."

"What exactly is the risk, Commander?"

"Liz's team was only able to obtain laboratory data on animal tests. The vaccine killed fifty percent of the cohort and created serious neurological problems in a number of the surviving animals."

"You can't play those odds, Commander!"

"The virus is universally lethal, Mr. President. Unvaccinated, I'm certain to die; vaccination gives me a small but fighting chance to survive. If it's alright with you, Sir, I'll opt for the latter.

"Before we conclude this call, there's one more matter we must address, Mr. President. I need your orders regarding the fate of the Prometheus. You are aware that the Chinese are ready to board her at a moment's notice. Our data is still highly vulnerable, at least the data that is currently being uploaded into the cloud."

"Your thoughts, Commander?"

"I recommend that we remove the remaining crew from their guard posts and scuttle the Prometheus the instant Mr. Hodges' upload to the cloud is complete."

"Have the charges been set?"

"Yes, Sir. Mr. Ramirez set them before we went in pursuit of the saboteur. They can be detonated remotely using a phone."

"And who has the access code, Commander, beyond you and Ramirez?"

"Mr. Kahn had access, but I asked Mr. Ramirez to change the code to prevent Kahn from using it."

"That would have been a convenient way for Kahn to dispose of you and Liz. He'd just need to get you both back on the Prometheus at the same time."

"I'm sure that was part of the plan."

"Give me the code, Commander. When I receive word regarding the data, I will order the three remaining SEALS to abandon the Prometheus, then deep-six her. That is what you are recommending?"

"Precisely, Mr. President."

"And if the Chinese move to occupy the ship before the data has finished uploading? What then, Commander?"

"We can keep them busy for a short time, after which the ship needs to be sent to its grave."

"Okay. Good luck, Commander."

"Thank you, Sir." Hart ended the call and summoned Ramirez.

"Well, Paco, you know full well what we're up against. Let's pray we live to fight another day."

"I have faith we will, Commander."

"And I have faith that the worst thing is never the last thing, Staff Sergeant."

CHAPTER 38

Brains on Fire

WHEN HART AND RAMIREZ ENTERED LIZ'S CABIN, they were surprised to see Lamott, Harding, Good, and Sitarski lined up in a queue. Though they were infectious, none of the men were wearing bioprotective suits. Hart saw they'd all been stacked in the corner. The men had their right sleeves rolled up to their shoulders, as Liz held an alcohol-drenched cotton ball in one hand and a syringe loaded with a green liquid in the other.

She turned to Hart. "Get in line, take off that suit, and roll up your sleeve, Commander. That goes for you, too, Mr. Ramirez. And be ready. I've got a feeling that this stuff packs a hell of a punch."

"What in the hell are you doing, Liz? Where's your suit? Why are you deliberately exposing yourself to the virus?" He fired off the questions in staccato.

"Sometimes there's no choice, Commander. Besides, if you go down, I'm right there with you."

When Liz finished inoculating the men, she rolled up her own sleeve, picked up the seventh syringe, and injected herself. Anticipating Hart's question, she added,

"I picked up five more vials and syringes while I was on the Prometheus. That leaves us three more as needed."

"Okay, Doctor, what now?" Hart asked.

"We get back into our bioprotective suits, go through decon, and then make our way to the isolation unit. I've already advised the staff to plan on manning it for the next five days."

"Why five days?"

"Because we will either be dead or well on the road to recovery by then," Liz responded.

As they navigated their way through the ship, it started to hit them; waves of intense nausea churning in their guts. The idea of puking in a bioprotective suit only intensified the anxiety.

"Just a few more feet," Liz advised them, directing the men into the unit. As soon as they were safely inside, everyone yanked off their hoods and promptly threw up into them.

"Guess I won't be putting that back on," Tommy Lamott remarked.

"Always the smartass, Mr. Lamott."

"Sorry, Commander."

"It's okay. Never a better time for a little dark humor."

Turning to Wilkins, Lamott asked, "Did you say this was the ship's morgue, Doctor? How convenient."

While Hart chuckled, Liz found no humor in his response.

"Mr. Lamott, the commander may find your humor funny, but I don't. So find a bed, lie down, and give it a break. The nurse will be in to check our vitals within the hour."

"Can you tell us what to expect, Ma'am?" Ramirez asked respectfully.

"I'm not sure that would be helpful, Staff Sergeant."

"I don't agree, Ma'am. I don't like surprises."

The remaining men, including Hart, nodded.

"Alright, if that's what you want. Remember, the vaccine has never been given to humans, at least not to our knowledge. Based on the animal trials, the majority of us will develop severe gastrointestinal symptoms—as we are already beginning to witness. Expect it to get worse, much worse. Some of you will likely experience painful cramps followed by copious bleeding from your rectum. Some may have your body temperatures soar as high as 106 degrees, causing either temporary or permanent changes to your neurological status."

"What does that mean, Ma'am?" Sitarski asked.

"Your brain will be on fire. Hopefully, your immune system, aided by the vaccine, will douse that fire, but there's no guarantee. If you manage to survive it, you'll have newfound empathy for the toll rabies takes on its victims."

"I would have rather remained ignorant, Ma'am," Sitarski commented wryly.

"Maybe you'll be one of the lucky ones, Mr. Sitarski, spared by the hand of God. Now, I want you men to do your best to get some rest. This is a type of battle you have never experienced before, with the sole exception of Commander Hart," Liz said. Hart had been exposed to a modified smallpox virus during a terrorist attack by the United Islamic State. The UIS had sought to create a worldwide pandemic, sparing only a select group of believers who had been vaccinated in advance against the disease.

"You'll need every ounce of strength and perseverance to get through the next forty-eight hours. God bless you all, and may I see you on the other side of this nightmare."

Liz took the bed next to her husband's.

The room went totally silent.

An hour later, a nurse outfitted in full bioprotective garb entered and walked up to the cot nearest the door. Jason Harding looked up at her with bloodshot eyes. She reached down and cinched a restraint around his right arm. Instinctively, he yanked at it.

"What the hell do you think you're doing?" he barked at her.

"It's for your own good," she said, both firmly and empathetically. "Now, please, let me finish my job." She reached for the other restraint.

It was too much for Harding to endure. Without thought, he swung his left fist and connected with the women's cheek, sending her flying backwards into the wall.

"What the fuck is the matter with you, Sailor!" Liz screamed at him. "That woman is putting her life on the line to help us! The restraints are to protect you in case you become delirious. The last thing we want is have you thrashing about and injuring yourself."

Despite the explanation, Harding's eyes still sparked with rage as he glowered at the nurse, who was huddled in the far corner of the room, blood visible on her face even through the hood of her suit. Then he heard the distinctive sound of a safety being removed from a pistol. He turned his head in the direction of the sound to see Commander Hart with a .45 caliber pistol pointed squarely at his forehead.

"If you touch that woman again, I'm going to put a bullet through your brain, Jason." Hart was dead serious. He watched as the tension flowed out of Harding's body and the man submitted, without incident, to restraints on his free arm and ankles.

Once everyone had been tethered to their hospital beds, the nurse used a remote reading thermometer to measure their body temperatures. Hart's was approaching 104 degrees, not a good sign.

"Do you want me to administer NSAIDS, Dr. Wilkins?"

"No, though it's counter-intuitive, the research suggests that the animals fared better when the fever was allowed to spike."

Ronny Good suddenly cried out in pain. He tried to double over, but the restraints held him flat against the hospital bed. Minutes later, the pungent odor of diarrhea filled the air, followed by a steady flow of blood. A second nurse was summoned to help clean up the mess. Mercifully, Good seemed to be completely out of it.

The next hours were like a swift descent into hell. Everything that Liz had promised, and more, became evident in the vaccine recipients. Still fully conscious, she turned towards the adjacent cot where Hart lay and said, "I'm sorry, Cowboy, it looks like I made the wrong call. I'm not sure any of us will be leaving this room."

"Have faith, Darling."

Liz nodded, "I'll do my best."

"No, there's no halfway with faith. You've got to be all in."

Liz chuckled wryly. "I never thought I would end up married to a holy roller."

Despite his trouble staying focused, Hart smiled. "I was a heathen for quite a while."

"I wouldn't say that. Just someone who momentarily lost his way."

"Amazing Grace, how sweet the sound . . ."

Liz completed the verse. "Who saved a wretch like me."

"We're going to get through this, Darling, I promise."

By morning, Harding and Sitarski were both delirious—shouting obscenities one second, then screaming at the top of their lungs as if in unimaginable pain. Hart seemed in a netherworld. Had it not been for the faint movement of his sheets, rising and falling with regularity, Liz would have thought him dead.

Somehow, she had escaped the vaccine's wrath—like the miniscule number of animals in the clinical trials that had remained asymptomatic. At first, she felt guilty, then realized that she'd been given a remarkable gift that would allow her to tend to others until they'd safely navigated the storm.

After thirty-six hours, it seemed clear who would make it and who would not. Sitarski and Harding were teetering on the edge of life. Good wasn't much better off. And Hart still lay immobile, showing neither symptoms nor much in the way of consciousness. Ramirez was clearly on the mend.

"I don't need these restraints, Dr. Wilkins." Ramirez volunteered. "I feel fine, and I can help you."

Liz asked the nurse to remove the restraints, and Paco bounded out of bed like a man with a second lease on life. "Just tell me what I can do to help, Ma'am."

"While I watch the commander, you could keep a close eye on Sitarski and Good. Let me know if there is any change in their status, Mr. Ramirez."

"Of course."

Twelve hours later, Ramirez summoned Wilkins to Sitarski's bedside. "I believe he's passed, Ma'am."

Liz felt for a pulse, but there was no need. His body was already cooling down. A glance over at Good convinced her that he was next in line. She pulled a sheet over Sitarski's head, said a silent prayer for his soul, then returned to her post at Hart's bedside.

"Come on, Cowboy," she said to Hart's seemingly lifeless body. "I know you can hear me. What did you tell me about faith? That it was something you can't do halfway? You've got be all-in. I'm counting on you, John, to have that faith—to be all-in."

She wept quietly, tears spilling from her eyes onto Hart's face. After a moment, she regained a measure of composure and wiped her tears from where they dotted his cheek. "Do no harm," she said out loud. "That was at the very heart of everything I've ever been taught in medicine. And now, I've killed my husband."

A low, desperate sob rang out from some deep recess within her. As it echoed off the walls of the room, she felt something tugging at her. It was Hart's hand, held back by the restraint. She uncinched the cord holding him back, and he reached for her face, as he slowly opened his eyes.

"The greatest good for the greatest number, Darling."

"Oh, John, I really thought I had killed you."

"You came pretty close, Darling," he said, before drifting off. It would be hours before he spoke again, but Liz knew her husband had turned the corner.

That afternoon, Hart raised his head off the pillow and turned to his wife. "I'm ready for my morning jog."

"Always the card," she said, as she removed his restraints, tears of joy sliding down her cheeks.

Hart said, with a softness in his eyes, "It happened again, Liz. I was in that place beyond pain. That place I'd been to once before. It's a peaceful place, Liz, where there is no suffering, full of light, where magical sounds form a sort of celestial music. But then I heard your voice telling me to have faith—faith that wasn't halfway, but full-in. That's why I'm back, Liz. Thanks to you and your faith. Let it be a lesson to me in conviction."

"Thank God you are okay."

"Yes, thank God, indeed!" Hart said looking upward. Then he looked at his wife. "You know you are the most beautiful girl I've ever seen," he said, his own tears rolling down his cheeks. "And the smartest."

CHAPTER 39

Deep Six

THE BODIES OF ROMAN SITARSKI AND RONNY GOOD were sealed in bio-containment body bags and prepared for burial at sea. Liz had wanted them cremated, on the slight chance that any residual traces of the virus might infect marine life, but no facilities existed within hundreds of miles.

The remaining men who had been vaccinated were confined to isolation until their viral counts zeroed out.

After seventy-two hours, Hart and Wilkins were summoned by the captain. They dutifully left the confines of the isolation room and headed to the bridge.

"I didn't think I'd see you alive again," Hamil said as they entered. "I'm so grateful you made it through."

"Not as grateful as we are," Hart said with a smile at his wife. "We understand that you wanted to see us, Sir?"

"I'm under strict orders to notify the president the instant we detect any meaningful threat from the Chinese. For whatever reason, they have been dormant since you entered isolation. But now, it looks like things are about to change." He handed Hart binoculars.

"I thought the president would have deep-sixed her by now."

"He decided to hold off as long as possible, waiting to see what impact the vaccine had on you and your crew. As I said, the Chinese have been quiet up until a few minutes ago."

"So, what am I looking for, Captain?" asked Hart.

"Three motorized dinghies being readied for launch from the rear of the aircraft carrier."

Hart lifted the binoculars and peered at the distant ship. "Got it. Looks like each one has a three-man crew, and they are heavily armed. We need everyone off the Prometheus this second. Let's get them onto a Knighthawk. We want them to be as far away from the ship as possible when it explodes."

"Agreed." The captain issued the order on a comm line, informing them a helicopter would pick them up from the deck in three minutes.

Anderson's second in command responded, "Sir, you must let us speak with Mr. Anderson. We understand that he's ill, but we are under strict orders not to abandon ship for any and all reasons, Captain."

"That's not possible, Sailor. Mr. Anderson is dead. Now get to the heliport and on that bird the minute it lands. That's an order!"

"Yes, Sir."

Moments later, a lieutenant entered the bridge. "Captain, I have the president on the line."

"Mr. President, I am here with Commander Hart and Dr. Wilkins. I'm going to ask the commander to brief you, Sir."

"Thank God you two made it!" The joy in Conner's voice was obvious. "Remember, Commander, you are not a cat, so don't count on nine lives."

"Yes, Sir. Mr. President, there are three dinghies full of armed Chinese sailors closing in on the Prometheus, presumably with the intention of boarding her."

"And the status of the remaining men onboard?"

"They were just evacuated by helicopter. I believe it is time to scuttle the Prometheus, Sir. You have the code."

Conner responded by reading off the string of numbers as he entered them into his phone. "0127558900012. Please verify, Commander."

"Verified, Mr. President."

Conner hesitated before pressing SEND. "You are sure our men are out of harm's way?"

"Yes, Sir. One hundred percent certain."

Conner pushed the button.

From under the ship, a massive bubble of smoke and fire burst forth from the ocean. For a moment, the entire length and breadth of the Prometheus was obscured by the fireball. The nine Chinese sailors, along with their dinghies, were vaporized by the blast.

The damage to the ship was catastrophic, causing it to break apart as if someone had cleaved it with a giant blade. The ship folded in the center like an accordion, raising its spear-shaped bow high in the air on one side and the stern-mounted propellers on the other.

The water churned like a boiling cauldron as the steel infrastructure screeched and groaned, then snapped violently. In mere minutes, the majority of the cutting-edge vessel was underwater. Ten minutes later, nothing remained of the Prometheus other than some debris floating on the sea and an ever-growing oil slick.

Paco Ramirez appeared, and asked permission to enter. Hart slapped him on the back, grateful to see him up on his feet. "You missed the fireworks, Mr. Ramirez!"

"No, Commander, I caught everything from the bow before coming up here. Just wanted to make sure you were happy with my work."

Hart burst out laughing. "Thrilled to death, Mr. Ramirez!"

"That goes for me, too," the president echoed.

"That's President Conner's voice, Commander."

"It certainly is," Conner responded, "And I'm damn proud of you, Staff Sergeant Ramirez!"

"Just doing my job, Mr. President." But he blushed from the compliment anyway.

Changing the tone, Hart addressed the captain. "I will need to interrogate the three men who were standing guard under Anderson's orders. It would be best if I did so in a tightly controlled environment, like the brig. I'll find out who we can trust."

"I didn't hear any of that, Commander," Conner commented. He didn't approve of many of Hart's methods, but knew he wasn't about to change the man and couldn't argue with the results.

"Understood, Sir."

CHAPTER 40

Ferreting Out the Truth

HART'S METHOD WAS SIMPLE BUT EFFECTIVE. Two burly MPs escorted the men, one at a time, into the sound-proof interrogation cell. They started with Joaquin Alvarez. The sniper was summarily shoved into a metal chair that had been bolted to the floor. Then restraints were affixed to his arms and legs.

"What the fuck are you doing?" Joaquin Alvarez demanded. But Hart remained mute as he brought a syringe with a clear liquid close to Alvarez's arm.

"Mr. Alvarez, you are about to become part of a grand experiment involving the deadly virus we confiscated from aboard the Prometheus." He proceeded to explain, in excruciating detail, what would happen to Alvarez's body in the hours that followed.

"Why are you doing this to me?" Alvarez cried out. "What have I done to deserve this, Commander?"

"You and Mr. Anderson conspired against the legitimate authority of the United States government and its Navy. You sought to cover up a black project that has been underway for decades, a project that not even our president was aware of. Accordingly, you have been sentenced to death."

"But I didn't do that," the man cried out as Hart approached him with the needle.

"Tell that to your maker!" Hart said with malice as he thrust the needle deep into Alvarez's arm.

The man sobbed, "I didn't do anything, Commander. I don't know what you're talking about."

"It's too late, Mr. Alvarez."

"But I didn't do anything, Commander!"

Hart stared into Alvarez's bloodshot eyes, trying to ferret out any trace of deception. Then, without explanation, he reached across and released the cords binding him.

"You're free to go."

"You just told me I was a dead man. Now you're telling me I'm free? What the fuck is going on?"

"I had to know if you were complicit in a conspiracy with Mr. Anderson. So I threatened your life. But, in reality, I injected you with normal saline. I'm sorry to put you through that, Joaquin, but there was no other way."

Alvarez fell to his knees. "Thank God, thank God," he wailed.

"Help Mr. Alvarez to his cabin," Hart instructed the MPs, "and bring in Mr. Latourno."

Hart repeated the process with Sammy Latourno and was met with almost identical results. It was now down to one man, and Hart wondered if he, too, would clear himself.

As the needle pierced Bob Bridges' skin, and the cool saline mixed with the man's warm blood, Bridges glared at Hart.

"You don't know what you're up against, Commander. Your life is going to end almost as quickly as mine, and there's not a damn thing you can do about it. And if you think unmasking Kahn or killing Anderson is going to make a difference, you are more blind than I thought."

Hart felt the fury rising in his gut. He leaped across the narrow metal desk separating him from Bridges and struck the man with every bit of strength he possessed. His fist shattered Bridges' nose, rendering him unconscious. The two MP's who had been waiting on the other side of the door rushed in.

"Drag his sorry ass into a cell. Don't engage with that man in any fashion. I will be escorting him to an undisclosed location in the near future."

"What about his face, Commander? This man needs medical attention."

"All that man needs a firing squad," Hart shot back as he walked out.

Hart returned to the bridge and was met by Captain Hamil. "I watched you on a live feed, Commander Hart. I understand why President Conner struggles with your methods. They are pretty unorthodox and, I suspect, not the kind of thing they teach you in the Naval Academy."

"I learned them in the sewers of the world, Captain, where there are no rules."

"I don't want any of this in the record. I've had the video scrubbed. No need to have any evidence that might hinder fair and appropriate punishment for that man's crimes."

"I'll make damn sure that he is court-martialed, if not shot. At the very least, he'll spend the rest of his life in a military prison for treason.

"Now. Can we talk about the Chinese, Captain?"

"We definitely kicked the hornet's nest. I assume you heard their flyovers. They are making a statement, but I don't think they'll strike. For the moment, their J-15's have returned to the carrier."

"Are we going to get any assistance out of Guam?"

"Funny you ask," the captain replied, pointing in a northeasterly direction, as a squadron of F-22's broke through the clouds. Hart could see the pilots lighting up their after-burners and descending on the Chinese fleet.

The captain flipped a switch, causing the pilots' audio to stream into the room. He handed Hart a set of binoculars. "Showtime, Commander."

"Niner, niner, bravo, I want you to skim the deck of that carrier, Major. Let 'em know we're not here to fuck around."

"Yes, Sir. Weapons are hot."

"I didn't say start a war, Major."

"Yes, Sir."

With that, one of the planes broke formation and headed straight for the carrier. Through the binoculars, it looked like the pilot was on a kamikaze mission, piercing the sky in a nearly vertical descent. At the last second, he pulled up, leveling off less than a hundred feet above the carrier's main deck. Hart watched as frightened sailors jumped overboard.

"That sure as hell woke them up," squadron leader Colonel Buzz Jeter remarked over the radio. "I think we should give them a little more to think about, Gentlemen," he said, as he set a heading for the destroyers. "I want you close enough to see the fright in their eyes," he ordered. "And I want missiles locked, just in case."

The squadron spent the next ten minutes wreaking havoc with the destroyers and guided missile frigate until they were finally interrupted by four Chinese J-15's that had been launched from the carrier.

"Let's have some fun," Jeter ordered as he set an intercept course for the lead plane. Switching to after-burners, it took only seconds to close in on the mid-section of the Flying Shark. Just as he was about to hit it broadside, the colonel banked hard left, then swept right, directly in front of the plane. He left behind a massive trail of jet wash.

The results were every bit as devastating as if Jeter had taken down the plane with a missile. Onboard the J-15, klaxons blared and warning lights flashed as both engines lost power. The pilot fought to regain control of the plane, which was now spinning like a top and dropping like a rock. But it was to no avail. It hit the ocean and disintegrated upon impact.

Realizing they were hopelessly outmatched, the remaining Chinese fighters broke formation, turned tail, and headed back to the carrier.

"Well, at least they've got some sense," the colonel observed.

"I believe the message was received, loud and clear, Colonel," Captain Hamil commented over the radio.

"I don't think you will have any further threats from the Chinese," the colonel responded.

As they were speaking, a lieutenant approached the captain and waited until he had his full attention.

"Sir, I thought you would want to know that the Chinese have begun to change course. It looks like they're headed home."

"That's good news, Lieutenant. Tell the helmsman to set a course for Naval Base Guam, and give me an ETA."

CHAPTER 41

Marital Discord

IT WAS A MODEST HOUSE by McLean standards but, when he purchased it in 1986, it was big enough to accommodate Marvin Kahn's growing family. Now, after thirty years, and with their children grown, there was no need for five bedrooms spread across four thousand square feet. It felt vacuous and eerily quiet. Still, moving was a tough topic for the couple to discuss.

Not only did Ingrid struggle with the idea of disturbing her nest, she couldn't imagine parting with neighbors who had become her cherished friends.

"You haven't touched your pot roast," Ingrid remarked as she observed her husband uncharacteristically pushing his food around with a fork.

"I paid our tax bill today. It was $14,000. Did you hear me, Ingrid? $14,000! Last week, I forked out $7,500 to repair the roof. You know how much I make, and it's not enough to keep up with these expenses."

With each word, his voice became more strident. "Every time we get hit with another bill, I ask myself, what are we doing here? Why don't we move into something smaller and more affordable? Then I remind myself that I've had this conversation with you on innumerable occasions, but it's really not a conversation, is it? No, I'd call it an exercise in futility."

There it was, the slap she had been waiting for. Her eyes glazed as she fought to keep her husband's denigrating words from penetrating too deeply. And she wasn't about to give him the satisfaction of evoking a tear. Struggling to compose herself, she dabbed her right eye with a napkin before speaking.

"Do whatever you feel is right, Marvin, but don't you dare treat me with contempt. I've been married to you for thirty-two years. Many of those years were happy years when we were busy raising a family. But things have changed. You have changed, Marvin."

"Changed? How have I changed, Ingrid?"

"You're not the loving, inquisitive man I fell in love with. You've become a cynical bastard."

Kahn's face flushed red and a look of shock flashed across it. Never had his wife confronted him so directly.

"Cynical bastard! Is that what you think of me?"

"Yes, that's exactly what I think." All of the pent-up frustration and anger suddenly spilled out of Ingrid Kahn. "Something eats at you day and night, and, like vitriol, it corrodes your soul. It seeps into all of your relationships, including with our children, and it poisons them. Maybe it's all the secrets you've had to keep through the years. I don't know. I just know I can't live with it any longer."

"That sounds like a threat," he growled.

"It's what happens when you finally push me to my limit."

They stared at each other, waiting to see who would be the first to blink. After what felt like an eternity, Ingrid reached out to touch her husband. It was a gesture of reconciliation. But, rather than accept it, Kahn drew back, pushing himself away from the dinner table and out of Ingrid's reach.

"On that note, I'm retiring to the guest room. Don't feel obligated to get up and have coffee with me in the morning. We'll continue this discussion another time."

But in her mind, there was nothing more to say. Ingrid knew that her marriage was dead and had been so for some time. She finished sipping her tea before walking slowly toward the bedroom, hopeful that sleep would bring some measure of peace.

The guest bedroom was just off the kitchen on the opposite side of the house. It wouldn't be the first night Marvin Kahn had slept alone. The closet and dresser were full of his clothes, and an extra dop kit resided next to the bathroom sink. He put on his pajamas, brushed his teeth, mumbled a few curses into the mirror, then headed for bed. In his hand was a copy of *Lion of Liberty*, a biography of Patrick Henry.

He switched off the overhead lights and turned on a small book-light. Despite the afterbirth of turmoil gnawing at his gut, he knew he would drift off into a dreamless sleep after a chapter or two. After ten minutes, his fingers loosened, and the book fell gently onto his lap. He awoke just long enough to extinguish the light.

As he navigated through a twilight space between wakefulness and dreams, three men clad from head to toe in black approached Kahn's house. Staying in the shadows and mindful of video doorbells and other surveillance systems, they made their way to a side door that opened onto the garage. A calculator-sized keypad was affixed to the right of the door, and a red LED glowed in the upper corner.

"She's armed, Major."

"How long?" the leader asked.

"Two minutes, Sir."

The man pulled out a small tool kit from an interior pocket, then removed what looked like a jeweler's screwdriver. In seconds, he had disassembled the alarm panel and turned off its primary sensors. With another tool, he successfully picked the lock on the door. They now had access to the garage.

The major removed a schematic of the house from his pocket. Briefly examining it, he said, "Gentlemen, the target should be in a bedroom just past the kitchen. It's where we saw the light on. It's approximately twelve feet from our point of entry."

He turned towards the door that opened onto the kitchen, but stopped. He pulled a small spray can of WD-40 from his jacket, giving the hinges a quick soaking. Then, with a nod, he signaled the men to put on their night vision goggles. They were going in.

The house was bathed in a surreal green glow as they moved, step by step, towards the guest bedroom.

As they approached, the third man in the group removed a cloth and a vial of clear liquid from his pocket. He poured the liquid onto the cloth just as the major opened the door.

Kahn rose in his bed with a start. "Who are you? What the hell are you doing in my home? Do you know . . ."

He never completed his sentence, as the damp cloth was placed over his mouth and nose. The overpowering odor of cloves filled his lungs, and he began to lose consciousness.

"Don't fight it, Mr. Kahn. We're not here to harm you," the man told him. "If we were, you'd already be dead."

Despite the admonition, Kahn resisted with all his might, grunting, thrashing, then finally collapsing on the bed. From behind them came a shrill scream. Ingrid Kahn stood in the doorway.

"My God, what are you doing!"

One of the men turned and grabbed her by the arm with one hand and covered her mouth with the other. He dragged her into the kitchen, shoving her into a chair and locking her arms behind her back with stay-ties. Finally, he gagged her with a dish towel. It would be hours before the cleaning lady found Ingrid and summoned the police. But it would be only minutes before Kahn was whisked away into the night.

Kahn came to with a splitting headache. The van into which he had been thrown was careening through God knows where. When it finally slowed, Kahn sensed that they were passing through a series of security gates. There was something familiar about the rhythm of their movements, the amount of time and distance between each stop. It wasn't Langley, but it was someplace he'd been many times before. He was sure of it.

Two men extracted him from the rear of the van and took him to a holding cell. There, he sat shackled and blindfolded, wondering if, finally, this was the end of the road.

CHAPTER 42

Director Rice

IT WAS LATE IN THE NIGHT when Conner received word from his Chief of Staff that Marvin Kahn had arrived at the White House.

"Get on the phone to CIA Director Rice. I want to meet with him immediately. Apologize for the late hour, but tell him it's urgent."

Twenty minutes later, a shaken Rice was standing in front of the president in the West Wing.

"Sir, it's 2:00 a.m. I'm not aware of any crises that would require such urgent intervention, though I mean that with all due respect."

"What if I told you that your organization had been compromised at the most senior level?"

"You're talking about a handful of men and women whom I trust implicitly, Mr. President. Begging your pardon, Sir, but I would tell you that you are crazy."

"And what if I then informed you that Marvin Kahn has been arrested and taken to a secure location where he is being held pending charges of treason?"

Rice looked stricken, as if the wind had been knocked out of him.

"Sit down, Mr. Rice," Conner ordered. The man lowered himself slowly onto the couch.

"What happened, Sir? What make you so certain that Mr. Kahn is a traitor to his country? That's a charge I find unimaginable."

"Before I answer that, I have to determine if you, Mr. Rice, are trustworthy. I feel pretty foolish having sat here every day for years receiving an intelligence briefing from your colleague, with never so much as a scintilla of doubt regarding Mr. Kahn's loyalty. That trust was ripped away from me this week by irrefutable evidence of the DDO's role in a conspiracy."

"How do I prove my allegiance to the office of the president and my country? What will it take, President Conner, or can it even be done after this level of subterfuge has happened right under my nose?"

"Would you take a polygraph, Allen?"

"In a heartbeat, Sir."

"And if I told you that Commander Hart was part of the conspiracy and I wanted him terminated, would you take care of it?"

Rice's pause was more than pregnant—it was pro-nounced. Finally, he spoke. "No, Mr. President, I would defy your order, Sir. I've worked with John Hart for more than a decade, and there is no man more loyal to his country than the commander. If that means you find me complicit, so be it, but I'm not taking down someone who I know is innocent."

Conner sat with his fingers laced studying Rice. His next move was crucially important.

"There won't be any need for a polygraph, Allen. You passed the test. It's thanks to Hart and his wife, Dr. Wilkins, that we uncovered this thing in the first place."

"Then what am I to do next, Mr. President?"

"Your job is to get Hart and Wilkins back to Washington in one piece. After that, I want them heavily protected until they can testify in an emergency session of Congress."

"I feel like I'm missing some pieces, Sir."

"Yes, you are," Conner said, and he began putting the puzzle together for a horrified Allen Rice, including Kahn's whereabouts.

"How will you contain this story? Something this powerful will leak out within minutes of the testimony, Mr. President."

"It won't leak," Conner responded.

"How can you be so certain?"

"It won't leak because the hearing will be open to the nation's media. I'm not about to be labeled as the president who whitewashed the most significant conspiracy in the history of America. We will spend the remainder of my term flushing out those loyal to the cabal and dealing with them systematically.

"So how do you plan to bring them back, Mr. Rice?"

"You've put your trust in me, Sir. Now, I ask that you leave the details up to me. I will deliver Commander Hart and Dr. Wilkins to the Capitol as quickly as it can be safely accomplished."

CHAPTER 43

The Odyssey

Twelve hours had elapsed since the USNS Mercy set sail for Guam, leaving twelve more hours until the ship docked.

Hart and Wilkins sat quietly in a pew in the ship's chapel, once more giving thanks for God's grace. Liz squeezed her husband's hand as they both bowed their heads in prayer, not for themselves, but for the very soul of America. As they rose to leave, they were surprised to see the captain standing by the door.

"There is someone waiting for you in my cabin."

"Someone, Sir?"

"He arrived by helicopter a few minutes ago. I've never met this gentleman, Commander," he added with a raised eyebrow. "He gave me his name, but I strongly suspect it's not the one that appears on his birth certificate. I believe he is here to begin the process of extricating you and Dr. Wilkins."

"Or terminate us," Hart said.

His words caused Liz to shudder.

"You don't really believe that, do you?" Liz asked her husband as the three of them navigated the corridors to the captain's quarters. He did not reply.

As Hart opened the door, an older gentleman with a graying moustache stood ready to greet them. He was wearing horn-rimmed spectacles and a perfectly tailored, charcoal-gray Hickey Freeman suit.

"You must be Commander Hart and Dr. Wilkins," he said heartily as he extended his hand.

Hart stepped forward but, rather than taking the man's hand, he shoved a semi-automatic pistol under his chin. Then, with an ominous 'click', he thumbed off the safety.

The man started shaking. "I was warned that I might not receive a warm reception, but I didn't expect this, Commander. Could you please put the gun down? There's no need."

"Who sent you?"

"Director Rice."

"With what orders?"

"I'm to make you disappear."

"That was a very unfortunate choice of words." Hart said, pulling the hammer back.

"No, no, that's not what I meant. My orders are to make you and Dr. Wilkins unrecognizable to even the most sophisticated facial recognition systems. Then, as soon as we arrive in Guam, I am to hand you off to a team responsible for your security en route to Washington."

"You want me to believe that we work for the same agency, but I've never seen you before."

"But you have, Commander. You just don't recognize me. My appearance changes with every assignment."

"Liz, check his bags," Hart ordered, pointing at the two over-sized cases.

Liz tried to press the square brass releases on the first case. "It's locked."

"Give her the codes!" he snarled as he pressed the muzzle deeper into the man's flesh.

"007," the man replied, "for both cases."

"Oh that's cute, real cute," Hart responded, rolling his eyes.

The snaps on the first case popped open, revealing a treasure trove of prosthetic devices, hairpieces, wigs, and make-up. Liz rifled through it, looking for a weapon, but there were none to be found. She repeated the process with the second case, which contained a full U.S. Navy uniform. Beneath it was an equally complete woman's outfit.

"I think he's telling the truth, John," Liz said at last.

But Hart was not yet satisfied. "Captain, step behind our guest and frisk him."

The captain methodically patted the man down. "He's clean, Commander."

"Do you, er, need further proof, Commander?" the man asked haltingly.

"No, I guess not." Hart lowered the pistol.

The man slowly exhaled. Then, after collecting his thoughts, he said, "You can call me Thomas. We don't have a lot of time. My work is slow and tedious, but when I'm finished, I can promise that your own mothers would not recognize you. Captain, do you have the two robes I requested?"

The captain nodded, "They're in the head."

"Excellent. I need you both to change into them. Then, when my work is done, you will put on the clothes I brought for you."

"What if they don't fit?" Liz asked.

"They'll fit," he said testily. It seemed he was not accustomed to having his professionalism challenged.

"Ladies first," Hart instructed, his eyes still riveted on the man. When Liz finished changing, it was Hart's turn to step into the head. He handed her the pistol. "If Thomas comes one step closer to you, put a bullet through his chest."

As Thomas had promised, the process of transformation was painstakingly slow,. So, too, were the final hours aboard the ship as it steamed towards Guam. Though Hart could not see himself, he watched as his wife's features morphed into those of a woman two decades older.

"If this is a preview of what's to come, I may be asking for a trade-in," Hart remarked.

"Not funny, John. Besides, you're not looking so dapper yourself, Sailor!"

Hart picked up a hand mirror that Thomas had laid out on the table. "My God, I look like I'm a hundred!"

"No," Thomas said, "but you do look like you're in your sixties. I'm going to have some work to do on the body. No 65-year-old man sports a physique like yours, Commander." He reached into his bag and pulled out a large, oval pad that was to become the Commander's new gut.

"And Dr. Wilkins, I'm afraid we need to lower your cleavage a bit."

Liz wrapped her arms around her chest. "No one's touching my chest, Mister."

Thomas handed her a prosthesis. "You can change in the bathroom."

An hour later, the couple looked as if they were ready to celebrate their fortieth anniversary.

"Just one question, Thomas," Hart began. "What in the hell would a couple our age be doing on a hospital ship? I thought the goal was to make us inconspicuous."

"You are retired Rear Admiral Henry Tate," Thomas said as he handed the neatly pressed dress uniform to the Commander. "Accompanied by his wife, Margaret," he added, as he handed Liz the second outfit from the case.

"With your permission, Admiral, I'm going to step out in the hall and allow you to change."

Hart nodded.

Before closing the door behind him, Thomas admonished, "Be careful not to disturb my work as you are dressing."

Once they were finally alone, Hart looked at Liz. "You still look as beautiful as ever, Darling, despite my little quip."

"And you, Sir, look quite distinguished."

"Despite my gut!" Hart said as he pressed on the padding over his abdomen.

"What are a few pounds between lovers?" she chuckled.

Decked out in their new attire, the couple looked the part. Thomas knocked twice on the door, requesting permission to enter. The captain was at his side.

As Hart opened the door, he watched the captain's jaw drop in amazement, followed by a salute.

"That's not necessary, Captain. Remember, I'm only a lowly Commander."

"Not anymore."

As the four of them congregated in the tight quarters, Thomas advised, "We're a few hours out from Naval Base Guam. I want you to remain here until I determine that it's safe to go ashore. There's no reason to raise any more questions than necessary among the crew."

"How will you determine that it's safe?" Hart asked.

"Ask me again when I return," Thomas answered as he and the captain exited the cabin.

Three hours later, and twenty minutes shy of docking at Naval Base Guam, there was a knock on the captain's door. Hart opened it and took an involuntary step back, stunned by what he saw. Liz, peering around her husband, gasped.

Standing in front of them was Commander John Hart, his bulging biceps visible under his uniform, and every hair perfectly in place. Without waiting for an invitation, he entered the cabin and closed the door.

"So what do you think, Admiral Tate? Convincing enough?" Thomas asked.

"You're good, you're very good," Hart responded. "Sorry for being so hard on you when we met."

"You responded exactly as you were trained to. I'm just glad you didn't pull the trigger. As for my disguise, hopefully it's good enough to attract the attention of anyone who wants you killed, at least long enough to get you safely out of Guam."

Hart's tone suddenly changed. "You know you're putting a red dot squarely in the middle of your forehead—where a bullet might follow. I can't let you do that."

"Commander, with all due respect, you have no choice. Like you, I accept my orders without question. These orders came from President Conner. So let me execute my duty, Sir."

Before Hart could respond, there was a second knock on the door. Thomas opened it and ushered in Liz's double. "The commander wouldn't be leaving his wife behind, would he?"

"Now it's my turn to object," Liz said. "The commander and I don't need anyone serving as our shields. If an attempt is going to made on our lives, we'll take the hit, not you."

The woman spoke. "That's not going to happen, Doctor. As I'm sure Thomas has explained, we're under strict orders—orders that we gladly accept as our duty, Ma'am."

Thomas began a series of instructions. "The captain will accompany you as you disembark. Two men and one woman will greet you at the end of the gangway. They will usher you to a waiting limo—normal protocol for a visiting dignitary. The limo is heavily armored and can take a hit from anything up to an RPG. From there, you will be transported to Andersen Air Force base, where you will board a G700 bound for Washington."

"Will the two of you disembark?" Hart asked.

"Yes, but only after you are en route to Andersen. Prior to that, we will stand at the ship's railing, making certain we are visible."

"Sitting ducks, you mean."

"If you will, but I'm confident that no one will take a shot. When we do disembark, that's when things may get a little dicey. It's our problem to worry about, Commander. All you need to be concerned with is getting on that airplane."

CHAPTER 44

High Anxiety

THE ADMIRAL AND HIS WIFE STOPPED at the edge of the gangway to thank the captain for his gracious hospitality. Then, arm in arm, they descended the short distance to the pier where three naval officers awaited them. The group saluted in unison while forming a protective shield around the couple.

"There's a limo waiting, Admiral, and we need to move quickly."

Once hidden behind the heavily tinted glass on the black stretch sedan, all three officers reached under their seats and removed short-barreled Uzi's, evoking a shudder from Liz.

"We don't mean to alarm you, Dr. Wilkins. We are just taking every precaution," the female officer tried to reassure her.

Liz nodded as she slowly exhaled.

Hart asked, "How long before we arrive at Andersen?"

"It's twenty-five miles, Commander. GPS is showing fifty-two minutes and change. We're not anticipating any delays."

Hart pressed the start button on his military issue chronograph. Then he took Liz's hand. "The nightmare is almost over, Darling. I suggest you get some sleep on the plane. We going to be hitting the ground running."

But Hart knew the nightmare was just beginning, a nightmare in which he could trust no one. Justice would be on his side, but hundreds of deeply entrenched pseudo-patriots would be out for his blood. They would put a bounty on his head, maybe even adding a bonus for inflicting tremendous pain and suffering before killing him. How would he and Liz resume any semblance of a normal life with such a threat lurking over them? But he knew there was no point in sharing such thoughts; they would only drive Liz's anxiety even higher.

We will do our duty to God and Country, he promised himself, and pray that God will watch over us.

As the limo ticked off the miles, a very different scene was evolving at the pier where the Mercy was docked. Thomas and his fellow agent, Erin, had just disembarked.

Out of the corner of his eye, Thomas saw sunlight glinting off metal. He ducked instinctively and reached for Erin, but not before he felt the searing heat of a bullet tear through his shoulder. Stumbling, he pulled her to the ground, attempting to shield her body with his.

But the assassin was thorough. He closed the distance in seconds, unloading his suppressed .40 caliber pistol into their heads. No sooner had he finished than he felt a barrel against the back of his head. The captain fired a single shot and dropped the man where he stood.

Seconds later, the news was communicated to the three-person security detail.

"I understand. I will communicate your message to the commander," the man riding shotgun said into a microphone.

The commander's heart began to race. "What was that about, Lieutenant?"

"Sir, we've lost two people on the dock. It looks like an assassination."

Enraged, Hart snapped, "I want someone to bring that assassin to me! Tell them to secure him and put him aboard the plane so we can have a little conversation en route to Washington."

"It's too late for that, Commander."

"Why?"

"The captain put a bullet through his head."

Hart slumped back into his seat. It had begun.

The remaining seventeen minutes were full of angst, as Hart realized that the security on Guam had been compromised. He prayed they would make it to the Gulfstream before anyone uncovered their subterfuge and came looking for them.

The security detail exited the limo and scanned the entire tarmac for possible threats before allowing Hart and Wilkins to step out into the hot, humid air. They rushed them to the waiting plane and stood guard while the couple ascended the staircase and the crew closed the hatch.

Hart and Wilkins sat in twin captain's chairs, affording them a view of the security detail. The three officers held a final salute as the pilot fired up the massive Rolls Royce engines and began accelerating down the runway.

"Welcome aboard, Sir and Ma'am." The captain stuck his head momentarily out of the cockpit. "I've got instructions to get you the hell out of here, and that's exactly what I'm going to do. Once we've reached our operating ceiling of 42,000 feet, I'll be back to speak with you."

"Are we going to make it, John?" Liz asked in an uncharacteristically weak voice.

"Of course, Darling." Hart's tone left no room for lingering doubt.

Twenty minutes after take-off, the captain returned as promised. He warmly greeted his passengers, then proceeded to describe the flight plan.

"Commander, Ma'am, we're flying two legs. The first will be to Edwards Air Force Base, which is showing at just under twelve hours. We'll refuel there, but not dawdle. I plan to be on the ground for no more than twenty minutes. Once we're airborne again, it will be a straight shot to Reagan National."

A perplexed look crossed Hart's face. "Why not Joint Base Anacostia-Bolling or Andrews, Captain?"

"Because we don't want any uninvited guests. We're breaking protocol to put down at the Reagan FBO, but we're hoping to appear to be nothing more than a corporate jet ferrying a wealthy couple. Which brings me to the instructions I've been asked to relay to you."

The captain turned to the flight attendant. "Would you provide our guests with their change of clothing, please?"

She returned a minute later with two boxes containing civilian clothes.

The captain continued with his instructions. "You are not to alter your appearance other than eliminate any signs of military involvement. In addition to your civvies, you'll find robes and pajamas. You're going to be on this plane for more than twenty hours, after which you will be escorted to the Capitol for an emergency Congressional briefing. I was told that the President wants you fresh and ready to rock and roll the minute we land, so I strongly recommend you get some sleep."

"Understood, Captain."

"I've taken the liberty of turning down the bed in the master suite," the flight attendant told them, as she pointed towards the rear of the plane. "There are beverages and light snacks waiting for you. I'll notify you when we are thirty minutes out from Edwards so you may return to your seats and buckle in. In the interim, don't hesitate to call on me if there's anything you need."

"Thank you," Hart responded with a warm smile. It felt good to be pampered in the midst of the storm.

"That goes for me, too," the captain added. "Don't hesitate to let me know if the folks in the cockpit can do anything to make your trip more comfortable." He tipped his hat and returned to his station.

CHAPTER 45

A Teetering Democracy

Liz was quiet as she pulled back the sheets just far enough to climb into the queen-sized bed, then curled up in a fetal position. Her back was to her husband.

"Are you okay, Darling?" Hart asked as he wrapped his arms around his wife and tugged gently until she yielded to his efforts, turning and resting her head on his chest.

"I can't stop thinking about them."

"Them?" Hart asked.

"Thomas and Erin," she said in whisper.

"They did their duty. They gave their lives, not for us, but for our country. If we are committed to honoring their sacrifice, then we need to do our part."

"And what does that look like, John?" Her voice was weak with uncertainty.

"We don't flinch when confronting the truth. We testify in front of Congress and the world about the rot that has seeped into our democracy. But it's going to get ugly, Liz. Very ugly."

"I thought you promised me that everything was going to be okay?"

He squeezed her tightly. "We always emerge from the darkness. You need to remember that."

"Psalm 23?"

"It would be a good place to start. Now, I suggest you try to get some sleep."

"I'll try." She draped her arm across him, her head still resting on his chest. But sleep remained elusive.

A chime in the aircraft cabin brought Hart back to the moment. Liz was lying with her eyes open.

"Did you get any sleep?" he asked.

She shook her head. "Not much."

He looked at his watch. Eleven and a half hours had passed in a heartbeat. "We must be about to land. You need to put on a robe and buckle up. I'm going up front for a moment to talk to the flight attendant."

Hart threw on a robe and moved to the front of the plane. There, the flight attendant was preparing a small breakfast for them.

"You look rested, Commander," she observed.

"Yes, thank you, but Dr. Wilkins didn't sleep. Do you have anything that might help her?"

"We have some Zolpidem."

Hart nodded. "That should help her relax."

The flight attendant walked over to a medical cabinet on the wall and removed a vial of pills. She dropped one into the Commander's hand.

"And you, Sir?"

"No, I'm fine. Thanks anyway." He turned and went back to Liz.

"What's this?" she asked, staring at John's extended palm. "It looks like Zolpidem."

"That's exactly what it is. As soon as we leave Edwards, I want you to take it and get some sleep. You should be able to squeeze in three or four hours." Hart waited for the argument that would follow, knowing that Liz was not one to take anything more than an occasional Tylenol.

But he was surprised when she responded with a "Fine."

As promised, the stopover at Edwards was brief. Within twenty minutes, they were back in the air and on course for Reagan National.

"I can't seem to shake the anxiety," said Liz. She sat on the bed, a mountain of pillows wedged under her back. "It has a real grip on me."

"I'd be more worried if you weren't anxious. You understand the magnitude of what we're up against, and the risks. For now, the best thing you can do is try to get a little sleep on the next leg."

"It won't change the fact that we seem to have a price on our heads."

"No, but it will make you more equipped to deal with it."

Liz reached over to the bedside table and picked up the small, brown pill. She examined it for a second before popping it in her mouth and washing it down with a swig of water. She settled back. "I'm going to start counting sheep. Wake me when we get there."

Conner had ordered his four most trusted Secret Service agents to secure the FBO at Reagan in preparation for receiving Hart and Wilkins. Once this had been accomplished, the lead agent notified approach control that the G700 was to be given priority clearance to land.

"You boys must have someone pretty special on that plane," the controller responded.

"He's a legend in his own mind," the agent replied. "Some former hotshot Admiral and his wife who've been on a naval publicity tour. Maybe you would call that exciting. We call it a pain in the ass."

"I'm glad we're on a private channel," the controller responded with a chuckle. "Request granted. She'll be landing on runway 2E in just under fourteen minutes."

"Thank you, Tower."

Back on the plane, the pilot turned on the intercom. "Commander and Dr. Wilkins, we're on final approach. We'll have you on the ground momentarily."

Hart and Wilkins had donned civilian clothes. A gray suit for him and a Burberry patterned skirt with a camel colored sweater for her. Liz pulled out her compact and unfolded the mirror. Then she quickly checked her prosthetics and make-up.

"You look ravishing, Darling," her husband said with a wink.

"And you look like the pride of the Navy," she shot back, "even without your uniform!"

"How are you feeling, Liz?" he asked in a more serious tone.

"I'm better, thanks."

No sooner had they landed than the four agents swept in and ushered Hart and Wilkins into a black armored Suburban. An agent sat on either side of the couple, with two more agents riding up front. Each man was heavily armed and covered in Kevlar.

Before the vehicle began to move, Hart spoke. "I want a weapon. I know that violates your policy but, frankly, I don't give a damn. If someone starts shooting at us, you'll be glad I'm armed."

The driver nodded to one of the men in the backseat, who reached under the bench seat and removed an Uzi. Handing it to the commander, he asked, "You do know how to use this, Sir?"

"Don't be a smartass," Hart responded as he checked the clip, then chambered a bullet.

What normally would be a quick ten-minute drive to the Capitol took twice that time due to the convoluted route they took.

"We're trying to stay under the radar, Sir," the driver explained. "We'll be pulling into a back entrance of the Capitol shortly."

Sure enough, the Suburban came to a stop a few feet from a rarely used access point to the House's Chamber.

"Let's go," the driver ordered. The two agents flanking Hart and Wilkins stepped out of the vehicle and checked the surroundings before instructing Hart and Wilkins to follow. Next came the driver. But the man in the passenger seat lagged a few seconds behind, giving Hart a queasy feeling in his gut.

As he heard the front passenger door finally swing open, Hart turned just in time to see a red dot from the agent's Glock moving up his wife's back. Without a second thought, he swung the barrel of his Uzi towards the man's head and squeezed the trigger. Twelve bullets streaked from the muzzle at a velocity exceeding 1,200 feet per second, followed by a waft of smoke. All of them hit their mark, ripping apart flesh and bone.

Liz froze as she stared into the empty sockets that had been the agent's eyes.

Hart reached up, grabbed her sharply by the chin, and turned Liz's face away from the carnage. "That man was about to put a bullet in your back."

The driver screamed, "Move it!" as he motioned towards the door.

They hustled inside. Once they were in the building, an agent led them up two flights of stairs, with the two remaining agents covering their backs. They emerged just feet from the House Chambers, which were packed to capacity. The lead agent escorted the couple to two chairs reserved for witnesses that were located near the front of the room.

A buzz resonated through the crowd as the participants in the emergency session failed to recognize the signature witnesses.

"Who are they?" the words could be seen forming on people's lips, only to be met with blank stares and shrugged shoulders.

Conner gave an almost imperceptible nod of acknowledgment to Hart and Wilkins before the President of the Senate brought down the gavel three times, calling the session to order. He then immediately yielded the floor to President Conner.

"I know you were given little notice before being summoned to this meeting. For that I am sorry, but we have a matter of utmost urgency to discuss. Before we begin, I wish to welcome and introduce our witnesses, who have traveled at tremendous personal peril to join us today." Conner smiled and gave a clear nod to Hart and Wilkins.

"Commander John Hart and Dr. Elizabeth Wilkins have just returned from an assignment in Micronesia.

What they have uncovered strikes at the very foundation of our democracy."

People were now shaking their heads in confusion, for Hart and Wilkins were nowhere to be seen, and the older couple sitting before them bore no resemblance to the Navy SEAL and his wife.

"Forgive my interruption, Mr. President," the Speaker of the House said, "But I think we are all a bit confused. Who are these people, and is it their intent to represent Commander Hart and Dr. Wilkins at this hearing?"

Hart looked at Conner, seeking permission to speak. Conner nodded.

"Mr. Speaker, I believe I can clarify matters." As he spoke, Hart loosened his tie, reached under the collar of his civvies, and begin to peel off what appeared to be skin. In short order, the entire mask covering his face was removed. Liz followed suit.

Gasps could be heard across the chambers.

"We were told, Mr. Speaker, that this was necessary for our protection, and since there have been two attempts made on our lives in the past twenty-four hours, the subterfuge may well have saved us."

The Senate Majority Leader interjected, "What's this all about, President Conner? If their lives are truly in jeopardy, have you not put us all in peril by bringing Commander Hart and Dr. Wilkins into the very center of our government?"

"Indeed, I have. But I believe that we will eliminate the threat by getting their message out, hence the presence of our nation's media. I'm going to ask that all questions be put on hold until our guests have completed their briefing. Commander Hart, Dr. Wilkins, the floor is yours."

With that, the couple began a chronological retelling of the events that had transpired since they had first learned of a problem aboard the Prometheus. When they finished, the Secretary of Homeland Security was the first to raise a concern.

"I find this to be nothing more than a fanciful tale, Mr. President. Eugenics? A cabal running ultra-black projects? This is the stuff of fiction. In this case, science fiction!"

Liz moved closer to the microphone. "We anticipated such skepticism, Mr. Secretary. And I agree, the assertions seem outlandish and can easily be dismissed as the overworked imaginations of Commander Hart and myself."

"You've got that right!" The Secretary nodded vigorously in agreement.

But Liz had not finished. "But what cannot be so easily dismissed is the mountain of data, going back decades, that supports our allegations." Liz signaled for a projector to be turned on.

"What you are looking at is the genetic profile of fetuses implanted in the wombs of female laboratory personnel who served as research subjects aboard the Prometheus," Liz explained. "These charts represent five children."

"Excuse me, Dr. Wilkins, but you know that is not possible," Senator Armand Legrand, a neonatologist by training, countered. "There are no embryos, fetuses, or children that possess identical genetic blueprints. Not even identical twins."

"I'm afraid that there are, Senator. And if you look at the genetic modifications, you will see that they follow a plan that was designed many years ago with the intent to develop a 'superior' race. The plan ultimately had to be shelved until science advanced to the point where it could support the twisted vision of those who sought that race."

"And you are saying that now it has?" Legrand asked.

"Yes, Sir. The Prometheus housed the most advanced genetic research laboratory on the planet."

"And the commander just informed us that this laboratory was sent to the bottom of the ocean."

Hart reached over and pulled the microphone in his direction. "It was either that or risk having all of our data fall into the hands of the Chinese. Would you have preferred that, Senator?"

Legrand grumbled something before switching off his microphone. The revelations caused a mad rush by journalists towards the exits, each hoping to be the first to break the stunning news.

The vice president slammed down the gavel. "Order, order! Let Dr. Wilkins continue."

Liz then showed scanned images of early data showing experiments that began in the 1920s. "Those of you who are students of history will remember a particularly dark chapter in America when major universities and foundations were on the front lines of those attempting to achieve racial purification."

"I think you have us confused with the Third Reich, Dr. Wilkins," Bill Edmundson, a notoriously far-right congressman from Virginia, asserted.

"No, Sir. The Third Reich learned about eugenics from us. We jump-started Hitler's program for racial purification and superiority at the cost of six million Jews and countless others."

"Fanciful bullshit, if you'll forgive my language," the man responded.

"Continue, Dr. Wilkins," Conner said, shooting a stern look at the congressman.

"Commander Hart and I are here to deliver irrefutable evidence that the Prometheus had a tripartite mission. First, to catalogue the genomes of all life on earth. Second, to develop new and highly lethal pathogens for use in biological warfare. And, finally, the ultimate objective, to develop the most *advanced* population on earth. One destined for world domination."

"Why are we just now finding out about this? Who knew about it before now?" the Speaker of the House asked.

Hart answered for the president. "Sir, it appears that the project was just the latest extension of a long line of projects implemented by a group that fancied itself a shadow government. Its existence was carefully concealed by CIA Deputy Director of Operations, Marvin Kahn, as our documents will reveal."

"No!" Bill Edmundson snarled. He stood up and turned to face Conner. "Thanks to you, Mr. President, we're no longer in the shadows. Today, we stand united as patriots fighting to protect this country from its dysfunctional government and its increasingly corrupt gene pool."

"Sergeant at Arms, arrest this man and remove him from my sight," Conner ordered.

Edmundson swung his fists wildly as a swarm of officers descended upon him, forcing him to the floor and cuffing him. As he was unceremoniously dragged out of the chambers, he bellowed one final proclamation. "The call is going out. The war for our country's future begins today!"

Conner turned to the assembled leaders, surveying the audience before speaking. "There can be no clearer validation of the treachery unveiled today than what you have just witnessed. Every one of you whose views and actions parallel those of Mr. Edmundson will find yourself subject to arrest and prosecution."

Before he could continue, dozens of individuals within the hall rose to their feet. Charlie Denim was the first to speak.

"We represent the people, Mr. President, the legitimate source of power in our democracy. You can't arrest us all, and the work we authorized will continue."

Conner nodded to the security forces, who swept in, arresting more than fifty senators and congressmen. Amidst the turmoil Hart and Wilkins were quickly dispatched by the Secret Service and taken to the president's motorcade.

When they were gone, the president concluded the session. "We must purge this infection that threatens the very life of our democracy and heal the gaping wound resulting from such treachery. I will be meeting with a group of you at the White House no later than 07:00 tomorrow morning."

With that, the president walked out.

Conner climbed into the limo across from Liz and John, shaking Hart's hand and reaching across to give Liz a hug.

"I didn't anticipate that reaction," he admitted. "I can't believe the audacity of these people. They are emboldened to do whatever they damn well please. I don't know what's scarier, the experimentation that took place on the Prometheus or the complete and total abdication of the rule of law by our governmental representatives. You do realize that this could tear our country apart, don't you?"

"Yes, Sir," Hart responded. Liz nodded her head in agreement.

"We've got to identify the heads of the hydra, Commander."

"What are you proposing, Mr. President?"

"A no-holds-barred conversation between you and Mr. Kahn. We need Kahn to reveal the handful of white nationalists waiting in the shadows for just the right moment to launch their insurrection."

"It's not going to be pretty, Sir. Mr. Kahn is not about to roll over and give up his most precious secrets."

"Do whatever is necessary to get the information, Commander."

"Yes, Sir."

CHAPTER 46

No Holds Barred

THE LAST TRACES OF DAYLIGHT HAD SURRENDERED to the night as the lights of the motorcade illuminated a path to the president's residence. Hart was on edge. He knew that no one outside of the occupants of the vehicle could be trusted.

"When we arrive, I'll have Mary help you get settled in for the night, Liz. The commander and I have no time to lose in identifying the conspirators behind this extraordinary act of treason."

"I understand, Mr. President."

As they walked into the West Wing, Mary Conner was waiting for them. She extended her hand towards the doctor, "You've had a hell of a day, Liz," she said, her voice brimming with concern.

"We both have." Liz reached over and squeezed her husband's hand.

Mary nodded knowingly. "The staff has prepared a suite for you and the commander. Why don't I show it to you."

As soon as they had disappeared, Hart spoke. "Where is Mr. Kahn being held, Sir?"

"The son of a bitch is in a holding cell in the sub-basement. I will personally escort you there and remain through the interrogation."

"I don't think that's advisable, Mr. President. His career may have been behind a desk instead of out in the field, but Mr. Kahn is one tough bastard. It's going to take much more than physical pain to elicit his cooperation."

"My presence isn't going to change that, Commander."

"What I have to do to Mr. Kahn may be repugnant to you. We've had discussions in the past about my methods. And, although you never argue with the results, you've made it clear that they are morally loathsome to you."

"That was then; now is now. I want to bear witness to every second. I'll escort you to the holding area. Oh, and remember, Commander, there are no limits. Do whatever it takes."

"Yes, Sir. Mr. President, the deputy has two grandchildren." Hart awaited the president's confirmation.

"Surely you are not going to involve them?" A look of horror crossed Conner's face.

"I believe you said, 'there are no limits,' Sir."

"Yes, but you can't inflict damage on innocent children. That would be barbaric."

"I need you to trust my judgment, Mr. President."

Conner studied Hart for what seemed an eternity before agreeing to his demand. He summoned an aide and ordered him to have Mr. Kahn's grandson and granddaughter picked up and brought to the White House.

"Bring the parents, too," Hart added, before the aide had departed.

"I never thought I would find myself fighting for the life of our democracy against an internal threat. Certainly not against what appear to be white nationalists."

"Nor I, Sir. Past threats have come in many forms and colors, but not claiming to be lily white with a long pedigree. Let's hope we can unmask the perpetrators, bring them to justice, and quickly mend whatever rupture they've opened in the fabric of our nation."

Forty-five minutes later, a well-dressed couple in their early forties, accompanied by two children, were ushered into the West Wing. Conner and Hart seemed to materialize out of the shadows. Kahn's daughter stared at them in disbelief.

"Mr. President, what are we doing here? And why is Commander Hart here? We were told that my father needed us urgently."

Hart stepped forward. "Susan, I know we have only met a few times, but you and Howard are going to have to trust me. Your father's life depends on it."

She recoiled. "What are you talking about? I saw my father yesterday. He was fine." She pulled out her cell phone. "I'll call him, and you'll see."

She punched speed-dial. The phone rang and rang, but there was no answer.

"Before I continue, I think it would be advisable for one of the staff to take the children into another room while we have a private conversation," Hart said.

Howard, a partner in a blue-chip conservative law firm, put his hands on his wife's shoulders. "I think we need to listen to Commander Hart, Dear."

As Susan nodded, a female secret service agent approached and, taking the children by the hand, led them out of the room.

"Susan, the reason your father is not answering his phone is because Mr. Kahn is being held in a detention cell two floors below us," Hart explained.

"What? I don't believe you!" A look of shock on her face.

"I'm afraid it's true, Susan." The confirmation came from the president.

She swayed visibly, as if about to lose her balance. Howard lunged forward to grab hold of his wife, not relinquishing his grip until she regained her equilibrium.

"I think you need to stop being so cryptic and tell us what the hell is going on," Howard said in a steely tone.

Hart nodded. "We have evidence that Mr. Kahn is part of an expansive conspiracy that has undermined the true rule of democracy for decades."

"Oh, come on, Commander," Howard sneered. "A deep state? That's ludicrous! I can't believe for a moment that you and President Conner would buy into such utter nonsense."

"Nor can I," Susan said, staring coldly at the two men. "My father is a loyal servant of the United States government. He'd give his life for this country. And now you are calling him a traitor?"

"Allow me to prove it to you." Turning to the desk, Hart spoke into a speaker there, "Cue up the video, please." A second later, a TV on the wall blinked on. "What you are about to see are edited video clips from Congressional testimony that occurred less than three hours ago," Hart explained.

Susan slowly raised her head and stared at the screen. After a moment, she turned away and muttered, "They've been doctored. My father would have no part of that."

"My patience is wearing thin, Susan. There's nothing doctored about the images you just saw. Your father may be a patriot in his own mind. In my book, he stepped off the path of righteousness, got lost, and ended up turning on his nation, though he won't ever construe it that way."

Facing the president, she asked, "What do you plan to do to him?" Her lower lip trembled as she waited for Conner's response.

"That depends. If he divulges the information needed to shut down the conspiracy, then he will be dealt with mercifully. If not, he will endure great suffering at the hands of Commander Hart and die disgraced."

That was too much for her to handle, and she fell to her knees in tears.

Howard comforted his wife, then looked up at the president. "What are you asking us to do?"

Hart explained, "I'm going to give Mr. Kahn a chance to come clean."

"Susan, are you willing to help us?" Conner asked, to which she silently nodded.

Hart continued, "You may not want to watch the conversation we are about to have. If he fails to cooperate, we will proceed to the next level of interrogation, which I will explain as necessary."

"I insist on watching!" Susan glared at him. "And if you hurt him, Commander, there will be hell to pay. We still have laws in this country against torture, as I trust you remember."

"Suit yourself," Hart answered, as he gestured toward the wall-mounted monitor and handed her a remote. "You can turn it off if it gets to be too much."

Hart left the room and, accompanied by a Marine guard, he proceeded to Kahn's holding cell.

"Mr. Kahn is in the second cell on the right, Sir," the Marine told him. "Good luck, Commander. He's one indignant bastard, if you ask me."

Hart nodded before moving quickly towards the cell. As he opened the door, Kahn grabbed him from behind, his right arm squeezing hard against Hart's windpipe. Without a second's hesitation, Hart reached up with his right hand and grabbed Kahn's wrist. He stretched his left hand towards the ceiling, then shifted his hips to the right, providing a clear target to Kahn's solar plexus. With stunning speed, he thrust his elbow backwards into the man's gut.

Kahn emitted an agonized moan as if his very soul had been crushed and slumped to the floor. Hart reached down with his left hand and grabbed Kahn by the throat. He lifted him off the ground just long enough to deliver a second blow, a powerful right cross that broke Kahn's nose.

Susan cried out as a torrent of blood engulfed her father's face.

"You don't have to watch this, Susan," Conner advised her.

Hart stared at his former boss. "You touch me again, Mr. Kahn, and I'll kill you."

"No, you won't. You need what I know," he said tapping the side of his head with a smirk as blood spilled from his nostrils. "There's a reason why you're still in the field while I serve as the DDO. You see, Commander Hart, the most important genetic trait is intelligence. Brawn is far down the line."

"Thank you for the lecture on eugenics, Mr. Kahn, but I don't have time. I'm under orders from our president to get the names of the people you report to. The leaders of the cabal."

"He's your president, Mr. Hart, not mine. I owe my allegiance to a different order, the successive generations of men who have seen the failures of our democracy as envisioned by its founding fathers and stepped in to make the necessary corrections. The smartest thing you and President Conner can do is just walk away. Let us reside in the shadows where we've been since before either of you were born."

A video-recording was capturing every word.

"Still have doubts?" Conner asked Kahn's daughter and son-in-law.

"This isn't happening," Susan said faintly.

"You really think we'd agree to be complicit to the most treasonous act in our country's history?" Hart laughed. "That's not going to happen, Mr. Kahn, not on my watch."

Kahn's tone softened. "I know you mean that, John. And you know I mean it when I say that there is nothing you can do that will make me give up the names of my colleagues."

"We'll see." Hart abruptly ended the conversation as he summoned the guard.

"What do you mean, 'we'll see'?" Kahn shouted after him.

"I'll be back," he told Kahn before exiting. He turned to the guard, "Clean him up," he instructed him. "You've got fifteen minutes."

As he entered the room where Conner, Susan and Howard were waiting, he beckoned the president over to him. "Sir, I'm going to ask for a high degree of latitude on this one. It's the only way I can see to break Kahn."

"Do what you have to do."

Susan's head hung low and tears dripped from her eyes as Hart approached her. Ever so slowly, she raised her head.

"I know what my father has sacrificed for his country. And I know that he would not do anything that was contrary to the long-term interests of the United States. That I believe with all my heart."

"Whatever his intent, your father's actions were horribly misguided. Regardless, he is guilty of treason by his own admission and can be executed."

"People would rally around him if you tried to convict him."

"We wouldn't try. He will die a slow and excruciating death in the cell in which he currently sits. Your father has hours to live, Susan."

She jumped off the couch and headed for Hart, beating her fists against his chest before being pulled off by her husband.

Hart gestured to Howard. "Sit her on the couch and listen carefully to what I have to say. You have one chance to save your father's life, and that's it."

"Commander Hart doesn't make idle threats, Susan," Conner interjected. "Tell them what they need to do, John."

"Mr. Kahn will sacrifice his life, but I don't believe he will sacrifice the lives of his grandchildren."

"How dare you threaten my children!" Susan bellowed.

"Your children won't be harmed, if you do precisely as I instruct you," Hart said with just enough malevolence to stoke her most intense fears.

"I'm going to give your father an ultimatum. Either he provides us with the information we seek or we execute his grandchildren. No man would want that burden upon his soul."

"And if he doesn't capitulate and calls your bluff?" Howard asked.

"He will witness what appears to be the execution of your children, starting with your son."

"Appears to be? Appears to be?" The volume of Susan's voice rose in horror. "What are you talking about?" she screamed.

"My gun will be loaded with wax bullets filled with a red dye. If I am forced to *shoot* your son, it will appear as though he has received a mortal wound. In reality, the bullet will cause nothing more than a bad bruise."

"His injuries may be superficial, but he will be scarred for life by the trauma. How many kids have a real gun pointed at them, then fired, Commander? Are you out of your mind?" Howard seethed with anger and contempt.

"I guess it comes down to whether you believe Mr. Kahn would sacrifice his grandson to protect his secrets."

"My father would never do such a thing!" Susan shouted. "How dare you even suggest it!"

"Then you have nothing to worry about." Hart turned to a Secret Service agent. "Move Mr. Kahn into the viewing room, and put the boy in the interrogation cell."

"You're really going to go through with this, aren't you, you sick bastard?" Howard spit out each word.

Turning again to the agent, Hart added, "And I want the little girl waiting in the wings for round two."

"I'm right behind you," the man said as he stood up and walked out of the room.

Conner knew that Hart had gone too far, but he couldn't stop him now. Instead, he could only pray for the children, their parents, and most of all Kahn, who he hoped would have the wisdom to capitulate.

As Hart and the agent descended a level to where Kahn was being held, Hart completed his instructions. "If Kahn calls my bluff and I am forced to take a shot at the boy, I want the interrogation cell to go dark three seconds after I pull the trigger. That will be long enough for the boy's shock and horror to register fully on Mr. Kahn. After that, get the boy out of there and put his sister in his place. I will be returning to the viewing room for a word with Mr. Kahn."

"Yes, Sir."

Hart stepped back as the door to the viewing room swung open. But, this time, there was no threat. Kahn, who looked like the victim of a gang attack, was slumped in a chair, his arms shackled to a table and his ankles chained to the floor. As Hart entered the cell, Kahn slowly raised his head. His face held little emotion other than contempt.

"It's good to see you, too, Mr. Kahn," Hart said sarcastically as he walked over and opened the blinds covering the one-way mirror that separated the viewing room from the interrogation cell holding Kahn's grandson. As he eyed the boy, Kahn's demeanor turned venomous.

"He's a child and he's a civilian. Get my grandson out of there, now, Commander."

It was the chink in the armor that Hart had hoped for.

"No, we still have some things to discuss, and I thought your grandson might provide a little encouragement for you to help us." Hart pressed a button activating a microphone that could be heard in the viewing room. "Have Tommy sit in the chair and wait for me."

He pulled out his .45 caliber pistol and removed the safety. "You know me, Mr. Kahn. And you've seen this routine before. I'm going in there and I'm going to give you ten seconds to start reeling off the names of your co-conspirators. If you don't, I will plant a bullet in your grandson's heart."

"Even you have your limits, Commander. You're not going to kill my grandson, not in cold blood. So, carry on with your little drama if you must."

"You underestimate me, Mr. Kahn."

Hart walked out of the viewing room and into the observation cell. "Don't move," he told Tommy with absolute authority as he pointed the gun squarely at the boy's heart. He pulled back the hammer, and looked into the mirror, knowing Kahn was on the other side watching his every move. Hart could hear Kahn's heavy breathing through the wall-mounted speaker.

"Ten . . . nine . . . eight . . ."

"Wait!" Kahn begged. "Don't do it, John. Let's talk."

"You're wasting my time. Start praying for your grandson's soul. Seven . . . six . . . five . . . four . . ."

"No, there has to be another way!" Kahn implored.

"The names, Mr. Kahn!"

"No!"

"Three . . . two . . . one . . ."

There was a deafening blast. The impact knocked the boy over, a thick red liquid oozing from the center of his chest. His eyes were wide open as if he were dead. Then the room went black.

A penetrating, unearthly wail arose from within the viewing room.

Hart waited a minute for the boy to be extricated and the girl brought in before confronting Kahn face to face.

As he entered the viewing room, Kahn strained against the chains binding him. "I'll kill you, you son of a bitch, if it's the last fucking thing I do." As he spoke, the lights went back on.

"Have a look, Mr. Kahn," Hart said, gesturing towards the mirror. His granddaughter sat on the other side.

"No, not Missy, not my Missy!" he cried out.

Hart once more pulled the pistol from its holster. "This time, I'm only counting to five, Mr. Kahn."

The Commander walked into the observation cell and wrapped his hand around Missy's upper arm. He then took the gun and pressed it against the back of her head, as he started to count. "Five . . .

"Four . . .

"Three . . ."

"Stop, I'll give you their names. Just let her go!"

The names spewed forth so fast that Hart could barely keep them straight. The list included a Supreme Court Justice, the Chairman of the Joint Chiefs of Staff, the presidents of two Ivy League universities, and a dozen others. Hart slowly lowered the gun. "Keep talking if you value your granddaughter's life," he said, and Kahn did.

Fortune 500 CEOs, major religious leaders, governors and mayors—Hart could barely believe his ears as the magnitude of the secret group grew. How could so many people maintain such a profound secret over a prolonged period, he wondered.

"There you have it," Kahn snarled. "You self-righteous piece of shit."

Hart didn't respond to Kahn. Instead he whispered something into the guard's ear. A moment later, Tommy reappeared in a clean shirt, seated where he had been when Hart fired the presumed fatal shot. Though he was crying and obviously terrified, he was very much alive.

Kahn was apoplectic. When he finally regained some semblance of composure, he turned to Hart. "You think you've won. That you're so smart."

"Brains over brawn, isn't that what you told me, Sir?"

"It's not over, Commander."

Hart left the cell with the two children in tow. "Lock him up," were Hart's final words to the guard.

Before returning the children to their parents, he asked the guard to cue up the video to where Kahn named names. He played it for Susan and Howard. "Your father only confessed after he believed that I had fatally shot your son. That's how far he was willing to go to protect his treachery and that of his co-conspirators."

Conner spoke. "I'm afraid you are going to be our guests here until we can detain all of the co-conspirators that your father identified. I cannot afford to risk having you warn them before they are arrested. We'll make you comfortable, and we have a physician tending to Tommy's bruise."

Over the next seventy-two hours, every man and woman named by Kahn was rounded up. The group was transported, en masse, to the United States Penitentiary Administrative Maximum Facility in Florence, Colorado, where they would undergo interrogation before awaiting trial.

Referred to as the "Alcatraz of the Rockies," the ADX was home to the worst of the worst, including such notable personalities as Theodore Kaczynski, the Unabomber; Robert Hanssen, the FBI agent turned Russian spy; and most recently, Joaquin "El Chapo" Guzman, the infamous drug lord.

Housed in concrete block cells for twenty-three hours per day, there was little for the prisoners to do but ruminate on a master plan—and a master race—gone bad.

Back at the White House, Conner, Hart, and Wilkins discussed next steps.

"What is your plan, Mr. President?"

"A Nuremburg-like trial. These people are war criminals. They masterminded a conspiracy that attacked our democracy with the intent to overthrow its lawful government. A conspiracy that has a lot in common with the former Third Reich."

"Agreed, Sir. How long before the proceedings can begin?"

"My hope would be within the next few weeks," Conner said.

"After we testify, Mr. President, it will be time for us to disappear."

"Agreed. I know you are well aware of the death threats against you and Liz; several hundred at last count."

"Yes, Sir. Liz and I are grateful for the security detachment you've assigned to us. But that can't last forever."

"Where will you go?"

"A quiet island, maybe in the Seychelles, maybe the Caribbean. Someplace where no one has heard of John Hart."

"What can I do?"

"We will need new identities, and new passports and drivers' licenses to go along with them. Of course, we wouldn't turn down one-way transportation to our destination."

"I'll have a Gulfstream fueled and on stand by for when the two of you are ready to leave."

"Three, Sir."

"What are you talking about, Commander?"

"I promised Liz that, if we survived, I would buy her a British lab and name it Nigel. It's the next thing on my list."

"I'm sure as hell going to miss you both."

"We won't be gone forever. Just long enough for the light you so often talk about, Mr. President, to overcome the darkness."

AFTERWORD

Thirteen hundred miles away, in a cabin not far from Gunnison, Colorado, a small group of men had assembled to plan the impossible. An exalted guest sat at the head of the dinner table, ready to preach to his compatriots.

As the meal ended, Alex Harner, the Director of the United States Prison System, began. "Every prison has points of vulnerability, and the ADX is no exception. The only difference is that the ADX's vulnerabilities have never been fully identified, nor exploited. Not until tonight."

Harner signaled to a man in the back, who turned on an LCD projector. An image of the architectural blueprint for the structure's first floor appeared.

"Gentlemen, you have weeks, not months, in which to liberate the true patriots of this nation, and my job is to draw the map that will allow that to happen."

So began a methodical plan to launch the greatest prison break in the history of America, a first step in rekindling the battle to reclaim the United States for its white majority.

Additional books in this series:

8 Seconds to Midnight

The 2018 IAN Book of the Year for Outstanding Thriller/Suspense;

Midwest Book Awards: Finalist.

The Wishing Shelf Awards: Finalist

Indie Book Awards: Finalist

BookLife Prize—2018 Semi-Finalist.
"Leifer's novel stands out among others that address terrorist attempts to launch nuclear and biological attack weapons on the U.S. Intelligent discourse, verisimilitude, and a full humanization of characters provide the novel exceptional depth and dimension."

Publisher's Weekly: "Well-developed main characters and plausible technical details help make a familiar plot fresh in Leifer's thriller. Fans of Tom Clancy and the TV series *24* will be riveted."

Paul F. Johnson for Readers' Favorite: "John Leifer grabs the reader from the first page and doesn't let go. The story moves along at break-neck pace, leaving the reader expectantly waiting to turn to the next page. Very good story, very entertaining. I highly recommend this book."

Catherine Langrehr for IndieReader: This is a great book if what you want is a vigorous, action-packed thriller with lots of suspense, dramatic last-minute acts of courage, and a clearly-defined right and wrong side. *8 Seconds To Midnight* is a thriller packed with energy, action, and suspense, which consistently delivers on the promises of the genre.

Terminal:

Amanda Rofe, Readers' Favorite: "I was completely captivated with the story line from the very first chapter. John Leifer writes effortlessly and eloquently. *Terminal* contains all the components of a blockbuster movie. This is a well-researched book which held my attention throughout. I highly recommend it."

IndieReader: 4.6 Stars. "*Terminal*, John Leifer's page-turning prequel to his book "*8 Seconds to Midnight*" in the Commander John Hart series . . . is supercharged and will grab readers by the throat, exhibiting the barely closeted global paranoia of modern times. There is no paranormal or horror story component, but this tale is unequivocally terrifying.

Booklife Review: "Leifer (*The Myths of Modern Medicine*) makes his fiction debut with this suspenseful and alarming kickoff to a trilogy."

Sinfully Wicked Book Reviews: "*Terminal*, by John Leifer, is a pulse pounding, edge of your seat terroristic thriller set against the backdrop of America and the Middle

East. Leifer's writing is so rich you will get lost between the pages, hoping for the story to never end. I was completely drawn in from the first page, and I can truly say this is an outstanding and thought-provoking story. I have a feeling each new book in the series will be all five-star reads for me. Yes, it is that good!"

Thou Shall Not Kill

Booklife Review: Leifer pulls out all the stops in his pulse-pounding third thriller featuring Cmdr. John Hart… President Jonathan Conner's go-to person in emergencies. Tom Clancy fans will appreciate Leifer's ingenuity in coupling suspense with a believable near-future scenario.

Ruffina Oserio for Readers' Favorite: *****Stars : "John Leifer weaves a narrative with powerful political themes. *Thou Shall Not Kill* is packed with action…Written in excellent and highly descriptive prose, this novel is both exciting and intoxicating."

Darryl Greer for Readers' Favorite. *****Stars. "*Thou Shall Not Kill* is a thriller of thrillers that really stands out from the crowd.It would be a sin if *Thou Shall Not Kill* does not make the bestseller list.

8 Seconds to Midnight

8 Seconds to Midnight takes the reader on a non-stop thrill-ride that begins with the clandestine transfer of nuclear material from a secure Pakistani military installation thirty miles north of Islamabad to a group of radical Islamists bent on the destruction of the West. It culminates in the streets of New York—minutes before the impending detonation of a fifteen-kiloton nuclear bomb. The city's survival hinges on one man, Commander John Hart, and his ability to ferret out the perpetrators, discern where the weapon is hidden, and disable it before midnight on December 31. Hart must rely on equal measures of brawn, brain, and prayer to stop the cadre of jihadists whose plan has been in the making for sixteen years. Should he fail, the job of healing America's potentially mortal wound will fall squarely on the shoulders of Dr. Elizabeth Wilkins. It is a job she did not ask for, and hopes never materializes.

Terminal:

In this chilling prequel to 8 Seconds to Midnight, the most devastating terrorist attack ever recorded on American soil begins and ends without spilling a single drop of blood. Four jihadists, armed with nothing more than a briefcase and a pen, walk nonchalantly through the country's busiest airports, killing time and killing people. A deadly mist, laden with a universally lethal virus, trails close behind them. Their goal: foment a global pandemic. Their vision: Armageddon, where only the Chosen Ones—those loyal to the United Islamic State—survive. The job of stopping them falls squarely on the shoulders of one man, Commander John Hart, but will he be in time?

Thou Shall Not Kill:

It was a beautiful morning graced by crystal blue skies as Kamal passed through the gate at Sapir Academic College, Israel's largest public university. Unnoticed, he merged seamlessly into the flow of bodies traversing the campus. At precisely 9:05 a.m. he began to recite his prayers. Two minutes later, he stopped, stared at the heavens, then shouted, "Allah Akbar!" before depressing a detonator. In a millisecond, scorching hot metal ripped through the flesh of anyone within Kamal's line of sight. Students dropped mid-stride. Dismembered bodies lined the sidewalks, and blood soaked the grass. Kamal's headless torso lay amid the dead and dying.

It was merely the first shot in a methodically planned, multi-pronged attack designed to "wipe Israel from the face of the earth." Its perpetrators included a combined army, 40,000 men strong, of Iranian, Syrian, Hezbollah, Hamas, and Russian forces—men who would stop at nothing to achieve their objective.

As the attack escalated from an act of terrorism to an existential threat, the words, Never Again echoed in the mind of Israeli prime minister Abraham Rabinovich. It was a promise by Jewish Holocaust survivors to never again be passive in the face of systematic annihilation.

With a single order, Rabinovich was poised to launch weapons capable of incinerating entire cities. Only two things stood in his way: his conscience and Commander John Hart.

✹

I hope that you have enjoyed this latest book in the series featuring Commander John Hart. If so, please consider sharing your thoughts with other readers on Amazon.com, B&N.com, Goodreads.com, and other platforms.

I would also invite your correspondence. Please write to me at: *johnleifer@aol.com*.

Finally, I encourage you to visit: *www.johnleifer.com* where you will find a great deal of additional information.

www.ingramcontent.com/pod-product-compliance
Lightning Source LLC
Chambersburg PA
CBHW031932110726
47902CB00001B/141